no easy

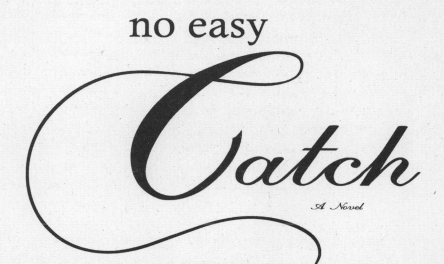

Catch

A Novel

PAT SIMMONS

no easy

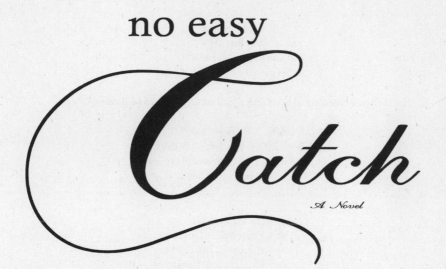

Catch

A Novel

PAT SIMMONS

WHITAKER
HOUSE

No Easy Catch
The Carmen Sisters ~ Book One

Pat Simmons
P.O. Box 1077
Florissant, MO 63031
authorpatsimmons@gmail.com

The author is represented by MacGregor Literary, Inc., of Hillsboro, Oregon.

ISBN: 978-1-62911-009-7
eBook ISBN: 978-1-62911-033-2
Printed in the United States of America
© 2014 by Pat Simmons

Whitaker House
1030 Hunt Valley Circle
New Kensington, PA 15068
www.whitakerhouse.com

Library of Congress Cataloging-in-Publication Data

Simmons, Pat, 1959-
No easy catch / by Pat Simmons.
pages cm—(The Carmen Sisters ; book 1)
ISBN: 978-1-62911-009-7 (alk. paper)– ISBN: 978-1-62911-033-2 (eBook)
I. Title.
PS3619.I56125N64 2014
813'.6—dc23   2014000599

1 2 3 4 5 6 7 8 9 10 11   ⨆   20 19 18 17 16 15 14

In loving memory of Francis Ronald "Rahn" Ramey, 1955–2013.

❧

Whew. I was stunned when I got the news that Rahn had passed away in June 2013. It's hard to say good-bye to a childhood friend, especially one whom I considered my big brother throughout my teenage years. How could my family have known, way back when I was in high school, that the same Rahn (aka Ronald) who hung out at our house, providing never-ending comedic relief, would go on to do great things? You never know a person's potential—never. Yet he suffered an illness unknown to me and died so young. Although it had been a while since I had seen Rahn do standup comedy, I was proud of him. Thank God for sending Rahn our way, with his charisma and unique sense of humor. He will be missed for years to come, but at least I have the memories.

ACKNOWLEDGMENTS

A special thanks to readers who have supported me throughout the years and to the many book clubs, bookstores, and libraries that have promoted my work.

Thanks also to:

Agent Amanda Luedeke at MacGregor Literary Agency.

Christine Whitaker at Whitaker House, for giving me the opportunity to tell the Carmen sisters' stories.

Authors Tia McCollors, Lisa Watson, and Vanessa Miller, who always checked in to make sure I met deadline. If folks only knew... Shout-out to Philly author Marlene Banks.

My Jersey Guilty captain, Mia Harris, for the epilogue.

Author Maurice Gray, for setting the record straight about the Charlie Brown baseball team...tee-hee.

My son, Jared, who has been a St. Louis Cardinals fan since he could walk.

My amateur assistant and hubby, Kerry, for giving me space to talk to my characters. I love and appreciate you.

My lovely daughter, Simi.

Bethesda Temple Church, and Bishop James A. Johnson and First Lady Juana Johnson—thank you for being shepherds for Christ. I love you, Bishop!

The descendants of Minerva Jordan Wade; Marshall Cole and Laura Brown; Joseph and Nellie Palmer Wafford Brown; Thomas Carter and Love Ann Shepard; Ned and Priscilla Brownlee; John Wilkinson and Artie Jamison/Charlotte Jamison; and others who were tracked down on the 1800s censuses and other documents; and my in-laws: Simmonses, Sinkfields, Crofts, Sturdivants, Stricklands, Downers...and the list goes on.

Jesus said unto him, If thou canst believe, all things are possible to him that believeth. And straightway the father of the child cried out, and said with tears, Lord, I believe; help thou mine unbelief.
—Mark 9:23–24

1

St. Louis Cardinals baseball outfielder Rahn Maxwell had made some wrong turns in life—women and money, to name a few—but this wrong turn could prove deadly if the pair of blinding headlights racing toward him in his rearview mirror didn't slow down.

He had just left a nightclub in downtown St. Louis, where he had met some friends. A construction sign had instructed him to detour off Interstate 64, and now his GPS attempted to recalculate. The darkness around him was thick as fog.

"Turn around when possible," his GPS kept advising, as if it sensed danger.

That would be a good idea, but at the moment, he had a more pressing issue. Since there wasn't time for Rahn to get out of harm's way, with a car speeding behind him, he braced for impact. Seconds later, the anticipated crash never occurred. An old Camaro shrieked to a halt alongside his pearl gray Mercedes-Benz G550 SUV, blocking his exit. Rahn experienced a bad gut feeling.

The front passenger window of the car descended, and a dark-skinned man wearing dark glasses snarled at him. Brandishing some type of machine gun, he ordered Rahn to lower his window. *Great!* And he had just declined the dealer's recommendation of armor-plated protection for his luxury vehicle. Now, Rahn wished he had followed his advice. How come hindsight couldn't be foresight?

Watching the gunman's movements, Rahn counted down the seconds until his life would end. He hadn't reached thirty-five, the age he planned to announce his retirement. Judging from the looks of things, his short-lived career was about to stop at twenty-seven. *God, I can't go down like this. Please help me.* Rahn had too many wrongs he needed to right, people to whom he needed to say his last good-byes, and babies he needed to kiss.

Exceeding his father's numerous awards in baseball would be the biggest missed opportunity. Even collecting a pension didn't sound too far-fetched at the moment. An induction in the Hall of Fame would be a plus, too. Now, all that seemed trivial.

All of a sudden, the driver of the Camaro jumped out. He appeared taller than Rahn's six-foot-three-inch frame. "Nice ride," he said, pointing his own gun at him.

Against the eerie backdrop of night, the man's fair complexion gave him the illusion of a ghost face with rows of silver chains weighing down his body. His bling shone like a neon light. "How about letting us take it for a test drive?" He grinned, revealing a gap in his bottom teeth.

Was the trigger-happy dude asking permission? Did Rahn really have a choice?

"You're moving too slow, man." Agitated, the gunman hustled closer to the vehicle as Rahn calculated the speed needed to back up without a bullet hitting its target. "Your life or your ride," he demanded.

Keep breathing, hands down, Rahn thought, more afraid at the moment than he could ever recall being.

"The fear of the LORD *is a fountain of life, to depart from the snares of death."* Proverbs 14:27 came to him as a whisper, as if God Himself was a passenger in his car.

The Scriptures never seemed like a lifeline until it was too late. As Rahn was about to plead for his life, his assailant bucked, his demeanor shifting to uncertainty.

"Hey, man—aren't you Rahn Maxwell?" He bobbed his head. "Yep, you are. All right, now. Whaz up, man? I remember that game against the Dodgers when the bases were loaded. I put a lot of money on that game. Man, oh man, when you cleared the bases with your two-run homer, it was cool." He snickered as if he was watching an instant replay.

Rahn was about to be murdered, and the man wanted to talk baseball? Rahn could barely recall his name, let alone the specifics of a game from last season.

This is your plan of escape, came the mental nudge from God.

Right. He took the cue. "Yep, couldn't let the Cubs gain ground—the Dodgers...the Dodgers." *Stay with the conversation, Maxwell*, his mind warned him. He swallowed, still on guard.

"Hey, y'all, it's Rahn Maxwell," the gunman shouted to his accomplices in the car. "Check him out." He still held his weapon erect.

Two thugs jumped out of the backseat. Scarves covered their heads, and bling drenched their bodies, which showcased tattoos splattered across their chests and arms.

Outgunned and outnumbered, Rahn pleaded with Jesus, *Lord, if You get me out of this, I'll clean up my act—promise.* Did he just make a vow? That left him no choice but to make good on it—not give lip service, as he had in the past.

One of the men rushed to his window and squinted at him, as if to verify his identity. He displayed a mouth full of gold-capped teeth. "A'wight, you won that game against the Dodgers with your two-run homer."

"Grand slam, fool," another one corrected him.

Actually, it had been a two-run homer, but who was Rahn to contradict a man with a gun?

The first gunman interrupted their impending argument. "Shut up, both of you!" He turned to Rahn. "Uh, could I have your autograph?"

What? Refusing to show that he was dumbfounded, Rahn obliged and put his John Hancock on the piece of paper he was handed. His captors-turned-fans admired his signature.

"A'wight." The head mugger patted the hood of Rahn's SUV and waved him back, as if he was a patrol officer allowing Rahn to cross the border. "We'll move so you can make a U-turn."

One of the accomplices nodded, then jumped in the car and backed it out of the way.

"Okay, take a right at the corner, and you'll be back on the highway. Be safe."

Really? "Thanks." Attentively, Rahn did as he was instructed. Once he was on the interstate, he tested his Benz's horsepower, surpassing the speed limit. He wasn't concerned about crashing or being arrested. He had escaped impending death. Either way, he was still breathing.

Thirty minutes later, Rahn turned down the narrow two-lane road to the gated community he called home. His strength seemed to drain from his body as he pressed the garage door opener. "I'm alive. I'm alive." As soon as he pulled inside and parked, Rahn rested his forehead on the steering wheel. Despite his natural strength, he felt faint. "Thank You, Jesus," he whispered before turning off the motor. Willing his legs to move, Rahn somehow slid out of the driver's seat, then steadied himself.

His heart continued to pound thunderously against his chest as he entered his house through the kitchen. He deactivated his alarm system. Now safely behind locked doors, Rahn scanned the familiar surroundings. He had never been so scared in his life.

Reaching for his cordless phone, Rahn fumbled with it until he had a grip. He punched in 9-1-1—something he should have done while speeding down the interstate. Rahn stuttered, speaking in broken sentences; Ebonics or even a foreign language might have slipped in before he was able to go into vivid details.

"Sir, I'll send an officer to take your statement," the frustrated dispatcher finally told him.

What? He huffed. He had sweated through the recap, only to have to suffer through it again. "Fine."

By the time the police—two of them—arrived, Rahn's mind had drawn a blank. This time weapons flashed before his eyes and he described the AK-47s better than he could the gunmen's faces. "When they recognized me, all they wanted to talk about was baseball and my autograph. The next thing I knew, one guy directed me out of their ambush. I never looked back...."

The questions continued for another twenty minutes. Finally, the shorter of the two officers advised him they would be in touch, and then he and his partner left. Alone with his thoughts, Rahn showered until the water chilled.

With no appetite or interest in television, Rahn collapsed on his bed. Although his body was tired, his mind was in extra innings. He continued to wrestle with the reality that God had spared his life. Maybe it had all been a dream.

~

"This is the most exciting weekend I've had since moving here," Shae Carmen told her younger sister Brecee.

"I thought a surprise visit would cheer you up." Dr. Sabrece "Brecee" Carmen had flown in from Houston, where she was completing her residency in pediatrics. It was almost midnight, and the sisters had just ordered dessert at a busy, posh restaurant tucked away near the Central West End.

Thank God for family. And thanks to her parents, Annette and Saul Carmen, for giving her three sisters: Stacy, Shari, and Brecee. After a painful breakup, Shae had quit her first job out of college, at a Nebraska TV station, and taken the first offer she'd gotten, at KMMD-TV in St. Louis, which had turned out to be a blessing. Not only was she a reporter in a major market, but she had added "weekend news anchor" to her résumé. Professionally, she had rebounded; personally, however, she was still struggling to pick up the pieces.

As far as Shae was concerned, three months hadn't been enough time to come to grips with the church scandal of a lifetime—her own. She was twenty-six years old, not a naive sweet sixteen. She was adamant about never dating again, even if it meant a lifestyle of singleness. She had church and family to fill in the void.

Shae relaxed in her seat at the booth. From the whispers and pointing of the other patrons, she knew some of them had recognized her from the ten o'clock newscast she'd recently anchored. That was preferable to the gossip and label of "home wrecker." She sighed and leaned forward. "You know, I still can't believe I was the other woman."

Brecee jabbed her finger at her. "You were never the other woman. *She* was."

"*She* was his wife." Shae shook her head. "I wanted to slide under the pew when that woman stood in front of the entire congregation and testified how her husband had patiently brought her back to the Lord. Alex never said anything to me about being married, separated, or divorced. Where were the church busybodies when I needed them to put a buzz in my ear?"

Brecee twisted her lips in disgust. "That two-timing married lowlife was leading you to believe you were the love of his life, pretending that God was the head of his life. *Puh-lease*. He was nothing more than a devil's decoy, a slimy church predator, conniving to deceive the saints."

Brecee's rant was as fervent as if she was the injured party. It would have been comical, if it wasn't for the fact that it was Shae's miniseries that was playing out. Growing up, the sisters had often been mistaken for twins because of their uncanny resemblance. However, when it came to their personalities, they were as different as powdery snow and hail. Shae was soft-spoken when she wasn't in front of the camera. Brecee, one year younger, was known for her unbridled tongue—a bad trait for a child of God, and she knew it.

"I can't believe I ranked at the top of my journalism class for investigative reporting." Why hadn't the stellar education given her the foresight in other areas? She cringed. Her gross error in judgment didn't bode well for her credibility as a television reporter. Her oath to uncover the truth, follow up on leads, and expose corruption had been compromised, just like her dignity.

If a boyfriend could deceive her and lie about being married, how would she know if a suspect, victim, or politician she was interviewing was telling the truth? How could she have been so clueless and so wrong about Alex's character? Before that fiasco, Shae had never second-guessed herself.

"Let that past hurt go." Brecee waved her hand as if she were swatting a fly. "Consider your East Pekin, South Pekin, or Whatever Pekin, Nebraska, experience as part of a well-rounded education on life outside the classroom."

Shae tapped her nails on the table. She had heard her sister say it all before.

"Look at the blessing that followed after what that trouser snake did. After you resigned from that overworked and underpaid reporter job, it took you only a month to land a better one. I call that checkmating the devil."

"Yeah." Shae curled her lips into a smile. Professionally, she had done well. However, her reputation had been blemished. It was hard to regain respect after a person's character was vilified in the public eye, even in a small town.

"You know what?" Brecee stole a flirtatious glance at a server as he swaggered past their table, then met Shae's gaze again, her face serious. "I think it was the power of suggestion that made you vulnerable."

"Huh?"

"Mother Stillwell got in your head, which allowed Alex to get inside your heart. She planted a seed with her whole 'Get that hope chest ready, sugar—your blessing ain't far away.'" Brecee's imitation of the eighty-something great-grandmother from their home church in Philly was spot-on, down to the crooked finger-pointing.

Shae rolled her eyes. Mother Stillwell had flagged her down in the church parking lot, in a car that needed a paint job and a new muffler. Even the driver's window seemed stuck in the "up" position, barely allowing enough room for a smoker to flip out a cigarette butt. Yet that hadn't stopped Mother Stillwell. Through that slit of an opening, she'd reminded Shae that "he's coming," as if she was talking about Jesus' return, as foretold in 1 Thessalonians 4:16.

"Here you go, ladies." Their server placed a mammoth-sized slice of cheesecake between them. Spying each other, the sisters locked forks, ready to battle to be the first one to sample the dessert.

"Only because you're treating me, I concede," Brecee said with a grin. "I know sweets are your weakness."

And it showed, too. The debacle with Alex Peterson had caused Shae's weight to fluctuate and her hair to thin in some places due to stress. Thanks to a hair weave, her tresses were on the mend. She would never snub her nose at any woman wearing synthetic hair again. But she would love to look like Brecee, who maintained her figure by working out, wore minimal makeup on her blemish-free skin, and had recently experimented with highlights in her long, brown mane—with stunning results.

Could it be true, what Brecee had suggested? Had Shae been so gullible as to allow an old church busybody to plant a bug in her ear?

Brecee helped herself to a bite of cheesecake. "I never mentioned this, but not long after you moved to Nebraska, Mother Stillwell was playing 'matchmaker missionary' again. This time, she had me on her radar. I dodged her as long as I could before she cornered me outside the restroom. You know, for an old woman with a cane, she gets around as if she's wearing shoes on wheels." Brecee chuckled. "Anyway, remember Brian Evans?"

Shae frowned as she slid another forkful of dessert in her mouth. "The name sounds familiar, but his face is fuzzy." Their home church in Philly had been huge. "Why?"

Brecee grunted. "Mother Stillwell said God had spoken Brian's name and my name in her ear. Right. Two days later, Brian was busted for buying drugs—another decoy in the church. Mother Stillwell apologized to me and retracted her earlier declaration, claiming she'd meant Evans Bryson and blaming the mistake on her blood pressure medicine. Then, remember—"

"Stop it." Shae cracked up and had to make an effort to keep her food inside her mouth. "You're really making me feel stupid that I might have subconsciously entertained her remarks." She sobered and looked away. "I'm so through with men in church. They're no different from the ones outside the temple walls."

"There are decoys everywhere. And you're anything but stupid." Brecee reached across the table and patted Shae's hand. "It's a known fact that sisters around Jesus Is the Way Church are praying to be next on Mother Stillwell's hit list for husbands."

"Sometimes I wonder, why me?" Shae propped her elbow on the table and rested her chin in her hand. Of course, there was no answer. Didn't the Bible say that God sent sunshine and rain on good and evil alike? At times, it didn't seem fair that the Lord would allow the saint to go through the same trials that she thought should be reserved for the sinner. She was definitely going to have to reread Matthew, chapter five.

Brecee leaned forward. "Listen to me, Sis. You can't let that jerk make you give up on your happily-ever-after. I'm praying that Jesus will release you from your mental bondage."

"Thanks." Shae smiled but didn't feel it.

"You're going to get back in the dating pool again, even if I have to push you in there," Brecee said, wagging a manicured finger at her.

"You better have a truck to assist you, because I'm not budging."

"But we're believers of Lamentations three twenty-three, remember? God's mercies are new every morning." Brecee patted her chest. "Just like God set aside seven thousand men in Israel that wouldn't bow to Baal in First Kings, I happen to believe that the Lord has set aside some good men for us—the women of God. My faith's in God, not men."

"My faith's in God keeping the wolves away."

"Amen." Brecee exchanged a high five with her, then signaled for the check.

Their server appeared, wearing a mischievous smile. "Ladies, your bill has already been paid."

Shae and Brecee stared at her in surprise. "What? Who?" they asked in unison.

Their server wasn't bashful about pointing in the direction of two good-looking, dark-skinned brothers waiting for a table near the lobby. Both men waved, and one of them winked, saluting the sisters with his glass of wine.

"Hmm-mm. Now, there are two possibilities," Brecee teased.

"I'll pass, but you go for it." Shae meant every word. She stood and gathered her purse and coat, and Brecee followed suit.

Shae was not in the mood for small talk, but it appeared their benefactors had other ideas. The men shifted their weight to a cocky stance as she and Brecee walked toward the exit.

"Gorgeous," Brecee mumbled, then flashed one of her flirtatious smiles that seemed to turn men into cartoon characters with tongues hanging out of their mouths, eyes bugging out, and hearts pounding outside their chests.

"Ladies," said one of them—definitely the better-looking one.

As if Shae no longer had a heartbeat to succumb to their charm, she simply nodded her acknowledgment and then pulled Brecee along before she could further encourage them.

"Hey!" Brecee exclaimed as they stepped into the brisk air. "It wouldn't hurt to say hello."

Shae didn't care how handsome they were. Okay, she did appreciate a good specimen; but the trust was gone. She wasn't interested in striking out again. As far as she was concerned, the game was already over.

2

The sound of gunfire propelled Rahn from sleep. Without a light to guide him, he was disoriented. His only thought was to get the pistol he had recently purchased, courtesy of Missouri's Concealed Carry Law, but never used. First time for everything.

Wait a minute. The noise that had startled him was actually his alarm. Groaning with relief, he fumbled on his nightstand for the remote that controlled the lights. With the lamps illuminated, Rahn noted his surroundings. He was safely nestled in his master bedroom.

Must have been a nightmare. Rahn peered at the clock. It was nearly seven thirty. He couldn't believe he had slept through the night, considering he had been shell-shocked when he'd arrived at home. Being someone who was not easily intimidated, Rahn was annoyed by his own freak-out behavior. He rubbed his face. "Get a grip," he told himself.

Minutes later, he had just settled under the covers again when his phone rang. "Yeah?" he answered. His voice was rough, his throat scratchy.

"Rahn, this is Greg Saxon, KMMD sports. A story came over the wire that you were involved in an attempted carjacking over the weekend."

He scooted up in the bed. News traveled fast. *Great.*

"Can you verify that?" Greg pressed on. "I was hoping you'd give me an exclusive interview."

Are you crazy? was on the tip of his tongue. Anything he said could be used against him. *Get a grip.* He was the victim, not the criminal. But did he want to make a public statement? Too late. This phone call indicated that word had already gotten out. So, the question was, how did he want to handle the aftermath?

The sports broadcaster was a halfway decent guy, making Rahn think twice about brushing him off. He was well respected and reported sports fairly. Rahn couldn't say the same about other media outlets, whose commentaries were often anything but objective. Not once had Greg ever tried to twist his words during post-game interviews, even when his performance on the field had been lackluster. And Greg was about to wed Janet Harris, who managed one of Rahn's charities,

Future Professionals, a nonprofit organization that helped boys in low-income families gain leadership skills.

After weighing his options, Rahn agreed. "Okay, man. When are you talking?"

"Tomorrow morning at eleven. Thanks, I'll see you then."

Once they'd disconnected, Rahn rolled over and closed his eyes. The last thing he remembered was a gunman dressed like a gold-toothed fairy godfather.

A few hours later, Rahn woke again, famished. He got up and eventually made his way to the kitchen, where he prepared two omelets and ate them with gusto. Next, he showered, shaved, and dressed, as if it was any normal day in the life of a baseball player during off-season.

Opting not to take his SUV, which would be history as soon as he returned it to the dealer, Rahn got into his Audi. Déjà vu kicked in as he headed downtown on Highway 40, searching for the detour signs he'd seen last night, which may as well have said "Death Trap." There was nothing. The construction crews had already removed them. Just thinking about the setup angered him.

In no time, Rahn arrived at the TV station. He parked his car but didn't get out right away. "I can't believe I agreed to this." He would've preferred not to rehash his humiliation. Then he remembered that he had forgotten to give Jesus His props once his impending death crisis came to an end. "I'm late, Jesus, but thank You for what You did last night. I will make a change in my life. I promised You that. Please help me to figure out how to do that." Rahn paused, wondering how drastic those changes would have to be. He didn't have time for further contemplation. He had an interview to do. "Amen," he said, postponing the rest of that conversation.

Once Rahn had gathered a degree of dignity, he stepped out of his vehicle and strolled through the revolving door into the lobby. He dead-ended into a massive black desk that blocked him from going any farther. A middle-aged security guard watched him closely but didn't say a word.

"Hello. I'm Rahn Maxwell, here to see Greg Saxon."

"I know." The guard gave a sheepish smile and slid a pass across the desk. "I'm a fan, Mr. Maxwell," he confessed, with a celebrity-stricken look of awe.

What impact would the incident have on Rahn's image? Would people be disappointed that he hadn't fended off the bad guys with crime-fighting skills worth replaying on YouTube?

"Glad to meet you"—Rahn scanned the man's name tag—"Thomas." He extended his hand.

Grinning, Thomas shook his hand, then picked up the phone and punched a few keys. "Mr. Saxon, your guest has arrived."

Rahn stuffed his hands in his pockets and glanced around the spacious lobby. After Thomas disconnected the call, he entertained Rahn with his favorite Cardinal plays.

He was rescued when a door opened, and Greg breezed through. "Hey, it's good to see you, man. Scary last night, huh?" He pumped Rahn's hand longer than necessary. "This way."

Rahn didn't answer but simply followed the short, muscular man into the newsroom. Writers, reporters, and other staffers spied him from behind their computer terminals. Some of the staff gawked openly at him. Why did he agree to this? To rehash the story would mean reliving the nightmare that professionals applied shock treatments to patients to help them forget.

Too late to back out now. Rahn was in step with Greg as they trekked down a long hallway, the walls of which were lined with the station's numerous awards.

It wasn't Rahn's first time down this corridor. Usually, it was for a post-game interview, recapping a bad play or discussing the mechanics of how his team had swept an opposing team—never anything as serious as facing death. Inside the studio, he followed Greg up a step to a circular platform, where two chairs and a table were situated for their live interview. An audio tech waited to pin microphones on their shirts.

After the sound check, the theme music of the midday show played overhead, and then the director cued Greg. Either the studio lights were too hot, or he was breaking out in a sweat, and the interview was just beginning.

⌒

Shae had just returned from a breaking news story about a grade school evacuation. On any given day, a handful of rumors circulated throughout the newsroom. Most were easily ignored, though some merited verification. But this morning, a doozy of a tale was gaining momentum when Shae walked into the newsroom. The Monday buzz was three gunmen had spared the life of a local sports figure because of his celebrity status.

"That's a joke, right?" Shae asked her colleague Diane Duncan, an investigative reporter, who shared one side of a spacious cubicle with her.

"Truth is stranger than fiction, I always say." Diane tapped out a few words on her keyboard, then stopped and spun around in her chair. "Get this: Greg snagged the first interview with Rahn Maxwell." She pumped her fist in the air.

"Go, Greg." Shae grinned and mimicked Diane, although she had no idea who Rahn Maxwell was or what sport he played. "We are the news leader." She took off her coat, draped it over the back of her chair, and got situated at her desk.

She removed her flurry ball hat and hooked it on a small hat stand she had assembled in the corner of her cubicle. The miniature hat store was a result of her rushing to work after the later church service. Since headpieces were second nature to her on Sundays, Shae hadn't realized that she was still wearing one.

The crystal-pleated, ruffled satin flowers and feathers hat had wowed her producer, who formed a grand idea for Shae to wear it at the end of the Sunday newscasts as a "kicker"—a feel-good story to leave with the viewers after all of the bad news they had been exposed to. Shae thought it was a silly idea, but hundreds of viewers had called and posted comments on the station's Web site applauding the gesture, so her hats had become commonplace on Sundays.

Absentmindedly, Shae finger-combed her hair, careful not to get a manicured nail tangled in the last remaining tracks of weave. With her hair growth, they would be coming out soon enough. They had been a headache since day one—evidence of the toll a bad relationship took, mentally and physically, on a woman. Whatever length she ended up with, so be it.

Once she booted her computer and signed in, Shae began logging her notes on the story as she waited for her photographer to load scene video into a master file. In less than fifteen minutes, she would be able to retrieve it, so her words could match the images prior to editing.

"Maybe it was a drug deal gone bad or something." Diane pulled Shae back into the rumor arena. "You know, there are always three sides to a story—his, hers, and the witnesses'. Nobody spared Christ's life, so I don't see what's so special about Rahn's."

That was an odd remark, considering Diane was a devout church skipper. Regardless of status, everyone's life had value. Christ didn't make distinctions. Shae was about to say as much but decided to leave her colleague's outlandish statements alone. Like Shae's sister Brecee, Diane didn't know how to bite her tongue. Neither did she put on a religious pretense in front of Shae.

Diane shrugged. "No disrespect. I'm just asking."

What was Rahn's purpose for which God had spared his life? Grace, of course, but what else? Shae didn't have the luxury of time to ponder someone else's purpose when her immediate need was to get her story ready for broadcast.

Shae had just refocused on proofing her script when Diane turned up the volume on her television. "Get over here and listen to his interview."

Honestly, Shae didn't want to, but she was nosy by nature. Her profession ruled out.

"He is one fine-looking brother." Diane nearly drooled. "Makes me want a bowl of chocolate pretzels."

"Snack food?"

"I'm hungry. Everybody looks like food to me right about now. Remember, my shift began at four, when you probably were rolling over in bed." Diane sighed. "Anyway, he's a catch."

"Welcome to *Sports Break*," Greg began. "Our segment today has nothing to do with the upcoming spring training, rumors of trades, or an early prediction of who will be in the pennant race. My guest is the reigning three-time MVP for the National League of Major League Baseball. Outfielder Rahn Maxwell is making headlines this morning, not because he saved a play, but because the sport saved his life."

A robotic camera turned to Rahn as Greg addressed him. "First, we're glad you're okay."

Linking his hands together, Rahn nodded.

Good-looking! Shae had yet to see a black man with a thin, trimmed beard who didn't turn heads. Yep, she'd give him a high score for looks, but one woman's dream was another woman's nightmare. Never again would she be sucked into that starring role.

"So, how did you become a victim of an attempted carjacking?"

He seemed to tense at the term. "It happened so fast. One moment, I'm on my way home after a function downtown, driving west on Highway Forty."

"About what time was this?"

"I'd say after midnight early Sunday morning. I didn't think anything was suspicious when I saw the detour sign, so I exited. It was dark. The next thing I knew, headlights sped toward me from behind. I had the strangest feeling something wasn't right. Why would another motorist race off the highway, not knowing what direction the detour would take him? Then the car blocked me in."

Greg listened intently, wearing a concerned expression. Shae always thought he was a great interviewer, causing his guests to forget about the cameras.

"I consider myself just as fearless as the next man, but I'd be lying if I said I wasn't scared. I anticipated the headlines would announce my death. At that moment, I realized that I was no longer in control of my destiny," Rahn admitted, for the whole world to hear.

"Unbelievable." Greg shook his head. "We checked with the police before the show. They said the detour sign was bogus. It's the latest crime fad popping up in cities across the country."

"So I was played. Great." Rahn looked disgusted with himself. "I guess that's why I didn't see any detour signs at the exit on my drive here. Anyway, I'm convinced that if it had not been for me playing professional baseball, and their respect for the sport, things would have turned out differently."

"Respect for the sport, but not life?" Greg's mouth twitched. "Did you give them the autographs they demanded?"

"I didn't wait for them to ask me twice. It was ransom for my life," he stated without shame. "I feel like God was using that as a way for me to escape harm, so I didn't hesitate."

Greg threw a few baseball questions into the mix before returning to the hot topic, and Rahn seemed grateful for the breather. "I hope the police catch those guys. You were lucky, man."

"No, I was blessed. I'm here today because there is a God who spared me and caused them to be distracted. I'll never forget this act of mercy for the rest of my life."

Shae had been about to tune out the remainder of the interview, but his confession caused her to remain glued to the monitor.

His acknowledgment of his fear stunned Shae. Humility was hard to find, especially among prosperous public figures, and his vulnerability spoke volumes to her heart. She'd felt a similar sense of helplessness when her fellow church members had made her feel ashamed of her relationship with Alex, even though she'd been clueless about his marital status.

Not only was Rahn good-looking, buffed, and strong; he appeared fearless, even though he'd acknowledged his fear. And he'd thanked God. That earned him a star in her book. His uncanny ability to recall the features of his would-be carjackers, under such stressful circumstances, was noted. Shae prayed he had given the police a detailed enough description for them to find the men before someone who didn't have a recognizable face or name got hurt or killed.

"Shae? Shae?"

"Huh?" Shae blinked at the sound of Diane's voice. She glanced at the screen. Rahn's interview had ended, and the producer was rolling the show credits.

"Girl, you're being paged. You better head back to the editing booth before your photographer comes looking for you."

"Right." Shae gathered her notes, leaped from her chair, and hurried down the hall as fast as her three-inch boots could move.

3

After Greg had made his closing remarks, ending the segment, and the director had cleared them, the tech reappeared and unclipped Rahn's microphone. They stepped down, and Greg asked Rahn a few more questions off camera as both men retraced their steps through the newsroom to the lobby.

Although they were engaged in a discussion, a woman who was heading their way caught Rahn's attention. As they drew closer, Rahn made fleeting eye contact with the most beautiful lady he had ever seen. He was a sucker for a baby-doll face with delicate features—she had both.

"Hey, Shae," Greg greeted her in passing.

"Hi, Greg." She smiled, then directed her attention to Rahn. "I'm so glad you're safe."

"Me, too."

Her soft, simple words were filled with sweetness and sincerity. But were they just a prelude to the jokes that were sure to pop up on late-night TV? No doubt many women would see his admission of fear as a weakness.

In the lobby, Greg shook his hand. "Thanks again for giving KMMD the exclusive. I owe you, man."

Talk about a distraction. Now Rahn couldn't get the image of Shae out of his memory. He didn't know what triggered this emotion—the moment frozen in time or her whispered words—but he felt something. "Who is Shae?"

Greg snickered, seemingly amused by his inquiry. "I guess you don't watch our news. Shae Carmen's been here a few months. She's is our newest reporter and weekend anchor—"

"I can get that from the station's Web site." Rahn reined in his frustration and lowered his voice. "Is she single, married, divorced, or seeing someone?"

"How should I know?" Greg shrugged. "Shae is cordial. She comes in and does her job—she's a great reporter, just an all-around nice person. By the way, I hope you received your invitation to my wedding."

Rahn took the hint that Greg had no more to say on the topic. *Fine.* He would take it from there. He shook the man's hand and bid him good-bye. Finding out more about Shae would give him something to focus on besides the instant replays of his carefree life that had almost been snatched away.

⌒

For some reason, Rahn Maxwell's confession that he'd been scared seemed to linger in Shae's spirit for hours after hearing it—during her entire shift, actually—and she couldn't figure out why. The man was human, after all, and anyone on the brink of death would be afraid. That ambush had changed him and altered his outlook on life. She could not only identify with that; she'd sensed it during his interview, which she'd almost missed.

It was after eleven that night when Shae arrived at the Westmoreland Condominiums, where she lived. The entrance was the size of a hotel lobby, with a lounge area that featured a showcase fireplace. Cozy tables and chairs were sporadically placed in front of a large window facing Forest Park. A side hall led to an adjacent restaurant, Turvey's on the Green, a sports bar known for live broadcasts and weekly jazz nights.

She waved at Mr. Chapman, who saluted her with a smile. The retired factory worker turned night security guard had adopted Shae as his daughter because she lived away from family.

"It's a shame about Rahn Maxwell. I watched the interview on your station."

"God spared his life."

"Yep, He did." Mr. Chapman nodded, then returned to a late-night talk show on TV as Shae walked toward the elevators.

On the fourteenth floor, Shae strolled down the hall to her condo. Inside, she flipped on the switch to illuminate her living room, making a conscious effort to switch *off* all thoughts of Rahn Maxwell. His interview had consumed enough of her time for one day, and she still felt the unexplained connection with him.

Shae performed her nightly beauty regimen, showered, and got into bed, Bible in hand. She frowned as she read that familiar passage in 1 Peter—chapter 3, verse 7—that didn't apply to her, since she wasn't a wife. She moved on to verse 8—*"Finally, be ye all of one mind, having compassion one of another, love as brethren, be pitiful, be courteous"*—and let that settle into her spirit before she drifted off to sleep.

A few days later, Shae found a small envelope, the size used for invites or thank-you notes, in her stack of mail at the TV station. The return address was from the elite suburb of Wildwood, Missouri. She didn't know anyone in faraway

West St. Louis County. Her small circle of new friends was limited to the station and church.

It was a good thing Diane Duncan wasn't around. With her suspicious mind and paranoid ways, Shae's fellow reporter would have strongly urged her to take the letter to the police to have it X-rayed or dusted for fingerprints. Shae undid the flap and slid out a small folded card. Confused, she squinted, admiring the artist's depiction of a woman resting her chin in her hand. She wore a dreamy expression, and she looked familiar.

Then she read the message:

Shae,

You make a man—me—glad that he's alive. Your smile and soft words were like a homecoming to my soul, which I prefer to my family and friends mourning my demise at a homegoing church service. I closed my eyes, and I saw your beautiful face. I sketched you from memory. I know I didn't do you justice.

Rahn

His passionate words knocked the wind out of her. She sucked in a breath, trying to recalibrate her racing heart. Shae blinked at the sketch again. He had captured her features: the pointy chin, the sculpted eyebrows, even the mole under her left eyebrow. How? Their contact had been nothing more than the blink of an eye.

He'd listed his home and cell numbers, in case she wanted to call him—which she didn't. Compliments were commonplace to people in the media. There was no reason for her to take this one personally, Shae thought, as she fed his note to the newsroom shredder.

4

*R*ahn couldn't believe it. His interview with Greg Saxon had gone viral, and it seemed as if everybody and his momma was reaching out to check up on him. Along with teammates and colleagues calling and texting, CNN, Fox Sports, ESPN, and NBC hounded him with media requests to rehash the same thing he'd told Greg.

"Why didn't Shae call?" Rahn questioned his close friend Marcus Evans, one of the starting pitchers for the Cardinals. Both had come from the Cardinals' Triple-A farm team, the Memphis Redbirds, the same year. Their personalities meshed, despite varying opinions on lifestyle choices. Although both men had gyms at home, they occasionally worked out together at the country club.

And why am I sulking about it? He kept that question to himself. "I'm telling you, man, in the briefest of seconds, we connected—at least, I thought we did. It was different—no lust on my part; no fan worship in her eyes, only genuine concern. When I got home, I couldn't get her out of my head." Rahn would have rubbed his face as a demonstration, but the weights in his hands were a deterrent.

After double-checking the room for privacy, Rahn lowered his voice and added, "I couldn't help myself from sketching what I saw to keep her doll face from fading in my memory."

Marcus added more weights to his barbell. "Yeah, and that blows me away. I've seen you do that only a couple of times in the eight years I've known you. That might be flattering if she knew you, but she probably thinks you're a stalker. Did you really give her all your contact numbers? That sounds like a scary, lonely person."

Rahn could see his point—sending Shae the sketch did seem a little excessive—but he blamed his irrational actions on her powerful allure.

"Now you're handling her rejection worse than the shattered invincible sports figure persona you built for yourself following the crime," Marcus said, going in for the kill.

"I wouldn't call it 'rejection,'" Rahn snapped harshly, mainly out of frustration. "Sorry...there's nothing I can do about the gunmen, but with Shae—" He paused and nodded to several newcomers in the weight room. "With her, one phone call, and things could happen. I almost feel like she's part of my life change."

"Something *did* happen to change your life—a gun and a prayer. If that wasn't life-altering enough, then I don't know what is. You admitted in that interview that God saved you that night. You owe Him big time. Don't let some woman distract you from fulfilling your debt to the Lord. You've dated enough of the wrong women to last years."

Rahn cut his eyes at his friend. "I know my social life hasn't been stellar, but I'm single, unlike you." Ever since marrying Yvette, his friend had worn the badge of husband proudly. Marcus was the model family man, especially now that he and Yvette had children.

While Rahn was happy for his friend, his status was his choice until he found the right woman. He was still holding out for that special someone and thought perhaps, just perhaps, Shae Carmen could be a candidate. But he wouldn't know that for sure unless they connected.

Marcus paused in his routine and faced Rahn. "Listen, I'm glad you're alive. All I'm saying is, don't forget about your brush with death."

That remark hit a nerve. "You better believe just because I don't want to talk about it twenty-four-seven doesn't mean I've forgotten. It's on my mind every time I drive down that interstate or see a detour sign anywhere." Resting his weighs, Rahn patted his chest. "I remember, so, for me to think about something pleasant, like a woman, doesn't mean my mind is in the gutter. There's just something about Shae that resonated with me."

Marcus backed down, holding up his hands in surrender. "I stand corrected. But you're like a brother. You know I've got your back, and I have no problem calling you out."

Rahn smirked. "True."

"I've seen Shae Carmen on TV a few times, and no question she's a beautiful woman. Whether she would be good for you or not, I don't know. My advice is, don't chase too hard." He laughed, breaking the tension.

"I won't." Rahn grunted.

They finished their workout and then hit the showers.

The next night, Rahn had just returned home and strolled into his master suite when his phone rang. He glanced at the caller ID—his mother again. Her constant checking up on him since the incident bordered on obsession. The combination of morning wakeup calls and nightly curfew checks, with random chats throughout the day, was driving him crazy. "Hi, Mom."

Eloise Maxwell looked for any excuse to call. After his father, Baseball Hall of Famer Ronald Maxwell, died of a massive heart attack seven years ago, his mother's mission in life had been to keep her two children, both adults, within reach—if not literally, then virtually, via the phone. As her only son, Rahn indulged her.

Years ago, his mother hadn't had any qualms about suggesting he and his older sister build a home on the sprawling family property. Rahn's answer had been a flat-out no. That would have been too close for comfort, not to mention how it would have hampered the lifestyle he enjoyed.

Thankfully, his mother seemed content that his older sister, Phyllis, her husband, and their twin sons had remained in Richmond.

"I was watching the local news this morning, and there was a shooting in the city." She gave him a play-by-play of the crime. "That's why I thank the Lord for sparing the life of my favorite son!"

Stifling a sigh, Rahn held his peace. He had grown accustomed to being called her "favorite son"—even though he was the only one—since he was a teenager. But he would give anything to erase that night from his memory.

He glanced out the French doors to the balcony off of his bedroom. The moon buffed the night sky, and his mind drifted to visions of Shae. Instead of stars twinkling at him, it was her mesmerizing brown eyes. What would it take to see her again and maybe enjoy a candlelit dinner?

"This is your testimony," his mother said, in a loving way just shy of a childhood scolding from the five-feet-something spitfire. His six-three stature didn't intimidate her. "You should never get tired of thanking God."

"And I don't," he said, walking away from the window. He picked up the remote, aiming it at the flat-screen TV in the adjacent sitting room.

"It's not too early to think about finding a wife and having children—"

"And how would that have prevented the attempted carjacking?" Rahn was amused that whatever problem was at hand, a wife and children were always her solution. After kicking off his shoes and peeling off his socks, Rahn flopped in his recliner. With little effort, he became engrossed in the NBA game: the San Antonio Spurs versus the Indiana Pacers.

"You would have been at a different place, maybe at home with your family. When it comes to God, our name has no value. Being Rahn Maxwell didn't save you from death, Son. God did. Don't let it be in vain. Have you gone to church since last week?"

Rahn closed his eyes. He had already committed to making a lifestyle change. Wasn't that enough? What did everyone expect of him—to stop living? He measured his words carefully. "I am praying more, Mom. Do you want me to park in front of the first church I come across, walk inside, and join?"

"Watch it," she warned. "Not every building that calls itself a church is a Bible-preaching, salvation-teaching center. Some are self-serving, having the appearance of godliness on the exterior only."

So, his philosophy was, why bother, since Sunday services were a programmable routine—in and out? His Bible, shelved in his home library, was more a showpiece, part of the décor. It didn't seem right for a household not to have one. However, the few times he'd picked it up, he'd felt no connection. Actually, he was surprised he'd heard God's voice the night of the carjacking attempt.

Half listening to his mother, Rahn turned up the volume of the game. Noticing both teams were playing hard, he stood. Although it was high-def, he would rather watch it on the 62-inch TV in his home theater. He padded down the marble spiral stairway to the first floor. Despite Rahn's wealth and fame, the solitary life he lived, in an effort to safeguard his privacy, was losing its appeal.

"Don't you think it's time for you to learn the difference between lust and love?" His mother *tsk*ed, transitioning with such finesse from the topic of church to women that she caught him off guard. "They're secondhand hoochie mamas that are available at bargain prices."

It was ironic how his mother and Marcus wanted the same things for him, but not in the same order. A family was his mother's priority; his friend felt God should be first. When his phone beeped, Rahn checked the caller ID. "Mom, Marcus is calling. I'll talk to you later."

"Tell that young man I said hello."

"Love you," Rahn said, then answered the other line. "Your timing is perfect, man. I was getting an earful from Eloise Maxwell. She basically told me to stop shopping at rummage sales for women."

"Ouch." Marcus hooted uncontrollably. Rahn wasn't amused.

Marcus tried to compose himself, only to start up another laughing binge. Finally gaining some control, he stuttered, "I'll add an amen to that one. You've got to love Mrs. Maxwell."

"Figures you would agree with her," Rahn said dryly.

"Great minds think alike. Since you're changing your ways, I'm calling to invite you to a gospel concert tomorrow night. Proceeds go to fund college scholarships. Yvette and I purchased twenty tickets to give away. Want to go?"

Rahn had committed to making changes, and he'd figured praying more and watching the slip of his tongue was a good start. But a gospel concert? That wasn't his choice of entertainment. "I hope I'll have other plans tomorrow night, after I call the station and ask Shae out to dinner."

"I see you're not going to drop that bone," Marcus conceded. "Then *bon appétit*, I guess."

"Yes, and get your praise on."

Rahn didn't waste time to follow through. Once they disconnected, he called the station. Just his luck, Thursdays and Fridays were Shae's days off. From habit, he was about to curse out his frustration but caught himself just in time. "God, I said I was going to change, but it's slow going."

What did she do on her days off, and with whom? Rahn pushed redial to KMMD-TV.

"Sports," Greg Saxon answered, once Rahn was transferred.

After the preliminaries, Rahn got to the point of his call. "Invite me back for a follow-up interview." It wasn't a request.

Greg's deafening laughter pierced his ear.

"What's so funny?"

"That's a first—an athlete demanding to talk to the media. We can get updates from the police. That's old news," Greg said nonchalantly.

Excuse me? "The threat on my life is now old news? It wasn't *that* long ago." Rahn felt disrespected. He needed that pity party to last a little longer. "Listen, man, I'd really like to see Shae again—"

"So, that's what this is about. You can see her on Saturday and Sunday at five and ten, then Monday through Wednesday, six and ten."

As if Rahn didn't know her newscast schedule. Since the day he'd first seen her, he had become a loyal viewer—not for the news but for the newswoman. Shae had already mesmerized him on Saturdays, then again on Sundays, especially at the end of her newscast, when she pulled out a hat like the ones his mother wore to church.

Shae's headpiece had sparked a lighthearted banter among her coanchors, but God help him if Shae didn't seduce him with her smile every time. The close-ups on his high-def television made him want to reach out and touch her, and Rahn had—at least, he'd placed his hand on the screen, as if it was a point of contact. Now who was the groupie?

5

As the newest media personality in St. Louis, Shae was expected to make appearances at local events. The station's strategy was simple: more visibility in the community might convince more viewers to switch to KMMD-TV for their weekend news.

This time, Shae waited backstage behind the thick velvet curtains at the majestic Fabulous Fox Theatre, smiling to muffle her screams of excitement at coming face-to-face with the night's main attraction. Tall and handsome Boris Hawkins engulfed her in a big hug. Stepping out of his embrace, Shae scrutinized the childhood friend she'd had a crush on throughout most of her teenage years. He was still fine, with his hazel eyes and dimpled smile. Last she'd heard, he had married. Hopefully, they were still together.

Boris gave her a slow appraisal. "You are looking hot, girl."

Shae blushed under his compliment, knowing there had been a few adjustments in her appearance since the last time he'd seen her. The Carmen sisters were a standout with their long hair, courtesy of their African and Italian heritages. Shae's mother always said it was a woman's glory.

Well, her glory had dimmed after the affair she didn't know she was having with a man she didn't know was married. Her hair length wasn't teasing her waist, as before, but at least it would spill over her shoulders again once she removed the weave. Plus, she was no longer a size seven.

That had been a long time ago. She had accepted her size ten with grace, but she freaked out when she had to slip into a size twelve garment like the red dress she was wearing that evening. Despite the size, Shae had liked the way she looked when she checked herself in the mirror before leaving her condo.

"Stop it," she teased, playfully punching Boris in the arm. Elated about seeing him, Shae couldn't think of a better way to spend her Friday night than at a gospel concert, and one that honored the memory of Dr. Martin Luther King Jr.

"Good evening, ladies and gentlemen." The event's organizer, Jodie Thomas, greeted the crowd, cutting into Shae and Boris's impromptu reunion. "Thanks for joining us tonight for the benefit concert."

"I wish we could catch up later, but I'm flying back home tonight," Boris told Shae. "Monica is pregnant with our first child." He puffed out his chest and grinned.

"Oh, congratulations." *Maybe someday, God will have a man who'll love me like that*, she thought.

"Please welcome our mistress of ceremonies for the evening, KMMD-TV's news reporter and weekend anchor Miss Shae Carmen, also dubbed 'The Hat Lady,'" Jodie said by way of introduction.

Shae gave Boris a quick hug before dashing off. As she glided across the stage to an enthusiastic applause, she could feel the excitement in the air. From the moment she entered the historic theatre, she experienced a taste of the nostalgia of an era long before she was born. The gold trim, marble pillars, winding stairs, plush carpet, and velvet upholstery spoke volumes of the caliber of its original patrons' pocketbooks. She briefly wondered at the entertainers who had wowed audiences in the theatre's heyday.

She stepped to the podium and smiled. "Good evening. It's an honor for me to be part of this festive occasion tonight. Shall we all stand to begin with a prayer"—she paused and glanced down at the program—"by Elder Ellis, followed by the congregational singing of the Black National Anthem, 'Lift Ev'ry Voice and Sing'?"

The minister gave an emotional prayer for tolerance and unity, which inspired the audience to sing the anthem with vigor. Afterward, Shae returned to the microphone, eager to introduce her friend. "Some of you may not be aware that I'm originally from Philly, so I know this group personally, and they can jam for the Lord. So, as they say, let's get this party started! Please welcome Boris, Brian, and Blythe Hawkins."

The brothers entered from the other side of the stage. Shae twirled around, preparing to retreat backstage, when, like lightning, Boris snuck up behind her.

"Oh no, you don't." He tugged her to the center with him. "Hey, St. Louis. It's true we go way back with Shae and her sisters, who were once considered Philly's musical prodigies. Don't let her broadcast voice fool you; this sister can croon, too."

"What are you doing?" she hissed, trying as gracefully as she could to loosen Boris' firm but gentle hold.

Coming from a family of musicians, she and her sisters had earned a reputation for their talents, locally and in several surrounding cities. Growing up, they tried to mimic the Jackson 5, the Winans, Sister Sledge, the Clark Sisters, the Newell Sisters, and other family singing groups. Stacy would command the keyboards, while Shari manipulated the high notes on the alto sax. Shae's role model had been Sheila E. as she'd perfected her craft on the drums. Brecee was out of control with her Chuck Berry antics on the guitar. But musical prodigies? She didn't think so.

"Do you want to hear her sing?" Boris coaxed the audience, ignoring her pleas to bow out.

The noise was thunderous until finally Shae conceded, but not without pointing a finger at Boris as she would a naughty child. "One song."

He laughed and then whispered his selection: "He'll Make a Way."

It felt good to use the gift God had given her as she hit the high notes. Boris and his brothers captivated the audience with their baritone melody, which blended with hers as if they were her backup singers.

The crowd remained on their feet, clapping and praising God, as Shae and Boris engaged in a "battle of the voices" duet. When the song ended, Boris linked his fingers through Shae's and urged her to take a bow, then stepped back for her to receive all the applause.

"Thank you." Shae smiled and waved. Boris rewarded her with another hug before she left the limelight, blowing kisses at band members she recognized.

As she approached the stage door, one of the photographers lowered his camera. It was Kevin, from work. Wherever a KMMD media personality was in the community, the station sent a photographer to shoot a few minutes of B-roll to air for its viewers as proof. "You're definitely in the wrong business." He gave her a thumbs-up.

Left alone in the shadows of the stage, Shae reflected on the memories of her childhood. She couldn't help but miss the countless times she and her sisters had performed at churches and family gatherings. Despite living separate lives and working in challenging careers, whenever they got together under one roof, they still jammed out a few songs with their instruments if they brought them along.

The piano in Shae's condo was a reminder of home, forcing her to fight back a bout of homesickness. Stacy was the true pianist. When Shae wasn't dabbling with the keyboard, she programmed a list of music just to watch the keys move as the songs played.

As the Hawkins brothers wowed the audience, it dawned on Shae that she hadn't sung "He'll Make a Way" since her disastrous breakup with Alex. But that was all right. That song had been a breakthrough. The past was gone, and she had to look to the future. Shae was no longer angry and mistrusting when it came to men. That didn't mean she was ready to date, only that bitterness no longer consumed her.

Overcomers inherit all things, God whispered His Word from Revelation 21:7.

Rahn boarded a plane to Virginia for a long weekend at home. His mother had been ecstatic when he'd called to tell her his plans. During the flight, he pondered what twist of fate might cause him to cross paths with Shae again. He prayed for another act of God, albeit one less threatening than a carjacking.

While he was enjoying an evening with his mother, sister, and nephews, Marcus texted him with a different twist of fate:

Getting praise on @ gospel concert. Guess who was the MC? Shae Carmen. Guess who can sing? Shae Carmen. Sorry u missed it. Hope u had a GREAT evening. LOL

6

Shae was an instant sensation when she walked into the newsroom the next day. Her producer, Terri Lane, folded her arms and tapped the toe of her shoe. "Hm. After watching the video of you at the gospel concert last night, I'm not sure if we should have you belt out a solo or stick with the hats at the end of the newscasts on Sundays. Maybe we should do both."

The scatterbrained expression on Terri's face indicated she was serious. The woman was known for taking risks if it would mean higher ratings than the competition. Shae doubted management would go that far, but stranger things had happened in the newsroom.

A bouquet of flowers rich in color seemed to lure her to her desk. "Wow." They were beautiful.

Diane snickered. "I'd say you were a real big hit."

Shae reached for the card. She flipped over the envelope and read aloud, "'Will you marry me? We can start with dinner. Raphael.' The man listed his cell number." She was flabbergasted at the fake proposition. "Do I have 'desperate' stamped on my forehead or something?"

"Nope." Diane shook her head. "But it is your first proposal since you've been here. Humph. A background check may prove he's a sexual predator." She rocked in her chair. "Don't get caught up in all the hype. I've been proposed to four times. I said yes twice, got married once, and got divorced a year later. I should've married the one I dismissed."

Talk about stats; it appeared her colleague had them. Diane had the personality and looks to get any man's attention. More than once, she used her assets to her advantage to make a person tell her everything she wanted to know. But romantic entanglements were definitely not her forte.

Shae laughed and scooted the floral arrangement to the side. "I won't, don't worry. He's forgotten already."

"Oh, and don't forget the Emmys deadline. KMMD loves awards banquets. You never know what story you've reported that will win."

"Okay."

A few hours later, Shae was in the middle of following up on leads about corner stores that were a cover-up for meth labs when she received another delivery from the florist. The multicolored blossoms reminded her of a rainbow. "I've never seen anything like this," she said in awe.

Diane stopped what she was doing and waited for the scoop. "Me, neither, so hurry up and see who sent them. I've got somewhere to be."

"Really?" Shae lifted a brow and waved the sealed envelope in her hand. "Then I guess this can wait until you get back."

Diane huffed and folded her arms.

"All right." To put her colleague out of her misery, Shae pulled the card out of the unsealed envelope and read silently. "Bummer, no marriage proposal." She tried to keep a straight face as she feigned disappointment. "It's only an invitation to a private three-day cruise."

"Now that would be hard to pass up." Diane gathered her things. She was almost out the door when she backtracked. "Scratch that. The dude probably doesn't have any money. He's looking for a sugar mama. See ya."

Reclining in her chair, Shae laughed at Diane's assessment. Moments later, her smartphone chirped twice, alerting Shae that her eldest sister had sent a text.

Thinking about my sisters. "And we know that all things work together…" Romans 8:28. Love, Stacy

It was a group text to her, Shari, and Brecee. Shae missed them terribly.

While some siblings grew apart as they neared adulthood, the Carmen sisters' bond had only strengthened, through thick and thin. They were there for each other, night or day. As long as there was United or Southwest Airlines, distance wasn't an issue.

Shae texted her back, **I believe that! Amen.**

Less than an hour later, Shae was interrupted again by yet another flower delivery. She was beyond annoyed, but she didn't take it out on the bearer of gifts. She thanked the guard for bringing the flowers to her desk. They were mixed with an abundance of greenery and could definitely be considered more a plant than a bouquet. Once he left, Shae frowned as she snatched the envelope.

It seems like I missed my blessing, in more ways than one, by skipping the gospel concert. I really would like to see you again. Please call me.

Rahn Maxwell

He'd listed his numbers again.

Her annoyance dissipated. The man had no gimmicks, no ridiculous proposal to a stranger, no bogus invitation to a suspicious dinner aboard a yacht. She stared at his phone numbers, actually debating. Should she or shouldn't she?

Granted, she was a recovering man-hater and didn't know what it would take to convince her to go on a date again. But there was something tempting about Rahn Maxwell, aside from his addictive looks and celebrity status.

Shae gnawed on her bottom lip as she fumbled with the card. Until she could figure out what it was about Rahn that drew him to her, she would play it safe. But, while she tossed his note in the trash with the others, she did give his bouquet preferential treatment on her desk, sending the other two to the lobby.

Shae survived the rest of the work week with no further deliveries. All she could think about was her days off, which began after her shift. She was unaware someone was standing at her desk until he cleared his throat. Startled, she looked up.

"I need a favor—a personal one." Greg Saxon from the sports department stood over her shoulder, looking frazzled.

"O-okay." Shae crossed her arms, waiting expectantly for him to continue. Outside of work, they really didn't know each other. Plus, the man was about to get married. What could he possibly want from her, and on a personal note, at that?

"My wedding is Saturday, and my soloist has been hospitalized with the flu. Is there any chance you could fill in? It's just one song, 'The Lord's Prayer.'"

Caught off guard, Shae opened her mouth, but nothing came out. "Uh, I work on Saturdays, remember? I'm sorry, Greg." Assuming that was the end of the conversation, she stood, preparing to check the board to see which story had been assigned to her.

"Wait." He pressed his hands together as if in prayer. "The wedding starts at two. If you leave right after you sing, you won't be late for work. I realize we haven't known each other that long, and I wouldn't have asked, but watching you on that video…"

The mastermind had it all figured out, did he? Shae decided to try reasoning with him. "What about someone in the choir? Anyone can sing 'The Lord's Prayer.' Besides, people are coming to witness you exchange vows. They won't care if the soloist is a little off-key." She hated to come out and say no.

Greg took the liberty of swiping Diane's chair and scooting it closer, trapping Shae at her desk. "My fiancée's friend sings like a songbird that stirs the soul, but my babe cried when she watched the clip of you singing. Not everyone has your gift. Please." He glanced around the newsroom, then looked at her again. "Listen, so many things have gone wrong with our wedding plans, and now this. I was hoping to lessen the burden by asking you."

Her colleague was laying on the guilt. Yes, Shae had heard horror stories about wedding day fiascos, and if she ever got married, she hoped not to experience one.

Stacy's text came to mind, and with it, Romans 8:28: *"All things work together for good to them that love God, to them who are the called according to his purpose."*

Was this part of God's purpose? Shae sighed. She really didn't have any plans for Saturday. And how would she get blessed if she didn't bless others? "All right," she finally conceded. "But I'm going to be in and out."

Greg exhaled as if he had been holding his breath for hours. "You just made our day."

Suddenly the Lord whispered Proverbs 18:24: *"A man that hath friends must show himself friendly."*

"Amen." Shae smiled as she watched her coworker walk away looking 100 percent relieved. Greg loved his fiancée; Boris loved his wife. Surely, there was a man out there who would love her unconditionally. Surely, someday, she would be the bride, not the wedding singer.

7

I hope you're planning to be at my wedding tomorrow." Greg Saxon's tone was almost taunting when Rahn picked up his home phone.

In all honesty, Rahn wasn't planning to attend. A generic congratulatory card, signed with his apologies and some money inserted, usually made up for his absence at those events. Why was Greg following up on RSVPs when he should be enjoying his bachelor party? "Actually, I have other—"

"I should've called you yesterday," Greg cut in. "I was in a jam, and to make a long story short, Shae is standing in for the soloist. It was a last-minute switch. I know you wanted another chance to meet her, so here it is. I suggest you take it."

Rahn was stunned by the breaking news, and his longing to see Shae again resuscitated. "I can make that." He could go car shopping with Marcus anytime. His friend already had a Jag. Now, where had he put the invitation? "Uh, you mind telling me the time and place again?"

Greg gave him the information, then said, "You can thank the flu bug for your good fortune."

"What?"

"Never mind. Janet is expecting her future husband to operate at one hundred percent, so I need my rest. Now we're even," Greg said before ending their call.

Rahn was so hyped that he barely got any rest after talking with Greg. He had another shot at convincing Shae to go on one date with him, and he couldn't blow it.

On Saturday afternoon, Rahn left his house, dressed to perfection from his tie to his socks. The blue suit was custom-fit, as was most of his wardrobe. A visit to the barber earlier that day had gotten him a precision trim on his mustache and beard, as well as the haircut he desired.

Rahn arrived at Rapture Ready Fellowship in record time. His determination to get to the church struck him as very ironic. Granted, his main motivation was a woman, but he figured he could receive a spiritual blessing, too.

Rahn stepped from his Audi with confidence, despite his doubts that everything would work in his favor. *Jesus, I know this is not the kind of prayer You're used to hearing, but I could really use Your help in this. Amen.* Taking a deep breath, he strolled to the entrance, nodding at other guests going in the same direction. He kept his sunglasses on, hoping to conceal his identity.

He opened the door for a few female attendees, ignoring their flirtatious smiles. His mind was set on one smile, and it wasn't theirs.

Once he entered the building, Rahn removed his shades. The church lobby boasted gleaming marble floors, with thick oak molding accenting the white walls. The artwork on several arched stained-glass windows was impressive. His heart pounded with excitement.

A young man approached him. He appeared to be in his late teens but had a thick beard like a grown man's. Wearing a tux, he was probably one of the ushers. "Did anybody ever tell you that you look just like the Cardinals outfielder Rahn Maxwell?"

"Every day." Rahn chuckled. "That's what my mother named me."

Tongue-tied, the usher pumped his hand. "Wow. Wait until I tell the others."

"Mind if I get comfortable first?" Rahn asked.

"Oh, yeah. Sorry." With a sheepish smile, the young man cleared his throat, straightened his stance, and fell back into his assigned role. "Please follow me." He clicked his heels, then spun around and led the way into the sanctuary.

The first thing that came to Rahn's mind was a winter wonderland with the abundance of white tulle decorating the end of each pew, as well as the altar at the front. It wasn't a large church, and the snug feel added intimacy. Yet Rahn shivered from the surreal sense of God's presence. The overwhelming feeling was a peace he hadn't experienced in a long time. Rahn wanted to cling to that emotion. *I need to belong to somebody's congregation.*

"What is your seating preference, Mr. Maxwell?" the usher asked.

Rahn blinked back to reality. "The bride's side."

He pulled out an envelope marked "Bride and Groom" from his inside breast pocket and handed it to the usher, thanking him for his assistance. As he took his seat, he overheard his name being whispered. In the past, the attention would have stroked his ego. But ever since the carjacking attempt, Rahn no longer had an ego—the Lord made sure of that. While some fans praised God he was alive, others tweeted or posted on Facebook that he'd used his name and fame to buy himself out of harm's way.

Money couldn't buy life. The rich and famous couldn't bribe death. If so, his father would still be alive. Rahn knew about privilege—he'd been born into it. The Maxwell name opened doors. But along with privilege came pressure. Rahn always found himself chasing after his father's record. The great power hitter had a .275

average and 300 home runs. During Ronald Maxwell's immaculate twelve-year career, he had clocked in 1,250 RBIs. Rahn wished he could say the same.

So, while it appeared he had been spared because of his family's name, Rahn knew it was God who had coaxed him out of danger and into safety. And nobody could convince him otherwise. Yet, to this day, the memory of Jesus' words in his ear was still sketchy, while the gunmen's threats were unforgettable. Being in church must have conjured up emotions he'd been trying to suppress.

He sat next to a bored-looking little girl who seemed more interested in her handheld video game than the nuptials about to take place. The child's mother smiled and murmured a greeting. It didn't matter if she knew his identity or not. Socializing was not the reason he'd come.

The minister entered the sanctuary and proceeded to the front. Behind him, Greg paraded in, his best man at his side. The groom's look of confidence outdid his tux. It might be a while before Rahn wore that look, unless Shae was the reason. None of his past relationships had made him remotely think of permanency.

The pianist struck the first chord, and Shae's voice preceded her appearance at the microphone stand close by. She was striking in her pastel outfit, and her hair was an attractive mass of curls. Even from a distance, she teased all of his senses. He couldn't take his eyes off of her. It was as if she had drugged him.

"She has such an angelic voice," the woman seated behind him whispered to her companion.

Rahn nodded in agreement, even though the comment hadn't been directed at him. Shae sang "The Lord's Prayer" as if it had been penned for her voice.

Long after Shae sang the final "Amen," the stirring music lingered in his ears. Draped in contentment, he watched as she stepped down from the podium. The next thing he knew, Shae was gathering her coat and heading for a side door. She was leaving already?

Soft instrumental music played as the mothers of the bride and groom started to process down the aisle. Glad he was on the end, Rahn exited the pew.

Rahn made a dash for the lobby, then froze, dumbfounded. There were several doors to the outside; Shae could have slipped out through any one of them. Huffing in frustration, Rahn looked one way and then the other.

That's when he got a glimpse of the bride, Janet Harris, and was temporarily distracted from his mission. Gone was her usual business persona. In her place stood a stunning woman with swept-up hair and a wedding dress that his mother would have approved as elegant. Beaming and beautiful, Janet waved at him.

He gave her a tender smile, inwardly chiding himself for forgetting that she was the reason he was there. Then his peripheral vision caught an image of a woman going in the opposite direction. *Shae.*

"Congrats," Rahn mouthed, then turned and hurried to intercept Shae before she could make a getaway.

At the door, Shae combed through her purse. There was no escaping him now. He admired how she stepped with the flair of a model on a runway. Whether it was intentional or not, he noticed. The dress showcased her shape and her nice legs, too. She was neither tall nor petite—a perfect fit, as far as he was concerned. His memory and his high-def plasma TV had done a poor job of capturing her beauty in the three weeks since he had seen her in person.

The intensity of his attraction grew with each step. He realized he hadn't taken a breath, so he exhaled. With keys in hand, she reached for the door, but Rahn was faster. She was the fly ball he had to catch. When she glanced up, her expressive brown eyes widened like a deer caught in the headlights. The element of surprise had definitely worked in his favor. "Hello, Shae."

Rahn Maxwell? Shae blinked. She had to remind herself to breathe as the larger-than-life man towered over her five-foot-seven frame. He was close enough for her to inhale his subtle cologne—nice. But where had he come from?

His black beard gleamed; his thick eyebrows dared her to touch, to see if they were as silky as they appeared. And his long eyelashes were a deal breaker. Why did they always look better on a man? Wow. How had she not remembered all of this?

She swallowed, but no words would come out of her mouth.

His gray pinstriped suit showcased the custom fit that restrained his muscles. There was no denying he was an athlete. If a man could be beautiful and handsome, he was the epitome of both. And his attraction shone brightly in his eyes.

Just then, she remembered the flowers, notes, and sketch he had sent her. She scolded herself for failing to respond.

She gave her head a mental shake and stepped back to break the magnetism. Maybe the wedding march playing in the background was sending a subliminal message, akin to Mother Stillwell's urgent promptings. Been there, done that. *A man is never so fine that his flaws should be overlooked,* she thought. And it seemed as if all men had faults—inside and outside the body of Christ.

"You never called." His voice was low and accusatory. "And I waited."

Despite his tough façade, he'd just shared another nugget of his vulnerability with her. It was usually the woman who waited. Shae bowed her head to gather her wits, then looked into his brown eyes. "I thought you were just being kind. In this business, I try not to take viewers' notes or flowers personally." She didn't say that his notes had started to wear down her resolve.

"Next time, Miss Carmen, please take my actions toward you very personally." There was no hint of teasing in his voice or on his face. "Why are you leaving so soon?"

"I have to get back to the station. I'm the weekend anchor."

Rahn chuckled and reached for her wrap. "I know. I've recently become a fan—a number one fan." When he held up the garment, Shae took that as a cue to turn around, so she could slide her arms into the sleeves.

Shae couldn't count the number of people who had claimed to be her number one fan. Yet, for some reason, the claim sounded different coming from him. A coworker exiting the restroom gave Shae the distraction she needed.

"One moment." She held up a finger, then waved to Sam to get his attention. Being a typical male, he acknowledged Rahn first, with a handshake.

"Excuse me," Shae interrupted. "Sam, if you're coming back to the station, would you mind bringing me a piece of wedding cake?"

He gave a nonchalant shrug. "I'll try to remember. No guarantee." Then he nodded to Rahn and headed back into the sanctuary.

Just like a man, Shae thought. Her coworker had probably forgotten her request already. She wanted that cake! As Brecee had said, sweets were her weakness, and wedding cake was near the top of her list.

"I'll be more than happy to bring you a slice," Rahn offered.

"Thanks, but I wouldn't want to trouble you. It was nice seeing you again. God bless you." She didn't want to address her avoidance of him. When she tried to move around him, Rahn pivoted and fell into step with her. It was comical, and she couldn't help but chuckle. "Where are you going?"

"I'm walking you to your car. Crime is up, you know."

"Yeah." She laughed. "That's what we report, but I'm on God's property, so I think I'm safe."

"Never can be too careful." He moved closer to her. "Consider me your bodyguard."

She could imagine him fending off criminals on her behalf. Even in that carjacking incident, he probably would have tried to protect her unto his death. That thought endeared him to her as he opened the door, and she breezed outside under his arm as if they were dance partners and Rahn was about to spin her around.

"Are you seeing anyone?" he asked.

Shae gulped. "I'm not available."

He seemed to shorten his strides to keep pace with her. "That wasn't my question."

This wasn't supposed to be happening. She had no intention of being lured into another relationship for years to come, maybe a lifetime; but the allure was tangible. When they reached her car, Shae faced him, ready to try to prune whatever was growing between them. "I'm sure you're a nice guy—"

"If that were the case, then you would give me an answer." His stare was so intense, Shae knew he wasn't going to back down. Nor could she dismiss him as easily as she had his notes.

Unfortunately, her heart and head weren't in sync. His scrutiny forced her to glance away. "I'm not in a position to find out how nice of a guy you are. I'm sorry."

When he appeared to have no comeback, Shae exhaled, feeling a mixture of relief that he had accepted her decision and disappointment that she had connected with his vulnerability. She unlocked her car, and Rahn opened the driver door for her. She smiled at him. "Thanks for being my bodyguard."

As she drove away, she found herself wishing again for a slice of wedding cake—her own. Like any single woman who believed in love, Shae wanted to be married, too. But she needed a little more time to sharpen her female instincts before she took another swim in the dating pool. The Lord knew she couldn't handle another decoy Christian.

8

*D*one. Shae unclipped her microphone from the neckline of her dress, stretched her arms, and stepped off the platform. It had been a long day, from serenading Greg Saxon's nuptials to anchoring the evening news.

Upon entering the newsroom, she spied several red metallic balloons, bearing the words "Thinking of You," bobbing in the air. They definitely hadn't been there before the newscast. Rounding the wall to her cubicle, Shae was surprised to see they were on her desk. She fingered the clear plastic box that anchored the balloons. It contained a chunk of chocolate cake with cream cheese frosting that was too much for one person, even for a cake lover such as herself.

Attached to the lid were a pink rose and a silver fork wrapped within a napkin. She loosened the card.

Shae,

Take this personally. I sensed your disappointment about wanting the cake, so I stepped up to the plate. Enjoy.

Rahn Maxwell

Her heart melted at his sweet gesture. Tears moistened her tired eyes, and she fanned herself to keep them at bay. It was a good thing she was alone in the newsroom. Her colleagues loved gossip, especially when it involved one of their own, but nobody stuck around after the Saturday night newscast. Shae sat down at her desk and removed the fork from the napkin. Then she bowed her head, said grace, and ceremoniously sampled her first bite. She closed her eyes, savoring the frosting.

You're making it hard for me to resist you, she thought as she slid another bite in her mouth.

"*Why try?*" she could hear Brecee say.

If only her baby sister wasn't working the overnight shift. Shae would love to call and discuss her conflicted feelings. Brecee would definitely argue that she should go for it.

Her office phone rang, interrupting her musings. She debated whether to answer or let it go to voice mail. It could be a viewer complaint, a compliment, or a hot tip. She was in no rush to get home, with no one waiting there, so she picked up. "Shae Carmen."

"Miss Carmen, you have a guest in the lobby," the overnight guard informed her.

Shae smiled. She didn't have to ask who it was. She suspected it was a tall, handsome male. "Thank you. I'll be right there."

❧

Under the watchful eyes of the security guard, Rahn paced the floor, waiting for Shae to appear. The guard had assured him Shae always left through this entrance when going home.

Shae's eyes were so expressive; Rahn wished he could have seen her reaction when she first saw the balloons. The more her pouty lips told him no, the more her brown eyes revealed she wasn't sure if she meant it. Her reservations and confusion were so raw that Rahn knew she wasn't playing games with him.

Finally, Shae emerged through the door. Her eyes weren't as bright as earlier—she looked tired—but it didn't detract from her beauty. Shae was just as pretty, and the evidence of her dining pleasure was in the way the corners of her mouth slanted up.

"Thank you for the cake," she whispered, meeting him halfway. "Did they serve chocolate at the wedding?"

Rahn took the liberty of wiping a dab of icing from her lip, and she blushed. He felt in tune with her, for some unexplainable reason.

"Busted. But I was told by the bakery that their cakes were just as good. I came to share, if you haven't devoured it already." Grinning, he pulled a fork out of his jacket pocket and waved it in front of her face like a fan.

She laughed, gifting him with the same engaging smile that infatuated him on camera, only it was electric in person. Jutting her chin out, Shae scrunched her cute nose. Did the woman know she was flirting with him? Rahn inhaled, taking in the scent of her perfume.

"You know I couldn't eat that whole thing on my own. Wait here while I get my things. We can sit and share it in the break room."

She returned several minutes later, trying to juggle her bag, the boxed cake, and the balloons. He came to her rescue, freeing her of the burdens, then followed her into a room that resembled a kitchenette/lounge/café, where he set everything on a table.

The ambiance of the break room didn't come close to the atmosphere he would have wanted for their first date, and he wasn't even a fan of sweets, but if that's what it took to woo her, he could manage.

While pulling out a chair for Shae, Rahn wondered what was going through her mind as she grabbed a plastic knife from a box on the counter and meticulously divided the slice in two. He covered her hand with his and helped her. The contact increased his heart rate. He glanced at Shae, but she didn't meet his eyes.

She forked off a piece of cake and stuffed it in her mouth, while Rahn sat back and folded his arms across his chest. He much preferred just watching her eat. "You said earlier that you're sure I'm a nice guy. What's wrong with nice guys?"

She kept her eyes averted, and for a moment, he didn't think she was going to answer. Finally, still focusing on the cake, she said, "I trusted someone when I shouldn't have—a nice guy, or so I thought. In hindsight, I believed I knew him—and myself—but I was wrong on both counts. It wouldn't be fair to jump back in and indirectly make someone else pay for the faults of another man."

Rahn's heart ached for her. His fist wanted to connect with the jaw of the jerk who'd misused her. But if Rahn wanted her—and he did—he had to be the better man. He had something to prove, and this time, he couldn't do it on the baseball field, where his talents were a given.

"I was reared in the church," Shae went on, "so all I know about relationships is the groundwork God has laid." Talking seemed to be her therapy as she chipped away at his side of the cake. "Plus, I don't date outside the body of Christ." She paused and gave him a pointed stare. "In your interview with Greg Saxon, you thanked God for sparing you. Has your commitment to God really changed since then?"

A pop quiz. Rahn was thoughtful about his response. Hoping she wouldn't protest, he took her free hand in his. "I'm not saying I've done everything right in my life, but I know God gave me a second chance with that carjacking." *And maybe with you, too.* "I'm confident I'm man enough to clean up another man's mess. Let me kiss and make it better—figuratively, until you say otherwise," he added quickly, seeing her raised eyebrow.

"He was a married man," she blurted out.

What? Rahn was shocked. Shae Carmen didn't come across as the type of woman who would compromise herself for any man, especially one who wasn't hers to begin with.

"But I didn't know it," she went on to explain. "I was humiliated in front of my whole congregation." She made a sweeping gesture with her arm.

"Ouch."

She nodded. "I was knocked off the pedestal I had created by my vanity, thinking I was 'all that' just because I was on TV. It was pure novice immaturity." Bowing her head, she seemed embarrassed. "I don't know why I'm telling you this."

"I'm hoping it's because you're willing to trust me. I don't have those types of skeletons in my closet that would hurt you," Rahn said, pleading his case. He leaned closer and lowered his voice to a whisper, even though they were alone, with no one to overhear. "Something connected between us the first time I saw you. I want to be an open book with you, Shae. I want to be the man who doesn't disappoint you."

She sniffed, then looked up. "Tell me about your relationship with God—the truth." Folding her arms, she sat attentively, like an expectant student.

Evidently his walk with God was really that important to her. "Fair question." He thought about the Scripture his mother had drilled into him and his sister whenever they'd gotten into trouble as children: *The truth shall make you free.* His truth was going to either win or lose his case with Shae. He took a deep breath. "I haven't always made the right decisions in my career and personal life. I'm sure God has a Rolodex of my wrongdoings, but the carjacking attempt was a wakeup call. Since then, I've been trying to read the Bible—but it's like empty pages with nothing to propel me, so I'm in limbo. I really want to feel I've made a change, but I guess, honestly, I don't."

She graced him with an unexpected smile, which was encouraging. "Salvation is a package of repentance, washing away your sins in Jesus' name, and receiving the Holy Ghost, which is an armor that the devil can't penetrate, and a spiritual strength to live a holy life."

He wanted her passion. "Show me this confidence you have in God. This is not a dare. Make a believer out of me, and I'll show you that God still has a few good men out there."

Shae narrowed her eyes pensively and glanced around the room, seeming to look in every direction but his. When she stood, so did Rahn, wondering if he had lost his case.

"I attend Bethesda Temple on Interstate Seventy," she finally said. "Service starts at ten thirty."

"I'll pick you up at ten."

"I'll meet you there," she countered.

"You don't have to drive in this relationship. Sit back and ride and let a real man show you how to pamper a woman." Rahn took her coat and gently helped guide her arms through the sleeves. "Nothing to say?" he whispered close to her ear, making her shiver.

"Bring your Bible and meet me in the lobby of the Westmoreland Condominiums on Union," she said with finality.

"I'll be there at nine fifty-eight."

"Make that fifty-six," she said, with a streak of mischief in her eyes.

"You just won't let go of that steering wheel, will you?" Rahn laughed. He was going to enjoy matching wits with the lovely Shae Carmen.

9

I've lost my mind," Shae uttered in disbelief. Perched on top of her velvet comforter, she stared at the remnants of her impromptu date with Rahn the previous night. Those helium balloons printed with "Thinking of You" were like neon signs flashing before her eyes. *Thinking of you...thinking of you...* With her phone in one hand and a strand of curls in the other, Shae closed her eyes and groaned. "I've lost my mind," she muttered again.

"And you woke me up to tell me that?" Brecee yawned. "Do you need a referral to seek counseling or something?"

Shae had needed to vent, so she'd reached out to Brecee—and to Stacy, Shari, and even her mother. All of them were on the conference line—Shari and her mother sharing a line, since they lived together—but Brecee was the only one who'd chimed in thus far. How she managed to possess a sense of humor after a twelve-hour shift at Driscoll Children's Hospital in Houston, Shae didn't know.

Most days, she welcomed her sister's wit. But now, just hours before Rahn was scheduled to pick her up for church, she found the sarcasm irritating.

"Maybe he drugged the cake, because I told him that I was the other wom—"

"There you go again," Brecee said in an exasperated tone. "You were never the 'other woman.' He was the jerk..." She ranted until she'd apparently depleted all of the adjectives in her mental thesaurus when it came to Alex, then took a deep breath. "Aah, that felt good. I should be able to sleep like a baby now that I know my big sister has left her comfort zone."

Stacy laughed. "Sis, you need to have your blood pressure checked. You're way too high-strung for this early hour. And I thought my husband was an over-the-top morning person. Ted has nothing on you."

"Shae, you *are* a good judge of character." Her second-oldest sister, Shari, jumped into the fray with her steady, well-reasoned attorney's tone. "This is a different city, different circumstances, different man. Besides, everything you want to find out about anybody, you can start digging into on the Internet, as if you didn't already know that. There had to be something about Rahn that caused you to open up to him. Maybe it's a good sign."

"Or a bad one," Brecee countered, bursting the balloon Shari was trying to inflate for Shae.

"Will you pick a side and stay on it?" Shae snapped at her baby sister. "You're the one who told me to get back in the ring."

"So what if I've got a little multiple personality thing going on here? This is the first time I'm hearing about Rahn Maxwell. And though I don't know anything about him now, I will. Like Shari said, you've got to love social media. All I have to say is, the brother better watch out, because the Carmen sisters will take him down if he steps out of line."

"Hush," their mother demanded, commandeering the conversation.

Everyone laughed, including Brecee, and then she yawned again. "On that note, I'm going back to sleep. Bernard is waiting for me."

"Who's Bernard?" Shae asked in unison with her mother and other sisters.

"The man in my dreams." With a *click*, Brecee exited the conference call.

"She got us on that one." Shae rolled her eyes. When it came to men, her younger sister's opinions shifted continually, depending on her mood.

"I do like Rahn," Shae admitted. There was no reason to hide her feelings from her family. Getting off her bed, Shae was drawn to the balloons like a magnet. She smiled, then knit her brows together in concern. "Do you think I have some type of dent in my spiritual armor that invites the enemy? Do I have an underlying weakness that makes me vulnerable to attract losers, abusers, cheaters, or bisexual men?"

"Sis," Shari uttered softly, "I believe you have a pure heart, and that's what draws good people, but sometimes, the devil tags along. Shake the devil off and keep steppin' forward."

"I've tried, but I keep having flashbacks to that moment when God chastened me. Jesus might as well have handed out a Revelation three seventeen T-shirt when Alex's estranged wife basically sang her husband's praises in front of the congregation."

"'*Because thou sayest, I am rich, and increased with goods, and have need of nothing; and knowest not that thou art wretched, and miserable, and poor, and blind, and naked,*'" her mother recited, then added, "God does chasten those He loves, so thank God He loves you. That was then, and this is now—like Shari said, different man, different situation. You said Rahn wants to prove himself to you. Let him. Church is a good place to start." She paused. "Personally, I think you're overthinking this and getting carried away when you need to be getting ready for church."

Shae sighed. "You're right." She checked the clock on the wall. She still had plenty of time before Rahn was scheduled to show up. "I'm just a little nervous because I do feel this connection to him. But I don't want it to cloud my judgment, since he doesn't meet the 'equally yoked' protocol."

"Daughter, many brothers are saved now because they were attracted to a woman in the church. Don't be so naive to think men don't want to live as men of God. Remember Brother Phillip Graves? He's a fine man today, but he was a common criminal until the day he walked into the church."

"You're kidding me!" Shari exclaimed, saying exactly what was on the tip of Shae's tongue. "Minister Graves, a criminal? Usually I can sniff those out, or I wouldn't be a criminal attorney."

They all chuckled.

"That's right, baby. Prison record and all. But his life of crime ended when he met Debra Cupples." Their mother paused. "Then, there's Pete Shepard, Henry Holmes, Al Price…the list goes on."

This discussion was truly a revelation about the men in Shae's home church in Philly, though most of the goings-on had occurred before she'd even been born. Two of the men her mother mentioned had already passed away, but they had been faithful to the Lord until their deaths, as far as Shae had heard from the church rumor mill.

Men can see only the outside of a person's appearance, but I see the hearts and will judge the good and evil, God spoke to her heart.

Shae knew that Scripture—1 Samuel 16:7.

"Baby, don't be afraid of letting God use you," her mother said, interrupting Shae's moment of reflection. "People don't come into the church already saved."

"Mother's right," Shari affirmed. "Maybe this is God's purpose."

"Let me just add a footnote here, as the big sister," Stacy inserted. "I don't think this is so much about Rahn's lack of commitment to God. I think you would have the same reservations about any man in the body of Christ, from the janitor to the pastor."

"And you should have some hesitation, not suspicion," Mother tacked on. "Yes, unfortunately, daughters, Matthew thirteen says that the tares do grow alongside the wheat. Pray that God will separate them and give you the right one this time."

"Amen, Mother," the sisters said in unison.

"Oh, before I forget"—Mother again—"Mother Stillwell says she's been thinking about you and lifting your name up to the Lord."

Shae was the first to groan, followed by Stacy and Shari. "Whenever Mother Stillwell starts thinking, it's not a good sign."

"But she's praying, sweetie, and no matter how misdirected our thoughts, Jesus can straighten them out."

The conference call concluded with their mother having the last word.

⌒

Rahn had thought his mother would be ecstatic to learn that he'd accepted an invitation to a Sunday worship service. But when he called her on Sunday morning, she cautioned him, "God knows the hearts of men that are deceitfully wicked. That's Jeremiah seventeen, verses nine and ten. Salvation has to be about you and you alone, not because another pretty face invited you to church."

As Rahn listened, he got dressed. He was determined not to be late, not because Shae had set the time but because he was going to take the lead in this relationship.

His mother continued her monologue. "Since everything has a purpose, God used those thugs to get your attention. Maybe your woman friend will point you in the right direction, so I'm glad you're taking advantage of the Lord's open casting call." She paused. "Remember, many are called, Son, but few are chosen. Strive to be a standout for God as you are in baseball."

A standout in baseball. Rahn didn't have time to dwell on his career. He had to go. "Thanks for the advice, Mom." They exchanged "I love you's" and ended the call.

Once he was satisfied with his appearance, he went to his library downstairs and located his Bible. Shaking his head, Rahn was ashamed he had never opened it. Since the attempted carjacking, he had signed up to receive a daily Scripture via e-mail, but he hadn't been reading it faithfully. "First time for everything." After setting his home security system, he drove to the Westmoreland Condos, arriving with seven minutes to spare.

He strolled into the building, admiring the décor and amenities. The security guard, an older, wiry gentleman, popped up from behind an executive-looking desk of thick wood. His eyes lit with recognition. He grinned, puffed out his chest, and extended his hand. "Rahn Maxwell. It's nice to finally meet you."

Rahn checked the man's badge. "Thank you, Mr. Chapman. I'm here to pick up Miss Carmen."

"Of course. She told me to expect you." Beaming, he lifted the phone receiver. "I'll let her know you're here."

"No, I'll wait. I'm early." Besides, Rahn wanted her to wonder if he was a man of his word.

The guard seemed pleased to have his attention for a few minutes. "I've been watching the Cardinals since I was a boy. I remember your dad. You're on the path to outshine him."

That comment gave Rahn pause. "My father was a tough act to follow, but I'm striving to be like him. I've had some rough patches on the road to get where I am today, but—" The elevator bell chimed, and Rahn glanced over his shoulder. His jaw dropped. "Shae." She looked exquisite.

Dismissing Mr. Chapman, Rahn straightened to his full height. He didn't know what to study first—Shae's smile, face, dress, shoes, legs, or hat. His eyes bounced like a pinball as she stood, rooted in place, waiting for him to come to her.

Without even trying, the woman was a temptress. From what he had gathered about her, Shae was a godly woman inside and outside. He was determined to protect her heart.

"You're early," she whispered.

"How could any man keep you waiting?"

Rahn waved to Mr. Chapman on his way out, then guided Shae to his car. He opened the passenger door, and she slipped inside. "Buckle up—my wife may depend on it."

Shae looked at him. "What?"

Rahn hadn't realized he had spoken out loud. "Your seatbelt." He pointed. "Buckle up. Your life depends on it."

Her lips form an *o*, and she fastened the seatbelt.

He rounded the car, got behind the wheel, and stole a few glances before starting the engine. Shae's perfume alone would make it a challenge to keep his hormones dormant. Jesus might have to gore out his eyes to keep him from lusting, and she wasn't even dressed to seduce him. *God, help me not to mess this up with You or her.*

During the drive, Rahn kept the conversation safe, asking Shae about her family, and whether she had any nieces or nephews.

"Only my oldest sister, Stacy, is married," Shae replied, "but she and Ted don't have any children yet. How about you?"

"Two nephews—twins—Julius and Julian." Rahn grinned. "Nobody was surprised, though, since my paternal grandmother was a twin."

"There are no twins in my family, as far as I know. But my sisters and I might as well have been quadruplets, being as close in age as we are."

"There are four of you?"

"Yes: Stacy, Sharmaine, Sabrece, and me."

"That's a lot of *s* names."

"It was my mother's way of honoring my father. His name was Saul."

"So, you were Daddy's little girl." Rahn could only imagine.

Shae angled her body to face him. "Yes, and so were my sisters, until the day he died, twelve years ago. I still miss Daddy."

"Me, too," he said, more to himself. The memories he'd made with his father were endless. Ronald had never stopped being a father, but, as Rahn had grown, they'd become friends, with Rahn feeling comfortable confiding in his father as such.

"This is it." Shae pointed to the Bermuda Drive exit, and Rahn turned off of Interstate 70. They inched along behind a long line of cars waiting to turn into a shopping-center-sized parking lot.

He snagged the first available spot, then grabbed his Bible from the backseat and helped Shae out. Despite the slight chill, Rahn didn't rush her to the door. He enjoyed their closeness as they fell into a comfortable unhurried stride.

Shae giggled.

"What's so funny?"

She bit her bottom lip, as if debating whether to share her thoughts, then shrugged. "You and me. Here I am with Rahn Maxwell, who is larger than life. It's like the captain of the baseball team taking me to prom." She giggled again.

"Not hero worship from you, too." Rahn groaned, then gave her a pointed stare to make sure he had her full attention. "Lady, I'll take you anywhere you want to go, but let's get one thing straight: When I'm with you, I know how to shut out everything else around me."

Shae didn't say a word but wore a faint smile all the way to the church entrance, where two men opened the double doors for them. Inside the foyer, a welcome committee greeted them with a hearty "Praise the Lord" and "Welcome to Bethesda."

Rahn received a few double takes, and they weren't all from the men. The females' expressions were that of wishful wonder, but none approached him, thankfully. An usher directed them to a pew, and Rahn helped Shae out of her coat.

As he took his seat, Shae knelt briefly to pray, then sat down next to him. "I'm glad you're here," she whispered, with sincerity in her eyes.

"I am, too." He held her gaze.

Their private moment ended suddenly with the click of two drumsticks. Cymbals clashed, horns blew, and the organist blended the instruments into an orchestra. Immediately, all of the people around him, Shae included, were on their feet, clapping their hands. Rahn didn't budge as he scanned the auditorium. It was a big church—not mega-sized, but he estimated a couple thousand members.

His foot caught the rhythm, and soon he was clapping along. The repetitive chorus seeped into his soul, and Rahn found himself singing the words to an unfamiliar song.

Cast aside your cares because I care for you.

Rahn caught his breath. In the midst of the music, he clearly heard the voice of the Lord, quoting one of his mother's favorite Scriptures. He bowed his head, acknowledging God's presence. It was the same feeling he experienced the night of the carjacking. Rahn shut out everything around him, his status, his family name, the money earning interest in his bank account, and the beautiful woman at his side.

If you don't praise Me, the rocks will cry out. I have created all things for My glory, God scolded him. *Have you not read Luke nineteen, verse forty?*

Rahn shivered. He remembered his mother sharing Bible verses along those lines, but he'd never read them for himself. And God knew it.

Without a defense, Rahn closed his eyes in shame. His hands seemed to lift involuntarily in praise—a gesture utterly foreign to him. He recalled the scary night that had set off the chain of events that had brought him to the place he was now.

As the music faded, Rahn seemed to float back to reality. *Whew.* He needed a few seconds to regain control before he let his eyelids flutter open.

A dark man of average height, wearing glasses, stepped to the microphone and introduced himself as Bishop John Archie, the pastor. "Welcome to Sunday worship at the Temple. Will our guests stand?"

Along with many others of the same status, Rahn complied. He was thankful he wasn't singled out as the congregation applauded heartily.

Bishop Archie waited for the auditorium to quiet, and then his voice boomed. "Your life will change today because the Word of God is aiming at your soul, and its precision is on the mark—not inches off its target but a perfect bull's-eye." He flipped through the Bible on the podium. "My sermon today comes from Isaiah fifty-five, and I want to focus on a public invitation. I'm sure you've heard the phrase 'Come as you are.' It's just a saying. It's not Bible-based. Don't kid yourself into believing that God will accept whatever you want to give Him. Cain and Abel are an example of that. What offering will Jesus accept once He extends the invitation? Nothing less than a complete surrender. The Bible says there is a time and a season for everything. Consider this the place."

Was God speaking to him only, Rahn wondered, or was this a generic message? His questions were endless as the minister's sermon drew him in.

Bishop Archie leaned on the podium, but he didn't seem out of breath. "Now is your appointed time for salvation; then, at an appointed time, the door will close. Don't let your own righteousness tell you you're okay. All of the ten virgins in Matthew twenty-five didn't think it was important to have the oil, or the Holy Ghost, as they waited for the great feast. Not to be prepared is foolish. Won't you come today and let the Lord fill you up? Time is not on your side. Won't you come?"

Rahn's heart pounded at the unknown and the what-ifs in his life.

As if in tune with his confused spiritual state, Shae touched his arm and whispered, "This church is a saving station."

"I believe it." Rahn shifted in his seat.

The pastor continued, "The Bible doesn't make any false promises. It says in Isaiah fifty-five, verse eleven, '*So shall my word be that goeth forth out of my mouth: it shall not return unto me void, but it shall accomplish that which I please, and it shall prosper in the thing whereto I sent it.*'"

Twelve minutes later to the second, Bishop John Archie closed his Bible. "It's time to get into position. If you choose God, He has your back; if you decide to stay with the devil, he will continue stabbing you in the back."

He urged everyone to their feet. "It's time to pray, saints. Somebody in here needs Jesus. If you want Him, repent where you are standing—there are no words for you to recite. This is a private confession between your soul and God. Then, step out and make your way to the altar, where ministers are waiting to pray for you, or help you prepare your body and soul for the water and fire baptism, in Jesus' name…"

Bowing his head, Rahn pieced together a genuine prayer of repentance. *Lord, what can I say but "I'm sorry"? It took a gun pointed at my face to make me realize that I'm not in control. Thank You for not allowing any of those thugs to pull the trigger. I'm honest in my intentions. I want a change.*

He was physically shaking as he felt Shae lean against him. She prayed softly until he made up his mind. "I can't leave here today without making a commitment."

"I feel that in my spirit." Her eyes were misty.

Taking a deep breath, Rahn disengaged their hands and began the journey down the aisle to the front. "Whatever it takes, I want the works to be saved," he told one of the ministers waiting for the baptismal candidates to come forward.

The man appeared old enough to be Rahn's father, and though his expression seemed stern, his eyes were filled with kindness. "It takes a complete surrender of your will. There is no guesswork with the Lord. After the baptism in Jesus' name, the evidence of His presence is revealed in a spiritual language. The power of the

Holy Ghost didn't cease in the book of Acts. That was just the beginning. The Lord will complete the course. Have you repented?"

"The best way I know how," Rahn replied, feeling foolish.

"God is the Judge." Nodding, the minister laid hands on Rahn's forehead and earnestly prayed for God to forgive him. Then another man escorted Rahn through a side door to a room where he was instructed to change out of his suit into a white T-shirt, pants, and socks.

Afterward, he joined other candidates in a waiting room, and together they began their journey to the pool. When it was Rahn's turn, he descended into the water. A short, stout man told him to cross his arms. With a firm grip on the back of Rahn's T-shirt, the minister declared, "My dear brother, on the confession of your faith and the confidence we have in the blessed Word of God concerning His death, burial, and grand resurrection, we indeed baptize you in the name of Jesus for the remission of your sins. Acts two says God will fill you with the Holy Ghost with evidence."

Rahn was dunked under with a force that surprised him. When he emerged, he was praising God uncontrollably, until he felt his mouth move like it never had before. His lips uttered a language he had never learned. What was going on?

10

$\mathcal{S}$hae quietly shed happy tears. For the most part, the sanctuary had emptied following the benediction, after the last candidate was baptized, but there were still pockets of groups hanging around. She had moved to a vacant seat near the side door where new converts would emerge after prayer and praise, and would remain faithfully at her post until Rahn came out.

It had been years since someone close to her surrendered to Christ. She never would have thought Rahn would walk down that aisle, wanting salvation—not on his first visit to Bethesda Temple. That's what she got for having an opinion about who God drew to Himself. Then again, she wasn't surprised. Rahn had said he wanted a change.

When Rahn reappeared in his suit, Shae dabbed her eyes. He displayed the same confidence in his stride, but his dazed expression was a sign that he had experienced something almost indescribable. They exchanged smiles, and she scooted over for him to sit. They both remained silent, as if waiting for the other to speak first.

"The Holy Ghost is really real," he finally said, with amazement, as if he was still not quite convinced. "I heard it…God's language, spoken through me, just like the Bible said."

"I know." Shae spoke softly, with reverence. Her hand trembled, and she refrained from brushing it against his jaw. Despite the attraction, they weren't a couple; plus, they were in a sacred place. "Congratulations. You are now a card-carrying member of Team Jesus."

"Thank you." His voice was tinged with emotion.

She was about to ask why he was thanking her, but she noticed the line of people that had begun to form behind him. She stood, letting him bask in the limelight. "You have company." She smiled.

He took her hand, restraining her gently. "Don't. Stay right here."

"Okay," she finally agreed, unable to deny his simple request. Shae took her seat again and discreetly checked the time as Rahn stood and greeted people. Although she didn't want to rush him, she had to return to her condo, get her car, and grab something for dinner—all before reporting to work. If they left within the next half hour, she could accomplish all that.

But this was Rahn's rebirth—a onetime event—so Shae prayed for patience while the other church members welcomed him into the body of Christ with hugs, handshakes, and a couple of pats on the back. A few of them requested a picture and an autograph.

The scene was touching, even as he switched gears into celebrity status. When his well-wishers and fan base scattered, Shae gathered her Bible and purse.

Rahn lifted her coat off the pew. He smiled but didn't say anything, instead regarding her with such intensity that she wanted to let down her guard and flirt with him.

"What?"

"I didn't get a hug from you." He opened his arms wide.

After a moment's hesitation, Shae walked into them. She indulged in a short snuggle, then stepped out of his embrace.

"Ready?"

She nodded and then led the way out of the sanctuary. In the lobby, Rahn was swarmed with more hero worship, mostly from young boys. "Do you mind?"

That he'd asked her permission was appealing. Most men would have been cocky and expected her to deal with it. He had moved up a notch in her esteem.

Shae shook her head. *He's so natural with children*, she thought, watching their interaction.

A few female church members strolled up to her. "Praise the Lord, Sister Carmen," one woman greeted her. Shae smiled at the unfamiliar but pretty face. She would even call the woman beautiful, with her hair, makeup, and clothes worn to perfection. "Was that the ballplayer who got baptized earlier?" She didn't hide her apparent infatuation with Rahn.

Suddenly Shae felt territorial. Was it because she wanted the crown God had promised for those who drew others to Christ, or was it because she was curious to explore a dating relationship with Rahn? In either case, it wasn't her call.

They had only shared cake, a brief conversation, and a church pew—and a hug. That definitely didn't qualify as a committed relationship, even if he had pursued her with flowers and notes. Trying to keep her expression unreadable, she answered slowly, "Yes."

"Praise God." Her sister in Christ seemed elated. "Is he seeing anybody? I mean, if you two aren't a couple."

"Sugar, it's sure good to see God bring men into the church," said an elderly woman who butted into the conversation with apparent indifference. Shae could have kissed her.

Leaning on a cane, she reminded Shae of Mother Stillwell—the false prophet of romance in Philly—with her vintage attire and pillbox hat, which had probably been stylish back before Shae could digest solid food.

As if on cue, Rahn came unexpectedly to her side. "Hello, ladies." He squeezed Shae's shoulders. "Sister..." He paused and glanced between the two women holding court with Shae.

"Alicia Davis," the younger woman filled in the blank.

"You can call me Mother Ernest, baby. Mother Mable Ernest." The older woman stretched her neck to make eye contact.

Mother Ernest? That was too close to Mother Ernestine Stillwell for Shae's liking. She gritted her teeth, bracing herself for the woman's personality.

"Mother Ernest," Rahn repeated, dazzling the senior citizen with a perfect smile, "and Sister Davis." His smile for her wasn't quite as engaging. "Shae and I are in the beginning stages of our relationship, just as I am in my walk with Christ. Will you pray for us?"

Whoa. That caught everyone off guard, including Shae. She didn't know what surprised her more: his keen hearing or his public statement. Evidently, he meant business about wooing her.

"Ready?" he asked her.

Still stunned, she could only nod.

With a wave to his newfound fans, Rahn escorted her out the door to his car.

"I wasn't expecting you to say all that back there," she confessed. "As a matter of fact, I'm surprised."

He shrugged as he disarmed his car alarm. "I know women. I wanted to make it clear I can't be tempted away from you. As of today, I'm officially in the body of Christ. I'm up for the challenge of keeping you from being disappointed by another church man."

Shae adjusted her hat and slid into the passenger seat, processing what Rahn had said. *Lord, did You save this man just for me? If so, I am loving Your choice.*

11

$\mathcal{G}$od blew my mind today." Rahn shook his head as he drove out of the parking lot. He was as exhausted from his up-close-and-personal experience with the Holy Ghost as if he had endured extra innings. "It's so hard to describe. It's almost mind-boggling." He released a hearty laugh because he was genuinely happy. "I'm glad I don't have to try and explain it to you. You already know what I'm feeling." He glanced at Shae, grateful to have her as his confidante.

It was funny how God had turned things upside down in his life. Just that morning, Rahn had needed all of his self-restraint to keep his eyes off of Shae, so that he wouldn't lust. Now, his eyes weren't a problem. His attraction was more than physical. "I'm convinced that I can live as a changed man after experiencing something so tangible yet so indescribable."

Removing her hat, Shae closed her eyes as she relaxed against the headrest. "The Holy Ghost is real. In order to walk with Him, you have to study God's Word, just as you do the game, and model your lifestyle as closely as possible after His stipulations. At Bethesda, we have Bible studies and new convert classes to help with that."

"I don't have a problem with learning the craft to be a sincere, practicing Christian."

Shae opened her eyes and glanced at him, then patted her chest. "You made my heart flutter with that statement." She grinned. "And my stomach just growled. You can drop me off at home, and—"

"You can't be hungry on my watch." He gripped the steering wheel. After what he'd experienced today, Rahn wanted her in his presence as long as possible. He would even go as far as to claim he'd started falling in love with her. Stranger things had happened. But he would rather wait and see where the relationship took them before he made such a life-altering declaration—one he had never uttered to any woman before.

"You don't have to do that," she protested.

"Shae," he said softly as he exited the interstate to Kingshighway, passing the route that would take them to her condo, "let me drive this. And I'm not talking about my Audi."

"Do I have to?" She puckered her lips in a mock pout.

It was an alluring gesture, but he checked his hormones and laughed. "Yes, madam."

It wasn't long before Rahn drove into the semicircle lane in front of The Chase Park Plaza on Kingshighway near Forest Park. The place had an impressive history, originally built as two separate buildings—The Chase Hotel and The Park Plaza. Besides its stately architecture, it could boast that the staff had hosted every United States president from the 1920s to the 1990s.

Now, the landmark housed executive apartments with an attached movie cinema and four restaurants. The Bistro was once a hot spot for national broadcasts of Big Band concerts, and Rahn thought it would be ideal to take Shae there, since Marcus and Yvette had raved about the service at Eau Bistro.

Valets opened their car doors as soon as Rahn brought his car to a stop. Shae turned to set her hat on the seat behind her when he stopped her.

"Don't. Please wear it. I've never seen a woman look so sexy in a hat. I hope I didn't offend you by saying that." He might be able to tame the testosterone from lusting, but his eyes could appreciate her beauty.

She blinked rapidly, then blushed. "You didn't. But I definitely need to be on Ashro's payroll. First the viewers, then my producer, and now you all like for me to wear them."

Shae reached for the sun visor to use the mirror.

"May I?" Rahn touched her chin and guided her face back to him. She trembled, and he was just as affected.

When she consented, Rahn studied her. In the briefest moment, he memorized everything about her, from the beauty mole near her left ear to her slight dimple on the right side. Then he positioned the fashionable headpiece to *his* satisfaction. "Perfect." He grinned.

"Okay."

He took that as a small sign that Shae trusted him on one more thing. Coming around the car, he escorted her along the carpet to the entrance.

The doormen bid them welcome, then pointed to the bank of elevators when Rahn mentioned where they were headed. During the ride to the top floor, Rahn was content to hold Shae's hand and keep his thoughts to himself. *God, help me to be a good Christian man for Shae and You.*

I will finish the work I've begun in you, God said, reminding him of Philippians 1:6, which one of the ministers at the church had quoted to him after his baptism.

The heightened spiritual connection he had with Jesus was definitely an adrenaline booster. How could he go wrong with God directing every segment of his life?

Shae leaned playfully on his arm as they stepped off the elevator. The host seemed to be waiting for them and promptly showed them to a table.

As he helped Shae remove her coat, Rahn inhaled the scent of her hair; then he pulled out a chair for her. The other patrons sprinkled throughout the restaurant didn't give them a second's glance, but he didn't mind.

"This place is beautiful." The elegance of the décor seemed to captivate Shae. He had to agree with her. "I can see why so many A-listers like Jerry Lewis and Sammy Davis Jr. dined here." She sighed, then lifted the menu off of her plate but didn't look at it. Her thoughts seemed elsewhere as she situated her elbow on the table and rested her chin in her palm. "I've jogged by this place so many times, but I didn't know its history until a month or so ago. A hip-hop artist and his entourage were staying here, and our TV crew couldn't get past the lobby. Talk about ultimate security to guard privacy. I've got to hand it to them."

She opened her menu, then glanced up. "What are you smiling about?"

Their server was about to approach their table, but Rahn motioned for him to give them a minute. "You. Watching you think, talk, and make the little gestures that are unique to you."

Lifting a brow that wasn't hidden under her hat, Shae curled her lips. "Well, this is what I'm thinking: Since I'm less than two minutes from home, I can get my car and drive myself to the station."

Leaning across his place setting, Rahn met her challenge. "Unless you feel threatened, I want the privilege of chauffeuring you. Besides Jesus turning my life upside down, you're the highlight of my day." He pulled his cell phone from his waist holder without taking his eyes off her, then checked the time. They had about three hours. "I can't think of anyone else I would like to share the experience of my new birth with than you. Plus, you know I'm already attracted to you. I hope the feeling is mutual."

The slight nod she gave would have to work. He didn't need a verbal confirmation of her feelings just yet.

"Then let's eat. All this intensity is making me hungry."

Rahn summoned their server once they were ready. Shae ordered the brunch special—turkey sausage patties and a pecan waffle—and a small glass of apple juice.

Their server was a middle-aged man who appeared to be of Mediterranean descent. His eyes lingered on Shae a little too long for Rahn's liking, and he cleared his throat to get the man's attention. "I'll take a large omelet with a side order of hash browns and a glass of cranberry juice."

"Yes, sir." He spoke as if giving Rahn a military salute. "And I'll get you a complimentary fruit platter while you wait." With that, the man was off to do their bidding.

More patrons entered the restaurant, but Rahn didn't let the crowd distract him from Shae. They chatted about the church service, her journey to salvation, and his satisfaction with his new life in Christ.

Then Shae changed the subject. "Were you always good at baseball, or did you just want to follow in your father's footsteps?" Her manner of asking questions made him feel almost as if he were fielding inquiries at a press conference.

"If only I could become the man my father was. My dad's skill came natural. I had to work hard at it."

By the time their meals arrived, the subject had changed a couple of times. Rahn reached for Shae's hand, ready to offer grace. "Jesus, I can't thank You enough for showing me the way. Lord, I didn't see any good coming out of what happened to me, but now I see—"

"Lord, bless our food while it's hot, in Jesus' name, amen," Shae interjected.

"Sorry," Rahn said, a bit embarrassed that he'd gotten carried away. "When I think about Jesus, I'm still in awe. Prayer seems more a conversation with God than reciting repetitious phrases I can recall without thinking."

"Don't ever apologize about your relationship with Jesus. I don't." Shae made an art of pouring syrup on her waffle.

He stared as she began to devour her meal with the same finesse as she had the cake they'd shared. "So, what are some of your hobbies?" He took a sip of his juice.

"Singing with my sisters, reading...I used to sew, but I stopped that after—" She paused.

What was she thinking? Before he could press her, Shae seemed to recover.

"Like any other woman, I like to shop." She beamed.

Their brunch was unhurried as they lingered at their table until Rahn checked his phone. It was almost time for him to drop Shae off at the station. He immediately felt the loss of her presence as he paid their tab, then escorted her back down the elevator and to his car.

Twenty minutes later, Rahn pulled up to the curb outside the KMMD-TV studio. "Here you go, Miss Carmen." He parked and helped her out. "I look forward to seeing you again in eight hours."

With a hint of bashfulness, Shae thanked him, gathered her things, and used her security card to open the door. Rahn sat there until she disappeared from view, and then he drove away, nodding to himself. His persistence had paid off. Rahn somehow believed that Shae Carmen was supposed to be in his life.

Not ready to return home, he called Marcus. "She could be the one," he told his friend as soon as he answered.

"I guess I don't have to ask who."

"No, you don't." Rahn couldn't help but smile. "I connected with her and with God today at church."

"You've been with Shae *and* went to church?" Marcus whistled. "I don't know which I want to hear about first. Why don't you stop by?"

"I'm on my way." To reach the Evanses' estate, Rahn had to take the same route he'd followed the night of the incident. When he passed the exit, amazingly, he no longer shuddered. In place of the trepidation he'd felt before, he rejoiced at what God had done for him.

In no time, Rahn arrived at the Evanses and parked in their driveway. Because of the security sensors around the property, the family was alerted to his arrival, as usual. Marcus Jr., aka MJ, and little Lannie—short for Yolanda—were standing in the doorway with their parents, waiting for Rahn as he approached from the front walkway. The children jumped in place, excited to receive company.

Rahn scooped them up, one in each arm. They squealed in delight as he hugged them. After setting them back on their feet, Rahn patted Marcus on the back and kissed Yvette's cheek.

They ushered him into the dining room, where a place setting had been added for him. Although he was still stuffed from brunch, he wasn't a fool to pass up a home-cooked meal, especially since Yvette was an excellent cook. He wondered if Shae possessed the same skill.

As was his custom, Marcus blessed the food. For the first time, Rahn really listened to his prayer. Then, as they ate, Rahn described his "Nicodemus moment," as some of the prayer warriors had referred to his baptism in water and then with Holy Ghost fire.

"Congratulations, man, on taking that step for complete salvation," Marcus said. "Finally! It took a woman to do the job that I couldn't do for years."

Yvette gave her husband a playful shove.

"What?" Marcus actually had the nerve to look confused.

"Be nice, Mr. Evans," she warned him.

Rahn grinned in amusement. He was accustomed to Yvette keeping Marcus in check. The pair was like family to him—Marcus, the brother he never had, and Yvette, his cheerleader/little sister.

Rahn slid a forkful of black-eyed peas into his mouth. "I considered myself as fearless as the next man until that incident. It didn't really click with me that missing heaven was an option. I either accepted God's way or no way. The thought scared me out of my seat and down that aisle. And I didn't look back."

"You were scared, Uncle Rahn?" MJ asked, his eyebrows raised in surprise.

Rahn looked to Marcus and Yvette to help him, but they both gave him a blank stare.

"Uh…" He wracked his brain for a response. How would he explain this if he were talking with his five-year-old nephews? *Lord, please help my mind on this,* Rahn silently prayed. "When you get in trouble at home, are you scared?"

MJ nodded.

"But since Mommy and Daddy love you, you know that after your punishment, they'll always love you. That's the way I felt with Jesus."

"Oh." The boy's chubby little face brightened. "Jesus loves little children, but I guess He loves big people, too," he said matter-of-factly, then resumed playing with the vegetables on his plate.

"Good answer, Son," Marcus said proudly.

Yvette's eyes twinkled with mischief. "So, what's Shae like? She's really pretty on TV. Is she nice?"

"Shae makes my heart beat when I'm with her. She's more beautiful than a person could imagine. But she was hurt by the fool from her last relationship, so she was a little hesitant about me."

Frowning, Yvette began to toy with her napkin. "Don't take this the wrong way, but please don't tell me your repentance was for show, to impress her."

"That was a low blow." Rahn schooled his expression to conceal his disbelief. "I've never played church—as a kid or an adult. You, of all people, should know that." *Lord, if I'm going to show anybody I've changed, I see I'm going to have to start with You and work my way down.*

"I'm sorry. It's a woman thing. I just needed to know. I'm pulling for you, but I'll get an attitude if you hurt her." Yvette lifted her chin with a look of authority he had seen her use only with Marcus.

Rahn shrugged. "I have nothing to hide. I've been more honest with Shae than I've been with any other woman."

When Marcus switched the conversation to the upcoming baseball season, Yvette excused herself, but not before patting Rahn on the back. "You're still my favorite slugger." She grinned.

"Hey, what about me?" Marcus feigned insult.

"Hmm. I guess you're all right," she teased, then ran out of the room to escape her husband's clutches.

His friend didn't take his gaze off Yvette until she was out of sight. Pure love shone in Marcus's eyes. Rahn wanted to experience that type of feeling.

Turning back to Rahn, Marcus snickered. "Wipe that grin off your face. We're legal. I can lust after my wife all day if I want."

"I haven't said a thing." Rahn did his best to keep a straight face, even though he wanted to laugh.

"Right. So, are we sharing the villa with Cisco again this year?"

"We always do."

Marcus and the other pitchers, as well as the catchers, had to report to spring training in Florida a few weeks earlier than Rahn and the rest of the team.

After a while, thoughts of Shae sidetracked Rahn, so he prepared to leave.

"Yvette and I are pulling for you," Marcus said as he walked him to the door.

Rahn shook his hand. "Thanks, man."

In his car, he called Shae. "Have you eaten?"

She chuckled. "You fed me earlier, Mr. Maxwell, remember?"

"And that was one of the best meals I've had in a long time, Miss Carmen. I'll have dinner delivered to you soon, then I'll see you after your newscast."

"I was just thinking about that. I can catch a ride home. You live a good half hour away."

"I'm offering to pamper you. When I report to spring training, I'll miss you like crazy, so let me do these small things for you while I'm still in town—please."

She was quiet for a moment. "I'm still trying to figure out how we went from a friendly chat over cake just yesterday to…I don't even know how to define what's happened between us in two days. I'm not trying to push you away, but can we slow this down? Please?"

Her request was soft and simple, but he had to read between the lines. It was a request that he had to respect. "We can, but if you're hungry, I'm going to feed you. I know that's somewhere in the Bible, so that's not up for debate. I've got this, Miss Carmen. Something tells me too much is at stake between us for me to strike out."

"Is this what I have to look forward to—baseball puns?"

"I'll try to keep them to a minimum, but I'm serious about showing you that I'm the one God sent for you."

12

With her phone cradled between her shoulder and her ear, Shae padded out of her bedroom, yawning, on her way to the kitchen. Spying the printed cushion on the window seat beneath the bay window in her living room brought back memories of the previous night, when, from her fourteenth-floor condo, she'd watched Rahn's car drive away.

He had picked her up from the station with a smile and a rose. "You look beautiful," he had complimented her.

And, despite her fatigue from a long day of church and work, Shae had somewhat believed him. When he'd delivered her to the door of the condos, he'd kissed the rose petals instead of her lips. Glancing up at the moonlight, Shae had wondered if she should give Rahn the green light to pursue a relationship with her.

"Jesus practically hands you Rahn Maxwell, gift-wrapped, with looks, money, and now salvation," Brecee said on the other end.

Shae now regretted having given Brecee the details when she'd called thirty minutes ago, waking her up. She prepared a cup of java, then headed to the window seat, where she could recall the fantasy of feeling like a princess. She took a sip of coffee and sighed. "The attraction is so consuming. Don't you think it's happening too soon?"

"Why are you trying to sabotage this?" Brecee asked, rather than answering her question. "Instead of eating that chicken Marsala dinner Rahn had delivered to you at the station last night, you should've been eating your words with every bite. God does have someone special for you."

Only her sisters could get away with throwing her words back in her face. Since Shae's personal life was considered family business, she put up with her sister's ranting. "I just don't want to get carried away. I can only hope he was sincere about his salvation. I think Bishop Archie scared him to death."

"Probably." Brecee yawned. Her sister was adjusting to those twelve- and twenty-four hour rotations at the hospital. "The few times I visited your church when I was there, I got the message loud and clear that your pastor focuses on getting people ready for Jesus' return and pursuing soul prosperity over financial wealth. Philippians two, verse twelve, does say, 'Work out your own salvation with fear and trembling.' Chalk it up to God's Word causing Rahn to tremble in his soul."

Stretching out her legs, Shae stared at her dark toenail polish, then shrugged. "It's hard for me not to be suspicious of a man's motives."

"As you should be. But it doesn't matter if Rahn had a cool stride to the altar or raced to the finish line, or whether he was willing or scared stiff; he came to Jesus, and that's all that matters. Case closed."

Brecee definitely should have been the attorney in the family. Gnawing on her lip, Shae was about to argue a point when God whispered Romans 9:15 in her ear: "I will have mercy on whom I will have mercy, and I will have compassion on whom I will have compassion."

Who could argue with God? Chastened, Shae banished any further doubts. "Amen, Lord."

"I'll second that." Brecee took a deep breath. "Now, with that out of the way, you should know that the fam has Googled everything we could find out about Rahn Maxwell."

"Of course. You all wouldn't be the Carmens if you didn't snoop. I did the same thing yesterday at work," she confessed. "I checked out his impressive sports résumé and his dad's. There was no hint of any type of scandal involving estranged wives or stalker ex-girlfriends." Shae rubbed her scalp. She couldn't wait for her hairstylist to take out her weave at her appointment in a few days' time.

"Then stop looking for kinks in Rahn's armor because of a certain scumbag in Nebraska."

Shae couldn't help but laugh. Alex Peterson was really becoming a fading memory. Rahn Maxwell had a way of bringing closure to a bad situation.

13

*T*here was something about letting go and letting God that was blissful. Shae had finally let her guard down, and Rahn had wooed her. They had explored St. Louis together and had even returned to The Chase Park Plaza and dined in the three other restaurants there, just for the adventure.

Shae found herself laughing more when she was around him, feeling secure and content, and finding him to be a prayer partner, which she cherished most of all.

On one shopping expedition, Shae refused his offer to buy her something she saw in a store window. Generosity was another one of his endearing qualities, not only with his money, but with his time when fans approached him.

As they sat in a café, enjoying a respite from browsing the stores, they somehow found themselves in a game of trying to read each other's thoughts. Shae smiled as she sipped her latte, her eyes on Rahn's as he enjoyed his espresso and watched her.

Rahn leaned forward as if coaxing her to meet him halfway to pucker up for their first kiss. He wasn't. His restraint was impressive, almost taunting her.

"Your presence has made my transition from just living to living for Jesus easier with our daily Scripture swaps. It's amazing the clarity I have since I received the Holy Ghost. I thank God for putting you in my life. You rescued me."

Shae's vision blurred as tears filled her eyes. "No, God rescued *us*," she said, her voice choked with emotion. "I've gotten clarity on some things, too." It didn't matter whether he could read between her lines or not. She was in a happy place, professionally and personally.

"Really?" Rahn smirked. "Your eyes tell me everything I want to know about what you're thinking." He stood and reached for her hand. "Come on, baby. Let's finish up your excursion in the shoe department."

Their time together began to run out, with Rahn scheduled to leave soon for spring training. The morning wakeup Scriptures and nightly chats had never meant as much to Shae as they did now. Finally, it came down to the last candlelight dinner they would share in a long while.

"Remember how I told you the first day I took you to work that I was going to miss you?" Rahn whispered. "That hasn't changed."

The ambiance of the restaurant and the sincerity on his face made Shae's eyes mist. "Me, too."

Rahn reached across the table, took her hand, and raised it to his lips. She shivered as he tickled each finger with soft kisses, then took her other hand and did the same thing, except that he kissed only one finger.

The gesture was far more seductive than Shae should allow, but she was enjoying it nonetheless. "Why did you stop?"

"Because each finger represents the number of weeks I'll be away from you at spring training—six—and six is the number of kisses I hope to collect before I go."

Six kisses. Shae doubted she could survive one kiss and not be drugged. She squirmed under his scrutiny.

Linking his fingers through hers, Rahn seemed ready to pour out his soul. "Know that every time I watch the local news, I'll think of you; every time I read my Bible, I'll think of you; and every time I hear a woman sing, I'll think of you and have the nerve to silently boast that you could sing it better."

Touched by his confidence in her, Shae blinked, and a tear escaped. Rahn's thumb was quick to catch it. If only she could package up his touch and retrieve it every time she missed him.

Shae did her best to recover quickly, so as not to become an emotional mess in public. She slipped her hand out of his grip and excused herself to the restroom. Once there, she fanned herself. "Whew." She didn't want him to go, but maybe they both needed six weeks to cool their hormones.

⤶

Once all the Cardinals players had descended on Jupiter, Florida, Rahn had to rehash the old news about his brush with death. "I got saved after that," he said, sharing his Nicodemus experience and referring his teammates to John 3 and Acts 2.

"I just bet you did," Cisco Martinez joked. The Dominican native was a great defensive catcher with impressive stats, and the team counted on him to make opposing players think long and hard about stealing bases. Like Marcus, he was Rahn's friend on and off the field.

Of course, Christ was the furthest thing from most of his colleagues' minds, so his audience dwindled in the locker room at Roger Dean Stadium until it was only Cisco and Marcus.

"Yep, the devil tried to set me up to take me down." Rahn grunted. "But God turned it around, and in the midst of the drama, I met the most beautiful woman."

Cisco roared with laughter and slapped Rahn on the back. "I'm glad you're safe, but you didn't need God for that. You've never had a shortage of hotties." He winked.

"No, I haven't," Rahn admitted. He would have to accept that it would take a while for people to forget his past indiscretions.

A few days into spring training, the Cardinals were ready to play their first exhibition game against the Miami Marlins. Begrudgingly, Rahn pushed aside all thoughts of Shae and put on his game face, ready to go to work.

Hours later, despite their hustle, the Redbirds lost 4 to 3. As usual, everyone engaged in a mental rehashing of the errors that had cost them the win. Fortunately, none of the games in the so-called Grapefruit League counted.

Once the team had showered, some of the players returned to their hotel rooms. Rahn, Marcus, and Cisco shared the amenities of the rented villa that was adjacent to a golf course and on the beach.

When the trio walked through the door, they sniffed the evidence that their housekeeper had already prepared them a meal. After dinner, they reclined on the patio, talking shop.

Cisco took a swig of his second bottle of beer. Although Rahn had been only a casual drinker before his pledge to Christ to live holy, he was tempted to ask their housekeeper to bring him one.

Go for it. They won't care. The thought floated in the back of his mind.

You are called to live sanctified. God's voice seemed to rumble in his head. *Study My Word. Second Corinthians ten, verse five: Cast down every imagination that tries to exalt itself over My authority.*

I can do this, Jesus. Rahn got to his feet and went inside. With a mind to stay focused on his salvation, he strolled into the kitchen and grabbed two bottles of fruit juice from the fridge. He blessed his beverage, took a swig, then swaggered back outside to the fellows.

Cisco eyed him with a wide Cheshire grin stretched across his face. "Marcus was briefing me on your media lady love until his wife called. Do fill in the blanks."

"Definitely. Shae Carmen is my favorite subject." Rahn matched his smile as Marcus stepped in the house for privacy. "She's a reporter during the week and a news anchor on the weekends. I'm serious about her. The buck might stop with this one." He set down his bottle and stretched his arms behind his head, flexing his muscles. "As a matter of fact, I'd rather talk to her now than you two."

"Right." Using his phone, Cisco searched the Internet for images of Shae and nodded. He scrutinized Rahn's woman too long for his taste. "Whoa. She is gorgeous. I could see myself getting dipped in some water and joining a church after that harrowing scene, but why would you want to stop sampling other fine specimens?" Cisco looked skeptical.

"Listen, my Santo Domingan brotha. I wasn't dipped; I was submerged underwater, leaving my sins buried at the cross. I had plenty of things to repent of, and now my bad behavior and misguided decisions have been done away with."

Rahn took out his cell phone and pulled up his Bible study application, then showed the screen to Cisco. "I want to live by this Book now. I can't chance God not stepping in to rescue me if there is a next time and I'm not living up to His standards."

Judging from Cisco's dumbfounded expression, it didn't appear that Rahn was getting through to his friend. "Shae's the one for me. One look in her brown eyes and I got lost there. As a matter of fact, I couldn't get her doll face out of my head, so I pulled out a pad and sketched her features in detail and sent it to her."

"He has it bad," Marcus said, rejoining them. Evidently he'd overheard their conversation.

"Um-hmm, until he sees another woman." Evidently Cisco couldn't accept that he'd changed.

"I believe Rahn on this one, my friend," Marcus said, backing him up.

"Really?" Cisco gave Rahn a pointed look, then finished off his beer.

"What more can I say?" Rahn exhaled. "She's beautiful, created just the way a man likes, or to my heart's specifications. She's got curves and legs. But what drew me in was her concern for me as a man, not a celebrity."

Not one to easily be swayed from his opinions, Cisco switched the subject and gave his predictions on which rookie from the Cardinals' Triple-A farm team would earn a spot on the permanent roster for the season.

"I watched Dudley Williams at bat today and yesterday. He's going to be some slugger," Rahn commented, and his teammates agreed.

Soon, Marcus was the first to call it a night. Not long after that, Rahn also abandoned Cisco for the solitude of his room, eager for Shae to get home from work so he could speak with her. Cisco had been right about his past. Rahn had never been one to have to wait for a woman. He'd always had plenty at his beck and call.

But that was then, Rahn thought as he stretched out across the bed and closed his eyes. His mind drifted back to the night when it had been Shae's brainy idea to take a stroll on the nearby walking trail in Forest Park, the pride and joy of

St. Louis. Million-dollar-plus mansions overlooked the popular tourist attraction, which was larger than New York's Central Park. Doctors, lawyers, and politicians preferred the proximity to the park's zoo, art museum, fish pond, ice skating rink, golf course, and the Jewel Box, a conservancy that also was popular for weddings and receptions.

Although it had been after eleven at night, he had obliged, taking her gloved hand in his. They had crossed Lindell at a leisurely pace and made a shoe path in the snow to the trail that circled the park.

"Cold?" He had scanned her attire from her hat to her low-heeled leather boots.

She'd shaken her head but snuggled closer, making him chuckle. They'd moved along unhurriedly, contemplating their own thoughts.

"Shae," he'd whispered.

"Hmm?" When she'd glanced up, Rahn had delivered his first kiss. Her lips had been softer than he'd imagined, and seemed to be the only cold spot on her body. They paused in their tracks and indulged in the briefest kiss he had on record. When her eyes had fluttered open, she'd playfully scrunched her nose at him.

"You cheated!" he'd teased.

Giggling, she'd rested her head on his shoulder, and they'd resumed their stroll. "How?"

"Your kiss." He'd waited for his heart to regulate. "It's a deadly weapon."

Rahn didn't know how long he was caught up in the memories, but when he returned to the present, the villa was quiet.

"Humph." He grunted. "I never did collect all six of my kisses."

He planned to rectify that the moment he saw Shae.

14

Shae, don't sit down," the evening assignment editor yelled across the room, not bothering to leave his coveted spot behind the semicircular half wall that served as the newsroom's information center. Every communication device known to man seemed to be housed there: computers, printers, scanners, fax machines, phones, and a whiteboard that listed stories and who was assigned to them.

"I have a maniac driving around the NorthSide randomly firing bullets. He's shot up a few cars, houses, and people. Take Jeff and get going—fast. I'll text you the details. Be prepared to go live at six. The live truck is already on its way."

The cameraman in question had his feet propped up on a nearby desk. Suddenly he came to full attention like a watchdog, ready to go on the prowl. He rushed past Shae so fast, she had to run to catch up with him. Minutes later, they were climbing into his white SUV.

Taking a deep breath, Shae prayed. *Lord, it's going to be one of those shifts. Please intervene.* Her adrenaline pumped as Jeff raced to the address the assignment editor had texted her. Pandemonium was in full force by the time they arrived. The oversized live truck bearing the station's logo was parked nearby, and its mast on top was cranked up, indicating that a satellite signal had been established back at the station.

Once Jeff had parked, he grabbed his camera. As a team, they piggybacked off each other for scene video that would tell the story. After speaking with several witnesses, they agreed on three interviews to feature in Shae's report.

With more than enough video and less than twenty minutes to spare, Jeff and Shae climbed inside the back of KMMD's live truck to the mini editing bay, where they selected the most compelling sound bites. Then, once satisfied with the one-minute reporter package they'd whittled it down to, Jeff fed the video and audio back to engineering at the station, where it would be cued ready to air.

Next, Jeff located a safe spot near some yellow police tape to set up his tripod for the live shot. Meanwhile, Shae paced the sidewalk, going over her script. More sirens blared in the distance. When Jeff stuck the microphone in Shae's hand, she stood in place and performed an audio check.

"We're coming to you in one minute," came the producer's voice through Shae's earpiece, which she had just plugged into her battery pack.

Shae strived to make her live shots intelligent, smooth, and compassionate for the victims, whether she had several hours or just several minutes to gather the news. Switching to "on-camera mode," she listened to the theme music, then waited for Thomas Greenley, the main anchor, to introduce the top story.

"Police are combing a North City neighborhood where a deadly shooting spree began. KMMD's Shae Carmen is live on the scene with more details."

"Good evening, Thomas. Witnesses say at least four men riding in a green midsized car fired shots in the thirty-seven hundred block of Kossuth. Families are searching for answers after two people are dead and five victims injured, one critically."

She paused to allow the station to play the video Jeff had edited, and watched the small monitor at her feet, waiting for her cue to go live again.

Thirty seconds later, she was back on camera. "The violence didn't stop there. The driver turned the corner at a high rate of speed, sending bullets flying on Lee Avenue. Then, at least three gunmen were seen shooting aimlessly three blocks away, in the thirty-seven hundred block of Penrose.

"Police have not released a motive or identified the victims, except to say they were young teenagers. We'll have the latest on this deadly drive-by tonight at ten. I'm Shae Carmen, reporting live on the NorthSide. Now back to the studio."

Once the producer had cleared them, Shae dropped her professional persona. "Sometimes I hate my job," she mumbled as she climbed into Jeff's truck. They both needed to get something to eat, despite the unappetizing piece they'd just put together. After a quick meal, they would return to the scene to interview more witnesses and get pictures of the victims.

Jeff turned the key in the ignition. "Yeah, folks don't like to watch the news because it's depressing." He grunted. "They *are* the news. It's just a reflection of their bad behavior. Wake up, people." He was about to pull into traffic when more guns discharged and sirens grew louder.

"There goes dinner," Shae murmured.

"Yep." Jeff shifted the gear into park again. They needed to verify if another location had been added to the crime scene.

Jesus, she cried within her spirit, *we need You!*

God whispered a Scripture in response: *"If my people, which are called by my name, shall humble themselves, and pray, and seek my face, and turn from their wicked ways; then will I hear from heaven, and will forgive their sin, and will heal their land."*

Shae knew 2 Chronicles 7:14 well. At that moment, she wished for Rahn's strong arms around her so that they could pray together.

15

$\mathcal{R}$ahn studied Shae's features as they chatted on Skype the following morning. He wasn't happy.

"I'm safe—really," Shae insisted, trying to appease him. "The police are at every crime scene. Plus, Jesus walks with me, remember, sweetie?"

Sweetie. How could Rahn be upset with her when she used such endearments with him? Her sultry voice made him remember the sweet kisses they'd shared—and made him long for the ones that were waiting in the wings.

As far as he was concerned, someone else could go into the trenches and cover the breaking news stories—not his woman. However, he held his peace. They'd had this very discussion not too long ago, on a different occasion when she'd been in the middle of crossfire. And Shae had held her ground. "This is what I was trained to do," she'd said. "I've won awards for my work, and recent stories have been nominated, but I'll be extra careful, in Jesus' name."

"Thank you, baby, in Jesus' name." That was the only name that could pacify him—somewhat.

"Well, I'm sorry you had a bad night at work," Rahn said as soothingly as he could.

Shae shrugged nonchalantly. "It's the news business. Unfortunately, a slow news day makes for a boring newscast for advertisers. But I'm okay. Really." She tried to sound convincing, but her acting was terrible. The weariness in her eyes betrayed her.

Rahn massaged his temples and silently prayed, *Lord, watch over her, please.* "I'm not happy hearing about this after the fact. The next time something like this happens, I want you to call me immediately," he told her. "Please," he added, to soften his demand.

"I didn't get home until after midnight, since I had to stay and write notes for the producer and the day shift reporters to follow up the next day, and I didn't want to disturb your sleep."

He didn't want to spend the little time they had to talk on a disagreement. Not once before meeting her had he thought about how the news affected the people who reported it. Shae's job was becoming too stressful for *him*. Once Rahn returned to St. Louis, he would whisk her away for a day of pampering, shopping, or anything else she wanted to do that would drown out the ugliness of the world.

"What about you, my baby?" he asked her. "How did you sleep?"

"I thought about you and how I wished I could hear your voice and get a big hug," she admitted softly.

"Done as soon as I see you."

Shae blushed and lowered her eyelids with a sweep of her lashes.

"Now, do you have a few minutes to swap Scriptures?"

"Yes." Her eyes brightened as she reached for her Bible.

"I forget what I last read to you, but what comes to mind now is 'I will be with you always, even until the end of time,' or something similar." He paused. "Baby, I care about you. I just can't seem to turn off my concern for your sake."

She chuckled. "I know, but somebody has to work. We can't all make money playing in a big yard with sticks."

Rahn laughed. The tension was broken.

Shae gave him a coy smile. "The Scripture you referred to is Matthew twenty-eight, verse twenty; it's talking about how, though we may not see Jesus physically, He's always there, even on the streets of St. Louis." She gave him a pointed stare. "My pastor back home once said, 'When fear comes knocking at your door, let faith answer it. Once the door is opened, fear disappears.'"

"I'll try to remember that." Rahn checked the time. Showing up late for practice was not an option. "Hey babe, I've got to run. But, for the record, I like boring news as long as you're bringing it."

Before signing off, Shae smacked a loud kiss on the monitor.

That gave him something to smile about as he, Cisco, and Marcus joined their teammates at the ballpark. Before they took to the field to face the Boston Red Sox, they came upon a large crowd of fans hoping for an autograph. Rahn and many of the other Cardinals players obliged. As usual, he gave priority to children over adults. When Rahn got into position in the outfield, he wore his game face, but his heart was in St. Louis.

In the bottom of the ninth inning, Rahn hit a two-run homer to tie the game. Now, Marcus and the others watched from the dugout as Matt Hammond walked to the plate. If anyone could bring the game to a close, it was the right fielder, and with a single swing. The pitcher threw a low ball, and Matt's bat made the game-winning connection.

The Cardinals celebrated as if the victory would put them in the pennant race. Regardless of the outcome, every win or loss brought Rahn one step closer to getting back home to Shae. The three weeks left to go felt like an eternity to Rahn. And the longing in Shae's voice when they spoke was evidence that the separation affected her just as much.

In the locker room, Rahn went straight for his phone.

Marcus shook his head as he opened his locker. "Man, you got it bad. Don't you want to shower first?"

"Nope." Rahn typed his message. "She can't smell me either way."

I miss you. Can we do lunch on Friday?

She texted back immediately.

You can get away????? Yes! Yes! Name the time and place.

Feeding off of her excitement, Rahn felt bad about teasing her—almost.

Your condo.

Shae's response wasn't as fast in coming. That didn't surprise him.

I don't think that's a good idea. We miss each other so much, the temptation would be too great. Name somewhere else—public, please.

He snickered.

Trust me.

He didn't realize Marcus had already showered until his friend bumped him on the bench. "Man, what are you doing? Writing a letter?"

Rahn shook his head. "Making a lunch date."

"When?"

"This Friday."

Marcus raised his eyebrows. "Is she coming here?"

Rahn stood and sauntered toward the showers. "Nope."

16

*H*ow can he ask me to trust him when I'm not sure I trust myself?" Shae gnawed on her lip, flustered beyond measure. The line was blurry when it came to her feelings for Rahn. Could she be in love with him, or was it lust? Either way, a lunch date of just the two of them—with those pent-up emotions—was asking for trouble.

She was connected with her sisters via Skype, but none of them had chimed in yet. Brecee in Houston and Shari in Philly looked concerned, but their oldest sister wore a whimsical expression. What was Stacy's problem? Shae had a real crisis going on in her life.

As Christian women, the Carmen sisters had been taught to avoid any entrapments that might lead to fornication. She should've insisted on a restaurant. "Stacy, aren't you listening? Don't you have anything to say?"

"Yes, I do," she said calmly, closing her eyes for a moment. Then she opened them wide and screamed like a madwoman. "We're pregnant! I couldn't hold it in any longer. I'm going to be a mommy!"

Shae and her sisters erupted in jubilant squeals and shouts of "I'm gonna be an aunt!"

"How many weeks' gestation?" Brecee asked, reminding them all of her medical expertise.

"So *that's* why you went to the doctor yesterday morning," Shari said. "Does Mother know? What did she say? How come nobody told me?" She sounded almost offended. She lived in Philly, just like Stacy, and probably wondered why she hadn't picked up on this sooner.

"What did Ted say?" Shae asked, putting her own crisis on hold. Her brother-in-law was so overprotective of his wife, he'd probably put her on bed rest immediately upon hearing the news.

Glowing with happiness, Stacy waited patiently until she had everyone's attention before answering. "I've been holding the news for days. Whew. That felt good getting it out. I'll call Mother when we're finished. Your dear brother-in-law got online and started ordering baby books and bookmarked Web sites about baby stuff. We may need a bigger house, with all the things he's planning on buying."

Shari *tsked*. "If you have a boy, we'll be in trouble. Ted is sure to have a child-sized car waiting for him the minute he learns to walk."

"But if it's a girl…I can't wait to take her shopping!" Shae was in awe. "I can't believe I'm going to be an aunt. Wait till I tell Rahn. He's already an uncle…" His name brought her back to reality. Wasn't Rahn the reason why she'd organized this Skype chat in the first place? She sighed.

Stacy must have heard her, because she straightened her shoulders and switched back to big-sister mode. "Now that I've gotten that out of the way, let's talk about you and Rahn. Personally, I think you're tempting your salvation threshold. One kiss or seductive look, and you're a goner."

Too late. Shae recalled their stroll in Forest Park the night before Rahn had left town. They had counted the number of kisses they'd shared, until Rahn had expressed concern that it was getting too cold for her. He'd said that they were one short, and that he aimed to collect upon his return. She tried to keep a straight face at the memory.

"Listen, Sis," Stacy went on. "You already know we have to save our bodies for marriage at all costs."

"Okay, let me jump in here," Shari said. "Garrett and I know what God expects from the people He has sanctified. If Rahn is truly walking in Christ, you two can double-team the devil and show the world that failing isn't an option for Christians. Remember, Jesus is able to keep you from stumbling and will present you faultless."

Shae caught the reference to Jude 1:24—it'd been the golden Bible text in the Carmen household. She admired her sister's steadfast determination not to sin in her relationship with Garrett. Somehow, Shari's input seemed the most relevant; like Shae, she wasn't married and probably experienced the same struggles, while their oldest sister had the freedom to do what married folks did.

"I need so much prayer, it ain't even funny," Shae mumbled.

"Okay, let's take a vote," Stacy said. "I vote no on Shae entertaining Rahn in her apartment. Change the location."

"I vote yes," Shari said. "Shae is grown and mature in the Lord. She's going to have to overcome this sooner or later. She can do this."

"Ooh, choices, choices—I could go either way," Brecee said. She tapped her chin. "I vote…can I have a drumroll, please?"

Shae rolled her eyes. Brecee's votes on sister issues were always unpredictable.

"I vote yes!" Brecee shouted, pumping her fist in the air. "Rahn knows he's on probation with God and you."

"Two in favor, one against, so it comes down to me," Shae murmured. All eyes were on her. "My vote is…I don't know."

"Then it's prayer time," Brecee stated, bowing her head. "Father, in the mighty name of Jesus, we come boldly to Your throne of grace, where we know we may obtain mercy. Jesus, Your Word says we shall receive power once the Holy Ghost comes upon us. We know temptation is part of life, and we ask that You would teach us to overcome sin and walk victoriously in Your salvation. Lord, please help us not to make You ashamed. In Jesus' name, amen."

Shae was the first to sniff. "I love you, sisters."

"Love you, little sis. No matter what you decide, we're all going to be praying." Stacy blew her a kiss and signed off. The others followed.

"I won't make You ashamed, God," Shae whispered.

She filled the remainder of her day off with personal pampering—first a hair appointment, where she had her weave removed, followed by a manicure and pedicure. While she was under the hair dryer, she couldn't help thinking about Rahn. She was touched that he would leave in the middle of spring training to have lunch with her. She also spent a great deal of time in prayer to the Lord.

Before she retired to bed, Rahn texted her.

Don't forget about our lunch date tomorrow, Miss Carmen.

How could she?

I won't. I miss you so much.

She debated whether she should ask for a change of venue, but she had to use the tools God had given her, and place her complete trust in Him—not herself or Mr. Maxwell.

I miss you more. Night, baby.

⌒

Early the next day, Shae woke with praise on her lips, not only because she would see Rahn, but in order to shame the devil back to his hiding place. She proclaimed James 4:7: "'*Submit yourselves therefore to God. Resist the devil, and he will flee from you.*'"

Although Friday was another day off, meaning she didn't need to report to the newsroom, she could be summoned to work in the event of breaking news—no exceptions. As a habit, she filled her idle hours until lunch watching different news programs on television. One of her pet peeves was the "news" talk show, which she considered an embarrassment to her profession. The hosts weren't concerned about presenting objective facts but only about asserting their opinions. That definitely wasn't taught in journalism school.

Shae prayed for peace and goodwill to all mankind on this day, even as she repented of her selfish reason for doing so: She didn't want anything to interfere with their date. When it was time to get ready, Shae scrutinized her reflection in the mirror. Rahn had commented on her "flawless" skin, so she took care to make sure her makeup kept up that illusion. Her hair had volume again, thanks to the curls her stylist had put in.

She slipped on a simple black dress with flirty ruffles and a pair of black heels, then got comfortable on her window seat, where she would count down the minutes until Rahn's arrival. As she watched for his car, her mind wandered. She imagined how devastatingly handsome he would look; how his deep voice would soften into a whisper when he said her name; how his nostrils would flare when his eyes locked with hers. It was always so mesmerizing, so tempting.

Then, there was Rahn's smile that made a woman wonder what he was thinking. Yet he never kept her guessing; he was up-front and honest about his intentions. Yes, she trusted him.

"It is better to trust in the LORD than to put confidence in man," God whispered, reminding her of Psalm 118:8.

She repented. "Okay, Lord. I trust in You."

When her intercom buzzed, Shae jumped. Her heart started pounding. She scanned the street below but didn't see Rahn's vehicle. She stood up, hurried to the panel near her door, and pressed the intercom button.

"Miss Carmen, I have some deliveries for you," said Mr. Chapman. "May I send them up?"

Deliveries? What kind of deliveries? Puzzled, she frowned. "Okay."

Finally, Shae heard a faint ding from the elevator down the hall. She smoothed her dress and then checked her reflection in the mirror, making sure her lip gloss wasn't smeared on her teeth. When she opened her door, two men greeted her—neither was Rahn. One was dressed in a white caterer's outfit and held a silver-domed platter. The other, wearing street clothes, leaned lazily against the wall as if posing for a CD cover. Suspended from a cord around his neck was a tenor saxophone—the same instrument her sister Shari played, along with their cousin Dino.

The elevator dinged again. Shae held her breath, expecting to see a handsome smile and confident swagger. Instead, when the door opened, the most beautiful arrangement of flowers was heading her way. It was so big, it hid the face of the person carrying it, but the deliverer was too short and too thin to be the man she'd been expecting.

Shae stepped aside and bid the caterer and musician inside. The caterer lifted a portable table that had been resting outside her door and carried it inside, along with the tray.

What was going on? If Rahn was going for a grand entrance, then he'd succeeded. She peeked down the hall again. Still empty. She turned her attention to the caterer, who had set up the table between her baby grand piano and the bay window and draped it with a white linen cloth.

Next, he fussed with the food placement like a skilled artisan. The man from the florist waited for her to direct him where to set the arrangement, and then he sprinkled pink rose petals on the table. Some of them fluttered down to her hardwood floor.

The saxophonist checked his watch, then positioned his lips on the horn's mouthpiece as the caterer punched in numbers on his phone. "All is ready, sir." When he disconnected, he pulled out the chair at the table. She hadn't seen it there. Why was there only one?

"What's going on?"

The three didn't seem obliged to offer her an explanation. So, she waited for Rahn to knock on her door or Mr. Chapman to announce him in the lobby. Instead, her cell phone rang, with a FaceTime request from Rahn.

"Where are you?" she demanded.

"Still in Florida, babe. We don't have much time."

"What?" Her heart sank. Yes, Rahn was wearing his uniform, verifying that it wasn't a joke. "I thought you were coming here." She tried to keep the disappointment out of her voice and the pout from her lips in front of her uninvited guests. She had gotten herself and her sisters worked up over nothing.

"You have no idea how much I wish I was there."

Angling her body away from her audience, Shae smiled and closed her eyes. "Me, too," she whispered, as the saxophonist began to play.

"This is the best I could do. I can't leave spring training unless there's an emergency. Although"—he winked—"I do consider seeing you an extreme emergency. Like the song?"

She hadn't realized she was tuning out the music. When she listened closely, she recognized the piece instantly—"I Wanna Be the Only One," by the all-female group Eternal, accompanied by gospel artist BeBe Winans, a song popular in the 1990s. "I love it."

"I stumbled across it and thought of you and me," he explained. "Enjoy your lunch, babe." In a whisper, he added, "You owe me a kiss." Then he disconnected.

Suddenly, Shae wanted to be left alone with her thoughts. She caught the three men staring at her. "Thank you, gentlemen." She eyed each one before dismissing them. "*Bon appétit.*"

17

When spring training was finally over, Shae was giddy with excitement. In celebration, Rahn sent a beautiful bouquet of flowers to the station. So much for not wanting to mix her personal life with her profession. The only nugget she'd given her nosy colleagues was a confirmation that she and Rahn were dating. Most hadn't realized how serious it was until the arrangement had shown up on her desk.

"There will be a pass waiting for you at the VIP gate for tonight's game," Rahn said when she called to thank him. "I can't wait to see you." It was the same voice she had listened to for six weeks, but it sounded richer, maybe because he was closer.

"I wish I had someone to tag along with me, so I won't have to sit there all alone."

"You won't be."

Even though she would see him in just a few hours, it was hard for Shae to say good-bye. Yet she had things to do and little time left to accomplish them.

Wanting to impress Rahn with her understanding of baseball, she had soaked up whatever she could learn by searching online and watching games on TV. She'd steered clear of the sports department at the station, though; Rahn was off-limits, and she was sure his name would surface if she asked too many questions. The bulk of her information came from the sports junkie of the family, Uncle Bradford. Her father's older brother, he was a walking sports almanac.

Along with her uncle's enthusiasm about baseball came his reservations about Shae dating a high-profile athlete. She wondered if her father would have given her the same counsel if he were still alive.

"My heart knows Rahn is the one," she told her uncle over the phone.

"God knows too, Shae," he reminded her.

Hours later, as promised, there was a pass awaiting her at the VIP entrance. Her heart pounded wildly. Despite her newfound knowledge of baseball and her excitement to watch the game, she would rather be smothered in Rahn's strong arms than sitting in an uncomfortable seat amid the other spectators.

The last time she'd gone to a baseball game had been when her father was alive. He and Uncle Bradford had taken all of the Carmen kids: Shae and her sisters and their cousins, Kevin and Dino. That had been so long ago.

Thanks to her uncle's briefing, she knew Rahn was off to a good start so far this season; the Cardinals had faced the Atlanta Braves, and in the series, he'd hit three home runs and earned six RBIs. She also had her uncle to thank for explaining that RBI stood for Runs Batted In.

Shae's heart pounded with excitement and nervousness as an usher showed her to her seat, in a row not far from home plate. An attractive woman scrambled to her feet. "Hi, Shae? I'm Yvette Evans. My husband, Marcus, is a good friend of Rahn's and also plays on the team. These are my children, MJ and Lannie." She gestured to a young boy and girl who were sitting there, sharing a box of popcorn. "We are your welcome committee." The children waved.

"Aren't they cute? It's nice to meet my welcome committee." Shae smiled and waved back, then relaxed.

With her teenage youthfulness, Yvette looked too young to be anybody's wife, let alone a mother of two. She sported a red Cardinals jersey, blue jeans, and a baseball cap, with her ponytail pulled through the opening in back. MJ and Lannie wore matching team jerseys with their last name printed on the back.

Shae had made an effort to look her best for Rahn without going over the top, but now she felt overdressed in her red shirt, floor-length floral skirt, and strappy, high-heeled sandals. She wished she was wearing one of Rahn's jerseys.

Yvette embraced Shae as if they were longtime friends, catching her off guard. "I'm so excited to meet you too. I love those hats you wear every Sunday."

Shae always felt a bit embarrassed when she received accolades about them. She grinned sheepishly. "Thanks. I guess more people watch our newscast than I thought. I receive so many compliments." She climbed over the children and took the seat Yvette offered next to her.

"Rahn hasn't stopped talking about you. He puts you just under any discussion of Jesus and right above baseball." Yvette giggled, then turned serious. "Marcus and I praise God for your drawing him…Rahn said you were special, and I agree. You two make a good-looking couple."

Shae felt herself blush as the woman rambled on. She didn't want to disclose more information than Rahn would like her to.

"Well, the feelings aren't one-sided. He has a piece of my heart, too." She felt comfortable enough to reveal that tidbit. Then she craned her neck, looking for Rahn.

"Here." Yvette nudged her with a pair of binoculars. "Extra pair."

"Thank you." Not only did she not look the part of a fan; she hadn't come prepared as one. *Note to self: Buy a jersey with Rahn's name and number. And a pair of binoculars.*

She peered through the lenses, scanning the outfield, then sucked in her breath. Rahn was standing in place, looking her way, as if waiting for her to find him. She could even make out his faint smirk, as if he could sense her eyes on him.

Oh, she missed him. *Lord, help me not to jump into his arms when we see each other.* She thought about how Whitney Houston had done that when Bobby Brown had been released from prison.

After the national anthem and the first pitch, Shae cheered and booed with the rest of the crowd. She prayed that Rahn would hit home runs every time he was at bat. He didn't, but she figured it was still worth asking for.

After the seventh-inning stretch, Shae tagged along with Yvette and her kids to the restroom. On the trip back to their seats, a few people approached her and asked for an autograph. She happily obliged them.

By the bottom of the eighth inning, the Cardinals were leading the Astros 4 to 1. Shae groaned when the Astros caught up, tying the game in the ninth. She was ready for it to be over, so she could reunite with Rahn after an agonizing seven weeks apart.

To everyone's relief, the Redbirds took back the lead and won their home opener, 6 to 5—in the bottom of the eleventh inning. Shae and Yvette exchanged high fives. As the crowd began to disperse, Yvette introduced her to some of the other players' wives. Shae also acknowledged some city officials who were in attendance, as well as a few familiar faces from church. But the anticipation of seeing Rahn caused her palms to sweat.

While Shae was speaking to a fan, she glanced over her shoulder, then froze. All her bottled-up emotions flashed before her as their eyes danced together until he was within feet of her. Without realizing it, she had memorized his swagger. She didn't know what to expect, because they had built so much of their relationship while he'd been away. Her answer came when he swept her up in his arms.

"I've missed you so much," Rahn said tenderly.

His hug was satisfying but short-lived. He released her with obvious reluctance and gathered her hands in his. "I want to kiss you," he whispered. "Will you let me?"

Shae shook her head, also with reluctance. "Too many prying eyes and cameras waiting to click and record."

Clearly frustrated, Rahn tightened his hold on her hand. "I don't have a problem putting on a show—on the field or off."

"I would just rather our sixth kiss be shared in private." She felt at liberty to flirt.

He grinned mischievously and had the nerve to look handsome while doing it. "Didn't you know those kisses were for the road? I'm home now, and we're starting over."

18

With an arm draped possessively over Shae's shoulders, Rahn escorted her to the private access door of the stadium. Once outside, they linked fingers and strolled in the direction of KMMD-TV's parking garage, a few blocks away.

"I'm in a perfect place right now," she said with a sigh of contentment.

Those were his sentiments exactly. Her presence filled the longing—the sense of incompleteness—he'd felt for the past month. FaceTime and Skype couldn't replicate this closeness or the scent of her perfume. Rahn halted his steps and scrutinized Shae. He brushed a finger against her cheek and wasn't surprised by her skin's softness. "How is it possible that you're more beautiful than when I left?"

Her eyelids fluttered at his touch, allowing him to admire her lashes.

The moment seemed surreal. Everything around them—traffic, pedestrians, birds—blurred in the background.

"What's wrong?" Shae smoothed his brows with her finger.

Capturing her hand, Rahn brushed a kiss on it. "I'm debating."

Her expression grew serious. "What?"

"When is the perfect time to tell you that I love you?"

Shae's eyes filled with tears. Her mouth opened slowly but closed again before anything came out. She didn't take her gaze away from his.

Rahn etched her reaction in his mind to make a sketch of later.

Then, as if in slow motion, she threw herself at him with such a force that he rocked on his heels. And she initiated a kiss that was both tender and passionate. Soon they had to separate, panting, to catch their breath.

"Baby," he said, trying to regain composure, "help me to read between the lines. Does that mean you love me, too?"

"Yes." She closed her eyes and smiled. When she looked at him again, her gaze was bright. "And it's scaring me how much I do."

This was the home run he hadn't expected to hit for years. "Shae, I've never told another woman that I loved her." He paused, gathering his thoughts, so there would be no misinterpretation of what he was about to say. "But you and I connect, spiritually and mentally. There is nothing about you that I would change.

Nothing. This is scary for me, too, but we have God, and I know He'll help us to keep our relationship pure."

Easier said than done. The devil came out of nowhere to mock his conviction.

I can keep him from falling. Jesus' voice chased away the saboteur.

Privy to the spiritual warfare within, Rahn was in awe of how the Lord was forever present to fight his inner battles. With renewed confidence, he entwined his fingers with Shae's again, and they continued on their way. "We can do this, baby—overcome any obstacle that tries to come between us. I believe that."

"I'll top your belief with my trust in God to help us." She looked up at him, her eyes sparkling, as she wrapped her arm around his. He flexed his biceps involuntarily.

A car honked. Rahn and Shae immediately looked for the offending driver. Yvette was in the passenger seat of Marcus's black Infiniti, giving them a thumbs-up. With a hearty laugh, Rahn waved them on.

Shae smiled. "I like Yvette."

"Good, because she was in your corner before you two met. She likes what you do to me."

They entered the garage and soon reached her car. Once Shae was behind the wheel, Rahn tugged on her seatbelt to make sure it was secure. When he squatted beside the door, Shae reached over and stroked his beard. "My protector. Thank you."

"Always." He leaned in for a quick peck on her lips, doing his best not to linger. "I'll follow you to your place." He straightened, closed her door, and patted her hood. Then he jogged the few blocks back to the stadium to get his Audi.

It took him no time to catch up with Shae at a traffic light. He tooted his horn.

She rolled down her window. "Show-off!" she shouted. When the light changed, she took off, and Rahn let her get a jump start. He had no complaints about trailing behind her at a snail's pace, relishing the knowledge that they loved each other.

When they reached Westmoreland Condominiums, Rahn parked a few spaces away from Shae, then got out of his car. Instead of heading his way, she started toward her building.

"Where are you going? I thought we would head straight to the restaurant to meet Marcus and Yvette." He caught up with her.

"I need to change first."

Scrutinizing her head to toe, Rahn shook his head. "You look perfect to me." He winked.

"You showered after the game. I just want to freshen up."

He conceded and reached for her hand, wondering when she would invite him up to her place. As they approached the entrance, Rahn stopped. Shielding his eyes from the sun, he surveyed the tall structure. "I know you told me once, but what floor do you live on again?"

"Fourteen."

They continued until Rahn opened the door for her and stepped aside.

Walking under his arm, she smiled flirtatiously before acknowledging the security guard. "You remember Mr. Chapman?"

"Of course." Rahn extended his hand, and the man accepted it. "Thanks for helping me pull off that catered lunch."

The older gentleman puffed out his chest and grinned. "Glad I could be of service. Anytime. Good game today."

Chuckling, Rahn accepted the praise.

Shae mouthed, *"I'll be right back."*

So, she wasn't ready to invite him in just yet. But soon she was going to have to trust him—them. Rahn was about to take a seat when the security guard seemed eager for his company. By the time Shae returned, twenty minutes later, Mr. Chapman had recited his own career stats and seemed clearly disappointed at her reappearance.

Rahn wasn't. Shae had changed into some sort of wraparound dress that hugged her figure nicely. Whatever his woman wore, she got his attention. His eyes followed her until she was within his grasp.

"See you next time, Mr. Chapman," he said.

"You bet."

Once outside, Shae tugged free of his hand. "I was hoping for a little time to stroll on the bike trail before we meet Marcus and Yvette for dinner." Her innocent expression was akin to that of a schoolgirl. "The weather is nice."

Rahn smirked, recalling the evening they'd spent together before he'd left for spring training. "You mean, unlike the chilly night almost two months ago."

Her eyes sparkled. "Yes," she said in a nearly breathless tone.

"We'll make time. I'm sure Marcus and Yvette will understand my indulging the woman I love." He winked.

"I love the sound of you saying that!"

"I love calling you my woman and saying 'I love you.'" He rubbed his nose in her hair, inhaling the clean, sweet fragrance.

Looping her arm through his, Shae leaned into him, and they wandered in the direction of the park. "I never thought I could miss someone the way I missed you." She paused. "The phantom lunch date was creative, sweet, and way over the top, but you made it special. I'm not complaining, but I would have been satisfied munching on a peanut butter and jelly sandwich if you'd been with me."

"That's good to know for next time."

She gave him a playful jab in the stomach, and he feigned injury. They crossed Lindell Boulevard but never set foot on the trail; Rahn pointed to a bench between two trees that had begun to shed their blossoms. He waited for Shae to sit, then angled his body to face her.

"Thanks for taking off to attend the home opener today. I felt like I was playing in Little League, showing off for my family."

Shae chuckled. "And I prayed for you to hit a home run every time you came to the plate. Talk about praying off-center. But I did learn some important things about baseball while you were gone."

"Really? Such as…?" Amused, Rahn tried to give Shae his full attention, but her gleaming white teeth distracted him, as did her faint dimple.

"The sport takes up two whole seasons before it's over, from April to September. And for the teams that make it to the playoffs, the season isn't finished until October. By the way, the Cards have won eleven titles, second only to the New York Yankees. And six weeks of spring training is totally unnecessary, since the games don't count. Just my opinion."

He laughed.

"However, it makes sense that the Grapefruit and Cactus leagues need the warm weather to practice. My uncle told me all about it, since Florida is known for its citrus fruits; Arizona, its cacti. It's still too far."

Was that a pout he detected? He liked seeing the carefree spirit she normally concealed beneath her professional persona.

"Correct. I'm loving your commentaries," he teased.

"The biggest injustice is the one hundred and sixty-two games—eighty-one are on the road—way too many frequent-flyer miles for me." She lowered her voice. "That also means I'll miss you eighty-one times."

Shae's vulnerability had him wrapped around her finger. His heart did a somersault. "I see it's going to be harder and harder for both of us when I leave for my road games."

Her eyes misted, and she glanced away. Rahn touched her chin and coaxed her to look at him, guiding her face closer to his. "Talk to me, baby."

She shook her head.

"Something caused your glow to dim. What is it, babe?"

She took a deep breath. "I never thought I'd ever get closure from my last relationship, since Alex was married. It's not like I could call him and ask why he did what he did."

The scoundrel. Rahn fought the rage building as his nostrils flared. A real man didn't mislead a woman, with his intentions or otherwise. "That man was a fool to toy with you, but I plan to cherish your love, and honor God in the process."

"I'm glad you don't have any skeletons like that."

"You can thank God for that. All my dirt was covered with the blood of Jesus when I was baptized, but I can guarantee you, I don't have any wives or children waiting to surface."

"It's a good thing, because I'm not into sharing when it comes to men."

"Ditto when it comes to women." He didn't blink.

Rahn meant what he said about sharing his woman. At the moment, he didn't even want to share her with his good friends. But Shae had insisted that they keep their dinner date with Marcus and Yvette for a little homecoming celebration.

19

$\mathcal{S}$hae had never been to Niche, even though it wasn't far from her condo. The restaurant was nestled in the heart of downtown Clayton, minutes from the city limits of St. Louis. One glance was enough to know the suburb had pricy real estate; the mature neighborhoods there screamed old money.

The hostess greeted them with a big smile, then blinked when she seemed to recognize Rahn. Her look of surprise quickly vanished as she moved to show them to their table.

Shae spied Marcus and Yvette waving at them, and she gave Rahn a nudge. "That's okay. We see our party. "

Too bad Rahn's chivalry demanded she walk ahead. Without question, some men liked to eye a woman's strut and lust like a dog in heat. Yet Rahn never made her feel he was undressing her. She still would have preferred walking behind him and watching his swagger—calculated moves like a jaguar, smooth, sleek, and predatory. His confident stride was an art form that commanded the attention of everyone in the room.

"Hey, buddy." Marcus stood and shook Rahn's hand.

Yvette kissed Shae on both cheeks, and Shae was wowed by the woman's transformation. Gone was the youthful-looking sports fan. The loose curls, carefully applied makeup, and form-fitting yet modest dress showcased her assets well.

"We didn't know if you two were going to make it after we saw you earlier," Yvette whispered.

Shae felt herself blush but said nothing. Rahn pulled out a chair for her, and she sat down.

Rahn scooted his own seat closer, and as they scanned the dinner options, he whispered compliments to her behind the cover of his menu.

Giggling, Shae shooed him away. "Stop it, Mr. Maxwell."

Yvette cleared her throat. "I didn't think to ask for children's menus, but perhaps we should," she teased.

Rahn groaned. "I haven't seen my lady in months. Leave us alone." He took Shae's hand and squeezed it. "At least you get to go home to a wife," he said to Marcus.

Their server appeared, introduced himself as Hanson, and stood ready to take their orders. "May I suggest the chef's tasting menu?" Hanson went on to explain that the custom menu featured samplers of all the entrees.

They decided to sample ten entrees among them.

"And may I recommend a wine to complement your selection?"

"We don't drink," Rahn stated, to Shae's delight. "How about iced tea or soft drinks?"

Hanson took their drink orders and then disappeared.

"So, how are you liking St. Louis?" Yvette asked Shae.

"More than I imagined," she answered honestly. She enjoyed her job and had fallen in love when she'd least expected to.

"I hope to be one of the reasons." Rahn gave her a pointed look.

"Most definitely."

Rahn brought her hand to his lips, and his mustache tickled her fingers. She squirmed in her seat, reminded that they weren't dining alone. "Stop it," she warned him gently.

She could barely think straight with Rahn by her side, yet she refocused to display her home training. "Sorry. Ah, yes, St. Louis is treating me exceptionally well, and it's much closer to Philly—my hometown—than my last job. As a reporter, I get to see the beauty of the city, as well as places I'd rather not visit by myself."

"Like shooting zones," Rahn interjected with a grunt.

Shae rolled her eyes. "Yes, we cover shootings, fatal car crashes, and fires, but we also celebrate youth achievements, company milestones, and amazing stories that only God could have orchestrated."

"No offense, Shae," Marcus said, breaking off a piece of warm bread, "but there's too much bad news that overshadows anything good."

"That's a fair observation. No offense taken." She heard that comment a lot, and she'd learned not to take it personally. "It's the viewers who tip off the media about the drug dealers and the shootings in their neighborhood before the police get to the scene. And unfortunately, those calls outnumber the ones about the great-grandmother who's turning a hundred or the comeback kid who survived a tragedy to graduate at the top of his class or the local grocer who is donating food to shelters instead of throwing it out."

The topic soon changed to faith, and Shae learned that the Evanses attended a sister church of Bethesda Temple. When their food arrived, they all joined hands, and Marcus offered an eloquent prayer, asking God to bless their meal, sanctify their minds, and help them to remember those in need. After a chorus of "Amens," they dug in.

During the meal, their conversation jumped from one topic to another until, somehow, Rahn and Marcus snuck in sports news, mainly baseball.

Yvette exchanged an amused glance with Shae. "You'll get used to it," she assured her. "I leave him to his sports, and when it comes to shopping, Marcus gives me free rein." She added in a whisper, "How about a girls' day out—shopping, a spa treatment, and lunch at a cozy restaurant—while they're on their next road trip?"

Shae didn't think the men were listening when she eagerly agreed.

"My treat," Rahn said, in a tone that meant Shae shouldn't bother turning down his offer.

"What about me?" Yvette asked her husband, giving him a sultry pout.

"You carry my checkbook everywhere. It's always my treat." Marcus snickered.

Yvette chuckled. "Oh, yeah."

After the dessert had been long finished, Marcus and Yvette said their goodbyes, saying they needed to get home and relieve the babysitter of her duties.

"Ready?" Rahn turned to Shae.

Her mouth said "Yes," but her heart longed for more time with him. It was still early. As they left the restaurant, he must have picked up on her somber mood, for when they got in the car, he said, "So, my little lady wants to go shopping? I know just the place."

"Now?" Shae smiled. "Honestly, I don't care if we go shopping at CVS or go for Ted Drewes' Frozen Custard…I just want us to squeeze in as much time as possible while you're here."

"Selfish, hm? I like that quality in my woman."

Rahn drove to the Galleria and led her into Nordstrom. Shae was surprised when the customers who clearly recognized Rahn actually left him alone—with the exception of two little boys who wanted a picture with him. He happily obliged them. *Yes,* Shae thought, *he is a true cheerful giver, just the kind God loves.*

At one point, Rahn perused the racks of women's clothes and shoes with no shame. To humor him, Shae tried on everything he selected, though she had no intention of buying anything or letting him whip out a credit card. But the experience was exhausting. They left only minutes before the store would close, each of them carrying a bag—the new wallets they'd bought for each other.

"You're going to have to let me be the man in this relationship and woo you like I want," Rahn said as he parked in front of her condo. He gave an intense look. "Thank you for the wallet, baby."

Her ears tingled, and she smiled.

"The next time we go shopping, don't bring your purse." Without a further word, Rahn stepped out, then came around to her door.

Inside the lobby, they strolled toward the elevators. Shae closed her eyes as she snuggled in his embrace. Their good-night kiss was short and sweet.

"Are you ever going to invite me up?"

She'd known the question was coming. Would she ever say yes?

Rahn squeezed her hand. "I'm not pressuring you, but you are my lady, and I have a right to make sure you're safely back in your home." He cupped her face with one hand. "All day my mind has been telling me, *I'm grown; I can do what I want*, especially when I'm in love with a sweet and beautiful woman."

His comments mirrored her thoughts exactly. Shae wrapped her arms around his waist and rested her head against his chest. "I agree we're two adults, but my salvation—our salvation—can't have been in vain. I don't want to have to repent for something that could have been avoided."

"I know." He sighed. "I know that if we fall into sin, there's no guarantee of another chance to repent. Ever since that carjacking attempt, that thought has scared me." He pushed the elevator button, then stepped back. "Go on up." He tilted his head when the door opened. "I'll stand outside and wait for you to wave from your window."

"We can do this, right?" She needed him to reassure her one more time.

He gave her a sad-puppy-dog look and slid his hands into his pockets. "We've got to," he said, clearly frustrated. "God knows I'm trying. Night."

You could lose a good man by playing games with him, the devil hissed in her ear. She shoved the thought away with a scowl, recalling Luke 9:25: *"For what is a man advantaged, if he gain the whole world, and lose himself, or be cast away?"* Mad at the devil, Shae marched out of the elevator, mumbling, "It's not worth losing my soul to keep a man."

Once inside her condo, she disengaged her security alarm and raced to the window. Rahn was leaning against his car with his arms folded across his chest. She waved to get his attention, and he waved back. Seconds later her phone rang.

"I see you, babe," he said when she answered. "Listen, I don't want to play games with God, either. I want us to be on the winning team. I love you."

Shae's heart fluttered, and she closed her eyes, as if doing so would make his declaration linger. What could be sexier than a man's sincere desire to walk with

God? Opening her eyes, she watched as he got into his car. Puckering her lips, she placed a loud, squeaky kiss on her phone's mouthpiece. "Thank you for my gifts."

"I might be going deaf, woman. You only let me buy you one gift."

"But you gave me you this evening. Good night."

20

*H*is woman was killing him with her sweetness. All she wanted from him was him. *Lord, thank You for my jewel.*

Once his ear stopped tingling from Shae's virtual kiss, Rahn placed a call to Marcus, holding his phone to the other ear this time. Marcus answered immediately. "What's up, man?"

"What would you say if I told you Shae was the one?"

"If?" Marcus barked, causing Rahn to fear complete deafness. "I would say you might be slow, but you're definitely not stupid. There is no *if*. She complements you, and I like who you are around her—yourself. Now, with that said, good night. I do have a wife." He ended the call.

Laughing, Rahn checked his rearview mirror before merging onto the interstate. "Yeah, I'm planning to have one of those, too."

A few nights later, at a restaurant with Shae, Rahn stared across the table at her. She looked beautiful, with her hair swept up and piled atop her head, her eyes sparkling with happiness. Her elegance matched the ambience of the restaurant. He loved her and could never tell her enough.

Both had worked the previous day—or, as Shae had put it, she'd worked while he'd played. He was about to depart for a seven-game road trip. It would be only his second one of the season, and already the routine was getting old.

A young man approached their table, breaking their trance. "Do you mind if I get an autograph, sir?"

"Sure." Rahn reached into his shirt pocket for a pen.

The young man cleared his throat. "I mean from Miss Carmen." He gazed at Shae, clearly smitten. "I've been a fan since you started at Channel Seven."

Shae graced him with a smile.

"You've got sixty seconds," Rahn answered for her. "We're on a tight schedule."

As far as Shae was concerned, Shakespeare had it wrong. *"Parting is such sweet sorrow"? No way.* There was nothing sweet about having to whisper good-bye to Rahn.

Shae had memorized the Cardinals' schedule before he left: a three-game series in Phoenix against the Diamondbacks; travel day; three games in San Francisco; back home. She was moping around her condo when Yvette called, lifting her spirits. It didn't take long before the conversation turned to Rahn. "I know you miss him," Yvette said.

"Yes, more than I thought I would." Shae sighed. "It's almost a tease." She flopped on the window seat and watched the rain pour down outside.

"It is, and you'll never get used to it. But there are ways of coping. Are you up for doing something fun tomorrow? Maybe lunch?"

Honestly, Shae didn't really care, and Yvette seemed to pick up on her hesitation. "I'll even let you talk my ear off about Rahn and still be your friend."

"Deal." Shae laughed because, deep down, she knew Rahn was all she wanted to talk about. Her sisters had pointed out as much, even going so far as to ask her to diversify her conversation topics during their Skype sessions. "Sure, I'd love to do lunch," she finally said.

The next day, when Shae left to meet Yvette, there was no rain in the forecast. The sunshine lifted her spirits even more, plus a brief phone conversation with Rahn.

He'd encouraged her with a Bible passage that was becoming their golden Scripture—1 Corinthians 13:4–7: *"Charity suffereth long, and is kind; charity envieth not; charity vaunteth not itself, is not puffed up, doth not behave itself unseemly, seeketh not her own, is not easily provoked, thinketh no evil; rejoiceth not in iniquity, but rejoiceth in the truth; beareth all things, believeth all things, hopeth all things, endureth all things."*

When she arrived at the restaurant, the two embraced, then Yvette suggested they dine on the patio. "It's gorgeous outside."

"I agree."

The hostess led them along a path around the common area to a side set of French doors that opened onto a magnificent garden of blooming trees and blossoming green plants. Even birds seemed to serenade patrons from their perches nearby. It was a perfect backdrop for the numerous wrought-iron café tables for two.

A soft breeze tickled Shae's ear as they took their seats. "This is nice."

"Isn't it?" Yvette said enthusiastically.

When their server arrived, both women ordered lemonades; Shae asked for a chicken salad, while Yvette went for a chicken salad sandwich.

Left alone, the two chatted about fashion, hobbies, and, eventually, baseball, until their food arrived. They paused to bless their meals and then picked up the conversation again.

"I have to ask," Shae finally said, "how you handle the long absences."

"I have two little ones to remind me of the man I love, but"—she wiped her mouth—"when they act up, I have no problem venting my frustration to their daddy after he finishes a game. If the team loses, though, I go easy on him."

Shae used her napkin to smother a laugh. "How long have you two been married?"

"Five wonderful years." Yvette beamed.

Did Yvette have any fears about Marcus's marital fidelity? Shae was curious, but she would never ask something so personal. She hadn't even asked her sister Stacy that question when she'd married Ted. Dismissing her curiosity, Shae switched topics as they enjoyed lunch. The time passed quickly until she had to leave for the station.

"Thanks for accepting my invitation. This really has been fun. My treat." Yvette paid their bill with her credit card. They walked together to the parking lot, where she gave Shae a good-bye hug and a piece of advice: "You and Rahn can make it. Rumors will abound about groupies sleeping with one player or another, but have faith in what you two have. And pray for him. Temptation can sneak up anywhere."

Shae's spirit lifted. "Are you saying that I have nothing to worry about?"

"Before Rahn's redemption, the lure was too great, and he indulged. After accepting Christ's salvation, my friend has a conviction that is unmovable, and he's in love with you."

"It's good to know I don't have to worry about the possibility of another woman." *Or of being the other woman.*

With one final wave, they went their separate ways.

At the station that afternoon, Shae hadn't even taken her seat when Diane bumped her chair against hers. "Hey," was her colleague's signature greeting. "The AP wire is reporting that there's been an arrest in Rahn's attempted carjacking case."

"Really?" Shae gave Diane her utmost attention. "That's great news." She quickly signed on to her computer and clicked on the Associated Press news tab to read the headlines and updates: "*St. Louis city police have arrested and charged three men from South St. Louis with the attempted carjacking of Cardinal slugger Rahn Maxwell…. Police set up a sting operation…*

Who says the media doesn't report good news? Shae thought, recalling Marcus's earlier complaint about the news business.

"You think he knows?" Diane peered over her shoulder.

"He's out of reach until after the game, but I'm sure this will make his day."

"Maybe he'll make *my* day and give KMMD his first reaction," said Greg Saxon, who'd appeared out of nowhere.

Shae eyed him warily. "Are you trying to use me to get to him?"

Greg exchanged a devilish grin with Diane. "It works for us," they said in perfect unison.

"The choice is his," Shae replied with a smirk. She refused to use her relationship with Rahn to earn brownie points with the station.

Besides that piece of breaking news, there wasn't much of anything else going on that was worth broadcasting. So, Shae collaborated with the producer and the assignment editor, Debra, in trying to drum up a meaningful story for her to report on. The upside of a slow news day was that Shae would be able to watch most of the Cardinals game while she updated a story she'd reported on a month earlier about the impact of a local food pantry closing its doors.

She switched the channel from CNN to the network that was about to air the game. Never had she appreciated a cameraperson's zoom lens more than when Rahn stepped up to the plate. Even in work mode, he was handsome, with his brown eyes and trim beard. Nothing he wore could hide his physique—a tailored suit, casual jeans, or a Cardinals uniform. Shae had to restrain herself from cheering out loud when his bat connected with the ball on the second pitch.

Although there was an unlimited number of interruptions from the staff and callers, Shae was able to keep up with the score. In the top of the seventh inning, one of the Diamondbacks' heavy hitters challenged Marcus's fastball. Shae pressed her palms together as if in prayer, and she didn't blink when the ball shot into the outfield. As the center fielder, Rahn had to make the call—try to catch it, or leave it to the right or left fielder. She willed his glove to go for it, but an emergency scanner shattered her concentration.

"Shae, we finally have something!" the assignment editor shouted from across the newsroom. She pumped her fist in the air. "Escaped prisoner in South St. Louis—yes!"

The timing couldn't have been worse. Shae leaped from her seat before the play was over and headed for the assignment desk. "What are the details?"

"The police say a black male dressed in a white hospital gown and wearing iron leg shackles jumped from a hospital window. Go figure why they can't spot him." Debra slapped her wide hips and scanned the newsroom for an available photographer. Then she picked up the phone. "Jeff to the assignment desk. Jeff Craig to the desk!" She twisted her lips into a scowl. "He's not doing anything but hiding from me."

When Jeff made his appearance moments later, he and Shae were quickly out the door and en route to the scene.

"Can you believe the security in this city?" Jeff joked, chewing on a straw as he drove. "The suspect should audition to be a stunt man in Hollywood."

"You know what they say...truth is stranger than fiction." Shae shook her head.

When they arrived at the location, Shae scrambled out of the news vehicle, carrying her microphone and notepad. Jeff followed with his camera. Her adrenaline pumped as she searched for an officer or a hospital spokesperson to interview. Of course, there were several bystanders eager to get some time in the spotlight. After they recorded a few interviews, Jeff shot video of the area, including the window the prisoner had jumped from. When the live truck with the editing bay arrived on the scene, Shae and Jeff got to work piecing together their story.

Forty-five minutes later, without a second to spare, they were ready with a video report, complete with scene images; the suspect's mug shot, provided by the police; and a handful of interviews. Stealing a minute for herself, Shae started to send Rahn a quick text about the good news on his case as her photographer set up his tripod.

Do you know

"Stand by," Shae's producer spoke through her earpiece, startling Shae and causing her to hit "send" before she was ready.

She stashed her cell phone in her pocket, cleared her throat, and mentally recited her opening line. Holding up her microphone, she waited for the anchor to introduce her story. "Good evening." She nodded to the camera. "The sheriff's department is advising residents in South St. Louis to keep all doors and windows locked tonight. A few hours ago, twenty-year-old Jesse Warner escaped from custody by climbing out of a third-floor window at St. Louis University Hospital. Warner is described as a black male, five feet seven, and bald. He has tattoos covering his right leg, and he was wearing leg shackles. Warner is wanted for selling and distributing narcotics and now for fleeing police custody. If you see this man, or have any information pertaining to him, notify the police. For Channel Seven news, I'm Shae Carmen, reporting live in South St. Louis."

"We're cleared," Jeff said. He looked around nervously as he removed his camera from its tripod. "Let's get out of here before this suspect decides to hijack our news vehicle."

Shae rolled her eyes. "Chicken."

"You've got that right. My job is to cover the story, not become part of it. C'mon, let's roll."

21

"*For even when we were with you, this we commanded you, that if any would not work, neither should he eat.*" Why did 2 Thessalonians 3:10 stand out to Rahn while he was reading his morning Scripture? The rule was a no-brainer that his mother had instilled in him and his sister when they were children.

Rahn loved his job—or "playtime," as Shae teasingly called it. But the fact remained that his livelihood was interfering with his love life. He lounged on his bed in the hotel suite he was sharing with Marcus, letting his mind drift, until his cell phone rang. The ringtone indicated it was Shae, calling to say she'd made it to her condo from work.

Closing his eyes, Rahn answered. "Since home is where the heart is, I'm homesick, baby."

Her giggle taunted him. "You've only been gone one day."

"Okay, Miss Carmen, you try to tell me it doesn't feel like one week apart."

"Guilty."

"Yeah." He exhaled. "Six more long days before we see each other again— Skype and FaceTime don't count. Speaking of the virtual world, I got your odd text earlier. What was that all about?"

"Oh, sorry. I pressed 'send' before I could finish the message, and we were at a scene, about to go live, so I didn't have time to correct it."

Rubbing his forehead, Rahn was afraid to ask what danger she'd been in this time, but her business was his business. "Please tell me there weren't any guns involved."

"Nope, just a boring old prisoner, escaped from a hospital window still wearing shackles. That's it."

Rahn let out a hoot. Marcus appeared in the doorway, frowning, evidently curious about the cause of his outburst. Apparently satisfied that he was okay, his friend shook his head and walked away.

Shae laughed along with him. Once they had composed themselves, she said, "I was trying to text you to see if you'd heard about the arrests made in your carjacking attempt."

"Yes, the police left a voice message that the bad guys confessed and are behind bars. Hopefully, that's the end of the story."

"Pretty much, unless there's a trial. I'm just so glad God intervened and spared your life, and that they'll be off the streets."

"Me, too," Rahn said, "though, in a sense, I owe those dudes."

"Are you insane? You could have been killed!"

"I know." Rahn shifted on his bed and glanced at the Gideon Bible on his nightstand. "But I recently read Genesis fifty, verse twenty: 'Ye thought evil against me; but God meant it unto good, to bring to pass, as it is this day, to save much people alive.' Although the devil had set up an ambush, God wouldn't let the gunmen harm me. That incident, bad though it was, brought me in contact with someone good—you, and Jesus. It was the best thing that could've happened to me."

Shae remained silent, though he thought he heard her sniffle. "Amen, in Jesus' name," she finally said. "It's because of my bad experience in Nebraska that I'm here in St. Louis. So, the Lord had my blessing awaiting me—you."

Her words hit home, making him miss her even more. They connected on so many levels. "I love you, you know that?"

"I do. And I love you, too."

Her attempt to stifle a yawn was ineffective—Rahn heard it, taking his cue to order her off the phone. "Get some rest, sweetheart. May God keep you safe and give you sweet dreams. We'll talk again tomorrow."

"If the Lord's wills it," Shae replied, as she always did. "Good night. I'll see you in my dreams."

His time away flew by, but no sooner had they reunited after that road trip than Rahn said another good-bye and was gone again. The days blurred after the Cardinals swept the New York Mets, then got pounded by the Atlanta Braves.

A lot more than the team redeeming itself after its losess was riding on the next series against the Phillies. This was personal. Rahn wasn't worried about his performance on the field; it was the impression he would make off the field, with Shae's family, that had him concerned. He arranged to have ten guest passes left at the gate of Citizens Bank Park in Philadelphia. He wouldn't be surprised if every one of them was claimed, which meant he would definitely be outnumbered by the Carmen family.

Shae had wanted desperately to be in her hometown and make proper introductions, but she couldn't get off work, since many of her colleagues were already on vacation. And that was okay with Rahn. He was a big boy and could handle the scrutiny. But he couldn't keep his mind from drifting while he waited in the dugout for his turn at bat.

At the top of the eighth inning, it was anyone's game, with the runs tied at four. The Cards had two outs, and Rahn was on deck to bat after David Freeman, but the third baseman struck out. Although the Cards needed to win, Rahn didn't look forward to extra innings. He wanted to get his long-awaited meet-and-greet over with.

Marcus struck out two of the Phillies' hitters, and Rahn caught a fly ball to end the eighth. In the ninth inning, Rahn was the leadoff hitter and managed a double. It wasn't long before the bases were loaded. But there were two outs when Matt Hammond came to bat. With the count at two strikes, Matt connected with a fast pitch and cleared the bases. Rahn was first to cross home plate. The Phillies couldn't duplicate the momentum in the bottom of the inning, and they lost to the Redbirds with a final score of 8 to 4.

In the locker room, teammates gave Matt kudos for saving the game and bringing an end to the Cardinals' losing streak.

"So, you nervous?" Marcus asked Rahn as they dressed after showering.

"What man wouldn't be? Family is important to Shae, and she's important to me. But I got this." Rahn slipped his feet into his shoes.

Ten minutes later, he strolled into the Hall of Fame Club lounge. Shae had texted him pictures and identified every family member she thought might attend. He recognized her mother right away. She was a striking woman with long, jet-black hair. Shae was definitely a younger version, only with skin the shade of honey.

Two equally beautiful women stood next to Mrs. Carmen—Shae's sisters. Both seemed happy to see him. He couldn't say the same for the four men towering over them like bodyguards. Two of them wore Phillies jerseys and eyed him with unreadable expressions.

An older, distinguished-looking gentleman approached him, smiling broadly. "Great game, Mr. Maxwell," he boomed. "I'm Bradford Carmen, Shae's uncle." He pumped Rahn's hand with a strong grip. The man had the charisma of a mega-church pastor, and that put Rahn at ease.

"It's nice to meet you, sir."

"Likewise," Bradford said, then made the formal introductions. "This is my wife, Camille, and my sister-in-law, Annette—Shae's mother."

Annette's eyes twinkled like Shae's. "Hello, Rahn. It's so nice to meet you." She gave his hand a soft squeeze. "My daughter said you were a great player. I agree."

Bradford laughed. "Those two don't know anything about baseball that I haven't told them."

"And they still don't know the difference between a strike and a foul ball," said a younger man, stepping forward. He was about the same height as Rahn. "I'm Ted, Shae's brother-in-law. This is my wife, Stacy, the oldest sister." His arm slipped possessively around her waist, and the loving gesture made Rahn wish for Shae. He admired any couple who seemed to be still in love after tying the knot.

"I'm Garrett," said another young man. Rahn shook his hand. "Good luck," Garrett added. "The Carmens are hard on a brother. This is my girl, Shari Carmen, Esquire." He beamed with pride at the woman, whose flawless dark skin reminded Rahn of an African queen.

Since the baby sister, Brecee, lived in Houston and was therefore missing in action, all the Carmen women had been accounted for. The two gentlemen who hadn't moved watched him with their arms folded. Rahn exchanged nods with them, but, judging from their body language, they weren't easily impressed. When Bradford cleared his throat, one of them stepped forward.

"Thanks for the tickets. I'm Victor, Shae's cousin." Victor offered Rahn a handshake. The darkness of his skin and features were almost identical to Shari's. Victor was clean-shaven and an inch or two shorter than Rahn.

"Dino. I'm his younger brother and backup." Built like an offensive tackle, Dino tilted his head toward Victor. His hair was straight, like Shari's, and he'd tied it back in a ponytail.

Hadn't that fashion craze played out a long time ago? Rahn wasn't about to ask. Instead, he watched with amusement as the pair sized him up. He wasn't easily intimidated—unless someone had an assault rifle pointed at him. "Nice to meet you."

Dino finally extended his hand and gave him the firmest shake of them all, squeezing hard as if he was trying to extract blood for the Red Cross without a needle.

Staring him in the eye, Rahn gave it right back, then turned to address the group. "I don't know about you all, but I've worked up an appetite. Since the team is staying at the Ritz-Carlton, I was hoping we could get to know each other over dinner at Del Frisco's Steakhouse, since it's right near there. My treat."

"That's expensive," Annette whispered, seeming to do a silent head count.

"It's not a problem, Mrs. Carmen."

"I'm rather starved, myself," Ted said, patting his own stomach and then his wife's.

Shae had told Rahn about her pending status as an aunt, so he congratulated the expectant couple. They beamed and thanked him before everyone filed out of the lounge.

"We'll need at least twenty minutes—thirty minutes, tops—to get through the traffic on Broad Street," Ted advised.

"I'll call the restaurant and let them know how many are in our party," Rahn told them. "See you there."

They walked out of the lounge together and parted ways at the curb. Rahn rode in the team's car service to the hotel, while the Carmens headed to the parking garage.

Half an hour later, the party of eight was gathered in a private dining room at Del Frisco's. Everyone ordered without much deliberation. It didn't go unnoticed by Rahn that they made conservative dinner choices. To him, that spoke volumes about their character. In his experience, most people splurged when a celebrity was picking up the tab.

A whirlwind of conversation circulated around the table while they waited for their meals. The men wanted to talk baseball, so Rahn fielded their questions, most of them centered on the day he was called up from the minor leagues to play in the majors. "I've been chasing my father's record ever since," he admitted.

"You're holding your own," Bradford assured him.

Annette and Camille were more concerned about his intentions toward Shae. "The Carmens have strong family ties," Annette informed him. Her voice was no longer soft but commanding. "My daughter doesn't recover easily from bad relationships. She may be a no-nonsense reporter, but she has a tender heart. The Carmen girls are a special breed. They're mine, and I'm a force to be reckoned with, even without these guys to back me up"—she gestured to the other men at the table—"if she suffers even as much as a hairline fracture to her heart."

Rahn took a deep breath. "Understood. I'm happy to say that I've repented in Christ of all my dirty deeds. Now, he whom the Son has set free is free indeed." Rahn smiled. "I can protect Shae's heart. She's very important to me."

"Good answer." Annette returned his smile, and for a second, Rahn thought he was staring into Shae's face.

"Speaking of protection," Dino broke in, "I guess a man of your status never thought you would be a crime victim, huh?"

Victor nudged him, but Shae's cousin didn't back down. Was his question laced with concern or mockery? Either way, it seemed Rahn wouldn't escape without talking about the incident.

"My life has forever changed," he acknowledged. "In an instant, I was knocked off my high horse, and while I was down, the sweetest, most beautiful, loving woman brought me back to life—your cousin. I love her fiercely and I'd protect her by any means necessary." Rahn shot Dino a pointed stare and forced him to blink first.

The women seemed pleased. The other men were quiet for a moment, and then they started applauding him. Soon everyone was clapping softly—even Dino.

Lord, thank You for winning them over…I think.

~

Shae twisted several strands of hair with her finger. Why hadn't she heard from Rahn or her family? The game had been over hours ago. Stuck at her desk, Shae was antsy. Her mind multitasked, reading the news feeds from various stations across the country and praying that her family liked Rahn. It wasn't like she had nothing to write. She had been assigned a two-part story on local pesticide companies that were using banned ingredients that caused customers and workers to fall ill.

When the quirky "your mother's calling" ringtone played, Shae jumped as she reached to answer her phone and learn the family's verdict on Rahn Maxwell. "Hi, Mother."

Evidently, she had been patched in to a conference line, because everyone was speaking at one time. "Okay, who wants to be the spokesman?" Shae's head was spinning as she tried to piece together the different assessments.

Uncle Bradford gave his animated recap of Rahn's every play, as if Shae hadn't seen most of the game on television herself. "I'm thinking about writing to the commissioner of baseball," he told her.

Uh-oh. "Why?"

"Do you know the Cardinals play the Pittsburgh Pirates seventeen times this season?" he practically whined.

"Okay…so?"

"The Phillies only get eight shots with St. Louis." He took a breath.

She still wasn't following him. Plus, she already knew all that. As a matter of fact, the calendars in her home were circled on the dates Rahn would return, and she'd programmed her cell phone to alert her accordingly. If all else failed, her heart had his return dates memorized. The downside was, when she calculated their time together, it was miniscule before he was off again.

"And the last three games are in hot and humid St. Louis," he ranted on.

"No worries, Uncle Bradford. My condo has air-conditioning. I guess you'll be meeting me in St. Louis, as the song says." One crisis averted. "So, what did everyone think about Rahn as a person?"

"We were all impressed," her mother said. "I think even Mother Stillwell would be pleased."

Shae frowned. What did Mother Stillwell have to do with this? "She didn't attend the game, too, did she?" She didn't want to link her happiness to the church mother who had a fifty-fifty chance of being a reliable forecaster of potentially blissful unions. Shae's relationship with Rahn had nothing to do with Mother Stillwell's self-proclaimed "gift." No, the fingerprints of a divine Matchmaker were all over her and Rahn.

"Oh no, dear. She always asks about you." Her mother's explanation didn't placate her.

"He's too much of a pretty boy for my taste," Dino asserted.

"Be nice," Stacy ordered on the line. Without any sisters to protect, Victor and Dino had never stopped stepping in since the Carmen sisters had reached an approved dating age.

"Do you expect her to date an ugly man?" Stacy silenced their cousin.

"Well," Uncle Bradford took the lead again, "I like him. Not easily intimidated, strong handshake, and personable. I'm sure he wanted to be anywhere but with a roomful of strangers without you to act as a buffer. I say you hit a home run." He chuckled at his joke; others groaned at his sports analogy.

"Me, too." Shae grinned. "I praise God that I didn't strike out again."

22

Rahn had flowers delivered to Shae at work before the Cardinals' chartered plane touched down at Lambert Airport. An invitation was included. Finally, his lady was within hugging, kissing, and praying together distance.

"I'd love to join you for an 'inspirational breakfast' in the morning, Mr. Maxwell," she cooed into the phone as he was driving home from the airport. Her professional voice melted away to a preferable softness whenever they talked. "I've missed you so much! What's so inspirational about it?"

"I'll be dining with you."

He imagined Shae's seductive smile when she sighed. Before he could further create an idyllic picture in his mind, out-of-control police scanners blasted in the background, shattering the moment. How could Shae stand all that noise?

"Hey, I've to go, babe," she said, her professional tone kicking back in. "Breaking news—a mob fight at a mall." She gave him a soft kiss.

"Be safe, okay? This man loves you."

"I know, and I love him back, and I always take Jesus with me." She disconnected.

"Lord, help me to always do my part to protect her heart, mind, and body, in Jesus' name," he prayed. "Amen."

During the rest of the drive home, for reasons unknown, Rahn did a quick assessment of his life. He had been a resident of Wildwood, a West County suburb, for years. He enjoyed the secluded estates away from I-64 and major streets. Whenever he returned from being on the road with the team, city-hopping across the country, Rahn always welcomed the sight of his stately house and the solitude it offered. It truly had been a man's castle, with high-end electronics at his fingertips and home-cooked meals prepared by his housekeeper. Not to mention a healthy, never-ending social life. Rahn had thought he had it all…until he had come face-to-face with Shae. Somehow, without her presence to share it, the multi-level, twelve-room house felt empty, despite the fine furnishings.

Minutes after walking into his home, Rahn unpacked, a task that took little effort. He sorted clean clothes from dirty, put his toiletries away, and rested his suitcase in the corner, open, ready to be refilled.

Usually, he liked to unwind when he got home, but his only desire was to see Shae. With a plan in motion, Rahn showered, changed, then grabbed his car keys again. After running some errands, he eventually ended up in the lobby of Shae's condo, chatting with Mr. Chapman as they watched the ten o'clock news. As the credits flashed on the screen, Rahn counted down the minutes until Shae's car pulled up to the curb.

The look of surprise on her beautiful but tired face when he acted as her doorman was priceless. He braced himself for the impact as she flew into his arms, then laughed as she squeezed him with all her might, and they rocked from side to side. "Now that is a welcome-home greeting any man would envy."

Few words were spoken as he indulged in her loving, until she abruptly broke free of his embrace. He frowned at the loss of contact. "Baby, what's wrong?"

"You," she ordered, pointing to the door. "Go home."

Rahn's jaw dropped. "Huh? A few seconds ago you were glad to see me."

"And a few seconds later, I still am, but I need a good night's sleep so I can look my best for my breakfast date with this good-looking man." She kissed him, then escaped inside an elevator. "Call me when you get home," she yelled as the doors closed.

"Hey, I'm that good-looking man," he tried to tell her, but she was already in flight to her floor.

"Miss Carmen was wrong for that." Mr. Chapman snickered.

Rahn stood there for a minute, shaking his head. "I know, but I wouldn't love her any other way." With a wave good-bye to the guard, he strolled outside, turned around, and counted the fourteen floors up to the dark window of her condo.

Shoving his hands into his pants' pockets, he waited. Seconds after the lights flickered on, Shae appeared as a goddess in the window. Rahn relaxed and grinned. She made a production of blowing him a kiss. In turn, he lifted his hand and moved to the right, pretending to catch it like a baseball in his glove. Whatever she threw his way, he wouldn't drop the ball on it.

⌒

The next morning, Shae was downright giddy as she talked to Brecee on speakerphone while getting dressed for her morning date. Anything she did with Rahn was exciting, as long as they were together. "We're having an inspirational breakfast."

"Judging from the way the family's been raving, you've definitely got a winner," Brecee said. "I'm so glad you got back in the game. Pun intended, if it worked."

Chuckling at her sister's sports allusion, Shae brushed a light bronzer on her face. "Yeah, you really hit that one out of the park." She and Brecee chuckled at her silliness.

"Please. Mine was better," Brecee argued, then added, "The happiness I hear in your voice proves my point that God still has good men out there for us sanctified sisters, and I hope I'm next."

Us? Shae froze, surprised by Brecee's statement. She had always thought her sister was too ambitious to surrender to love. "I pity the poor man. He'll be trying to tame a tiger, with your in-your-face loose lips. I've got to go."

Humming a familiar gospel tune, Shae gathered her hair on top of her head. With the weather forecast predicting heat and humidity, she chose a colorful sundress and sexy sandals to highlight her recent pedicure. She scrutinized her looks from different angles. By the time she was satisfied with her reflection, Rahn's ringtone alerted her to his call. She answered in a singsong tone, "I'll be ready and waiting!"

Silence. She frowned when he didn't interject one of his witty sayings. "Is everything okay?"

"N-no..."

His stuttering scared her. "What's wrong?"

"My sister called. My mother was just rushed to the hospital by ambulance. She was unconscious."

Shae gasped. "Oh, no! Is she okay? What happened?"

Rahn sighed heavily. "Baby, I don't know, but I've got to take the next flight out."

"Of course." *He needs me.* Since Shae had chatted with his mother several times on FaceTime, she hoped her presence would be welcomed. She would have taken the day off, but that wasn't possible during February, May, or November sweeps, especially since Channel Five had edged out Channel Seven in ratings. Since then, everybody at KMMD-TV had been working hard to regain the lead. No vacations were scheduled; even sick days were questioned.

But she had to be there for him. "I'll come with you. It's early enough that I can get back in time for work."

23

You can't. You'd never make it back in time," Rahn said, remembering the wise adage *"The best laid schemes of mice and men often go awry."* "Planes are definitely not the fastest way to travel when you really need to get there."

Rahn couldn't keep the frustration from seeping into his voice. "I'm catching the first flight out, but it has a layover in Atlanta. So, I'll arrive in Richmond one hour earlier than the next nonstop out of here."

"Do you need me to take you to the airport?"

He was touched by her offer as he exited onto I-270. "Thanks, but no thanks. I'm already on the way." Plus, she had no idea where he lived.

"Then I'll meet you at the airport before you go through security." She continued to grasp at straws, and he loved her determination to be there for him. Her concern was comforting, and Rahn craved a moment with her, even for thirty seconds. But where? He knew she wouldn't want a public display of affection. He wracked his brain. "How about the cell phone lot? That way, I'll be—"

"See you in twenty minutes tops." *Click.*

Even without her saying it, Rahn felt her love, and he needed it, because his thoughts were jumbled. *Lord, I can't even pray right now.* Rahn hadn't cried since his father had died. *God, help me not to break down before Shae sees me.* Driving on autopilot, Rahn found himself at Lambert Airport in no time. He followed the directions to the cell-phone lot, where he was surprised to find Shae already waiting.

She got out of her car as he pulled in next to her. If his mother hadn't fallen sick, nothing would have kept him away from her. She looked gorgeous—lilac was her color—and her smile was bright and warm as she opened her arms. Rahn stepped out of his car and walked into her embrace. It was the soothing balm he craved—her touch, her whispered words, and her sweet fragrances, which normally excited him but now seemed to calm his inner turmoil.

Reluctantly, Rahn pulled away from her. "Sorry to cancel." He gritted his teeth. "It'll be more than a week before we can see each other again. When I got

117

the news, I had my agent take care of a two-day leave of absence request for this family emergency."

"*Shh.*" She brushed a kiss against his lips. "You only have one mother. Go see about her. James five, verse sixteen, says, '*Confess your faults one to another, and pray one for another, that ye may be healed. The effectual fervent prayer of a righteous man availeth much.*' Know that I'm praying fervently for her recovery and your peace." Closing her eyes and bowing her head, Shae whispered, "Father God, in the mighty name of Jesus, we come boldly to Your throne of grace, where we might obtain mercy..."

Rahn doubted he could utter any words without breaking down, so he just listened. After losing his father, he didn't want to think about his mother not being in his life.

"Jesus, we know the power of life and death is in Your tongue. We ask that You command the condition to be removed from Mrs. Maxwell's body. Raise her up, give her a testimony of praise, and comfort Rahn's heart. Give him peace in this storm, in Jesus' name. Amen."

"Amen," Rahn said, his voice cracking. "You give me peace." He rubbed her arms, not taking his eyes off her.

"Everything is going to be all right."

He nodded. "I know. I keep telling myself that. When my dad died of a brain aneurysm seven years ago, my sister, Phyllis, and I became concerned about mom's medical history. She's borderline diabetic. Maxwell might be a big name in some circles, but our family is small. Honestly, we have more friends than family. I want to change that." He was about to disclose something he had never shared with any woman. "When I marry, I want to have at least three or four children as my contribution to the Maxwell dynasty."

"That sounds like a good number. I hope your wife agrees to that." Shae did a poor job of keeping a straight face.

Her tease made him smile. "I think I can convince her."

"I'll be rooting for you." She giggled. "I can't imagine a happy childhood without more than one sibling. With three sisters and two close cousins, we had each other's backs. We still do. It's up to Victor and Dino to carry on the Carmen name."

Rahn gathered her hands, brought them to his mouth, and planted soft kisses on them, then guided her arms around him. Without saying a word, he enjoyed their last embrace. "I'd better go."

Shae's eyes became misty. "Remember James five sixteen. '*The effectual fervent prayer of a righteous man availeth much.*'"

"I'll remember." Stealing one more glance at her, Rahn got back into his car. As he drove off, he braced himself for whatever bad news awaited him yet prayed for something good. *Lord, I've confessed all my faults to You, so please hear my prayers.*

He parked in the long-term lot, slung the strap of his duffel bag over his shoulder, and then, with his boarding pass in hand, cleared security. Ninety minutes later, he was fastening his seatbelt. Closing his eyes, Rahn couldn't think about his mother being rushed to the emergency room without reflecting on his father's final journey to the hospital. *Lord, let Mom come back home.*

It seemed as if the flight had taken a day and a half before Rahn's plane landed at Richmond International Airport. He texted Shae as soon as he was permitted to turn his cell phone on again.

I made it, babe. Talk to you soon. Be safe on the job.

Once he debarked from the plane, he walked through the terminal, his steps dragging with dread of the unknown—of seeing his mother in a state he didn't want to imagine. Phyllis and her husband, Louis, were waiting for him as he rounded the corner. His big sister met him halfway and clung to him when he hugged her.

It was the same ritual that had happened when Rahn had gone home in January after the attempted carjacking. Phyllis hadn't wanted to let him go. With a sad expression, Louis shook his hand and patted him on the back. It was déjà vu.

"How is she?" Rahn asked with his arm around his sister's shoulder as they walked toward the parking garage.

"She's conscious. The tests showed she is no longer a borderline diabetic... she's crossed over to full-blown diabetes. Her blood sugar level was nearly four hundred and fifty!"

"What?" Rahn gasped, choking on his own air.

Phyllis nodded. "Praise God she's okay. You better believe I gave her a serious scolding about her diet and the insulin injections that she *will* be taking." Petite in stature, Phyllis possessed the attitude of a giant. She didn't mince words when it came to having her way. Even her five-year-old twins jumped at just one look from her.

"I want to go see her right now." Rahn had two days to talk some sense into his mother. Be it by threats or incentives, she would change her lifestyle. He needed her to be around to see those grandchildren he wanted to give her.

Eloise Maxwell's eyes lit up as Rahn slipped quietly into her ICU room at Virginia Commonwealth twenty long minutes later. Although the IV restricted her movements, his mother was able to lift her hand. Rahn kissed her forehead before dragging a chair closer to her bed. He felt a sense of relief that she looked better than he'd expected and that her heart monitor had a steady beat. *Thank You, Jesus.*

"Mom, your options have run out. You're past the pill stage. You must give yourself daily insulin shots."

She turned her head away from him like a defiant child. When she faced him again, her eyes were glossy. "I'm sorry to worry you and make you miss your games." Her voice was weak.

"The games will be played, whether I'm there in center field or not. I've only got one mother"—he recalled Shae's phrase—"but you've got to take better care of yourself. Do I need to get you a live-in caregiver?"

"Hush," she said, gathering strength from somewhere to become indignant. "Young man, I'm very capable of taking care of myself." Her rant seemed to drain her, so Rahn held his peace. Once she settled down, he grabbed her hand and quietly prayed as he watched her, hoping she would drift off to sleep. Of course, she didn't.

Rahn's stomach growled, reminding him he was hungry. He stood and rubbed his mother's arm, careful of her IV. "Shae is praying for you."

"I want to meet her," she mumbled, closing her eyes.

"I want that, too, Mom." He kissed her forehead, then stood over her bed as she finally dozed off. Exhaling, he exited her room and took advantage of the opportunity to speak with her doctor, who happened to be coming to check on her.

"Your mother will live a long, healthy life if she makes some drastic changes to her diet and monitors her blood sugar levels," the doctor assured him. "She admitted she hadn't been doing that, and she is going to need someone to hold her accountable. She was lucky this time."

"My mother was blessed," Rahn corrected the physician. He and his sister would double-team their mother to follow the doctor's orders. After thanking the doctor, Rahn headed toward the exit of the intensive care unit.

As he was about to push the button to open the double doors, a familiar voice grabbed his attention. It belonged to St. Louis native Joe Buck, who had interviewed him many times in the broadcast booth after a game.

Rahn paused and listened to the sports announcer give a play-by-play on a baseball game against the Colorado Rockies. He was reminded that the Cardinals would be playing without him for the next few days.

Since the curtain wasn't completely shielding the patient, Rahn peeped inside the room, expecting to see an old soul. To his surprise, a young man who looked barely a teenager was hooked up to numerous machines.

Although the patient seemed drugged, he made eye contact with Rahn, pointed at him, and struggled to speak. His movement got the attention of an older man posted at his bedside, who gawked at Rahn. With two pairs of eyes staring at him, Rahn stepped closer to the room but didn't enter. "Hello."

"Are you...are you Rahn Maxwell?" the man asked.

"Yes, sir, I am."

"Really?" The patient struggled to prop himself up on his elbows.

"Watch it, Son," his father cautioned him, then motioned for Rahn to enter. Rahn approached the bed. "How ya doing, buddy? What's your name?"

"Benjamin...I'm sick," he said, speaking slowly and slurring his words.

"He had a sickle cell episode a few days ago, on his eighteenth birthday," Benjamin's father explained.

Eighteen? He definitely didn't look his age. Rahn had never met anyone with the disease, which was surprising, since it affected people of color at a higher rate than other ethnic groups. Benjamin seemed fragile. "Get better, buddy. I need all the fans I can get," Rahn said, trying to cheer him up.

He thought about the three autographed baseballs he traveled with, to give to any young fans he might encounter. It was one of those odd habits his dad had passed down to him. Rahn had continued the tradition as a way to honor his father's memory following his death. "A young child could become a fan for life," Ronald Maxwell would always say. Even some of Rahn's teammates had started doing the same thing. Benjamin would get one.

Pray for him, the Lord spoke to Rahn's heart, giving him an overwhelming yearning for the teenager.

Me? He had no fancy words, as a minister would, so he hesitated. Praying at home behind closed doors, with Shae, or at her church, in unison with others, didn't qualify him to publicly pray for a stranger.

Pray for him. God's command was clear.

Rahn swallowed, then decided to ask the father for permission. "Sir, do you mind if we say a little prayer?" When the man consented, Rahn took a deep breath and bowed his head. He waited. Was Jesus going to give him the words to say, or would He direct him to intercede with tongues?

"In the name of Jesus," Benjamin's father began.

Then the words seem to flow out of Rahn: "We come before You, Lord, with thanksgiving for a new day...also for Benjamin. Jesus, we know that Your blood works for healing and salvation. Please cover his body with Your blood and command the sickness to flee. Although we don't know Your plan for Benjamin's life, please give him the strength to praise You and the faith to believe in Your Word. Thank You, God, in Jesus' name. Amen."

"Amen," Benjamin mumbled.

"Thank you so much, Mr. Maxwell." Benjamin's father wiped his eyes.

"Thank God," Rahn said. It was the second person he'd had to correct within an hour. *Jesus, I know miracles still exist because You performed one the night You spared me. Benjamin could sure use one now.* "If you would like an autographed baseball, I'll bring you one when I return tomorrow to see my mother again," he told Benjamin.

Benjamin mustered a smile, but the excitement didn't reach his eyes.

Seems God is adding to my prayer burden, Rahn thought as he left. Not only did he have his mother on his prayer list, but now Benjamin, too. His mind was elsewhere when he joined his sister and brother-in-law in the family waiting lounge.

Phyllis and Louis stood. "Well?" Phyllis said. "Did she seem to listen to you?"

"I added my two cents, and I'm praying to God that He gives her a mind to want to live a long, long time. Come on. I'm drained and hungry."

"I'm still not used to my baby brother—"

"He's hasn't been a baby since he gave up his training pants," Louis snickered.

Phyllis playfully stuck out her tongue at him. "I know that." Then she ignored him, turning back to Rahn. "Anyway, I'm still getting used to you putting God in the mix of situations. I admire your sincerity. You seem so natural with your salvation and not ashamed. Momma's scare is forcing me to up my prayer life, too."

"That's all God," Rahn said. "Plus, being with Shae has made the transition easy."

"I can't wait to meet her." Phyllis smiled mischievously.

"I can't wait to get back to her, but I have to make sure Mom is okay first."

Their destination was his sister's spacious ranch house, where Rahn had decided to stay, instead of at his own Virginia home. For this short period of time, he needed to be close to family. When he arrived, Phyllis's twins, Julius and Julian, greeted him at the door. The babysitter squeezed past, waving good-bye.

Rahn braced for his nephews' customary tackle, feigning helplessness by yelling for his brother-in-law. And, as always, Louis deserted him, forcing Rahn to ask for a time-out. His nephews enforced the penalty of dragging him to their shared bedroom, where they showed off the latest additions to their baseball card collection and their new catcher's gloves.

"Do you have a girlfriend?" Julian asked. He grinned, showing a gap from a missing tooth.

Before Rahn could answer, Julius bumped his brother out of the way. "Are you going to have babies and give us cousins to play with? Aunt Mary only has stupid girls." He gagged as if he was going to vomit.

Julian picked up his glove and struggled to wiggle his small hand inside. Rahn helped him. "Uncle Rahn, can we come live with you in your mansion?"

"Come eat!" Phyllis called from the kitchen. Rahn couldn't ask for better timing to escape their inquisitive minds.

As expected, the boys asked about their grandmother, and then Julian repeated his request: "Can we come and live with you, Uncle Rahn?"

"Say the word, and I'll pack their bags," Louis joked. Or maybe he was serious. It was an entertaining dinner, as always.

After everyone had finished, Louis helped his sons with their homework, while Rahn brainstormed a plan of action with his sister. "So, we agreed on a medical monitoring service?" Rahn recapped.

Phyllis nodded. "Yes, in addition to me stalking her and you harassing her over the phone. And you know she doesn't want to come and live with me, so I think we've got it covered. Now that we've got that out of the way, do I hear wedding bells?" His sister grinned.

"It's possible." He shrugged. Baseball season was a terrible time to start a relationship, but he and Shae were putting in a lot of effort to make it work. "As a matter of fact, I'd better go text her."

"I'm surprised you lasted this long." She gave him a goofy grin.

Retiring to the guest bedroom, Rahn did just that.

I saw Mom. She's okay, but she has full-blown diabetes and will have to take medicine for the rest of her long life. Miss you and love you forever.

Smiling, he hit "send." Regardless of what city or time zone he was in, Rahn drew comfort from knowing they would always talk before the night was over.

Rahn showered, dressed in a fresh set of clothes, and read a few passages from Hebrews. A while later, his cell phone played Shae's distinctive ringtone. He hadn't realized he had closed his eyes. "Hey, baby."

"You sound tired."

Yes, he was, but Rahn wasn't about to fess up to it. After recapping his discussion with his mother's doctor and the plan he and Phyllis had decided on, he told her about Benjamin's struggle with sickle-cell anemia.

"Jesus, please perform a miracle in his body," Shae whispered. "I did a story months ago on how diseases affect certain ethnic groups, broken down by age and sex. My heart ached the entire time I worked on that piece. I'll keep praying for your mother and Benjamin, too."

"I knew you would." Their conversation was cut short when, this time, it was he who did a poor job of muffling a yawn.

After a restless night, the morning came too soon. Back at the hospital, the doctors were confident that his mother could be discharged if she agreed to follow a strict daily diet and exercise regime. Neither Rahn nor Phyllis batted an eye, to show her they meant business, so their mother agreed. Next on Rahn's agenda was Benjamin. However, when Rahn checked, the young man was no longer in his room. He inquired after him at the nurses' station.

"Benjamin Cross was moved to a regular room earlier this morning," the nurse informed him. "He's on the sixth floor." She gave him the room number.

After thanking the woman, Rahn rode the elevator down with his mother and the hospital staff member who was pushing her wheelchair. He got off on Benjamin's floor, while his mother continued to the lobby, to wait for his sister to bring the car around.

Rahn sauntered down the hall, checking the numbers by the doors.

"May I help you?" a nurse asked. Two other nurses looked up at him, and one gave him a seductive glance.

Shaking his head, Rahn spied room 612 and pointed. "Thanks." He tapped on Benjamin's door before proceeding inside. This time, a woman sat at the bedside. Her weariness was evident by the dark circles under her eyes. By contrast, Benjamin appeared more alert today than yesterday.

"Mr. Maxwell. Hello." She stirred in her chair, about to get up, but Rahn stopped her. She seemed relieved as she leaned back. "I'm Denise, Bennie's mother. My husband told me you offered a prayer for him. Thank you. As you can see, prayer does change things. My son's improved condition is evidence of that. He's been expecting you."

"And I've been looking forward to seeing him, too." Smiling, Rahn pulled out the autographed baseball from his inside jacket pocket. He personalized it, then handed it over.

"Thank you," Benjamin said, with awe in his tone, his voice stronger than yesterday. He even threw out a few of Rahn's stats.

Rahn was about to leave when Denise stopped him. "Mr. Maxwell, please don't stop praying for him."

"I'll remember." As he retraced his steps back to the elevator, a smile tugged at his lips. *Yes, Jesus, prayer does change things. Thank You.*

He and his sister got their mother settled back in her home in no time. Rahn double-checked the instructions with his mother to the point that she'd become irritated. "I know how to take care of myself," she snapped. "I took care of two children and a husband."

"Okay, Mom," Phyllis conceded.

As Rahn prepared to leave that afternoon to rejoin the team in Atlanta, the family linked hands for a group prayer. Again, Rahn waited on God to speak to him, as others looked to him to take the lead. He said a simple, heartfelt prayer for healing and wisdom.

"Amen," they all said together.

"Next time you come home, bring Miss Carmen," his mother demanded with a smile.

"I will." Rahn winked, then kissed her cheek before leaving.

Phyllis dropped him off at the airport. He texted Shae before he boarded the plane.

I'm leaving. Mom's doing better. Wish I could detour to St. Louis to see you. Love you.

His sister had asked him about wedding bells. Maybe it was time for them to start ringing. Shae was interwoven in his heart and world.

24

$\mathcal{S}$hae was spoiled—and it was Rahn's doing—but she wasn't complaining. As a matter of fact, he had established a protocol, and now she expected flowers to be delivered at the station whenever he returned from a road trip.

Diane Duncan inhaled the fragrance of the latest floral showpiece gracing Shae's desk, then stated the obvious: "Umm, Mr. Maxwell must be home."

"Of course!" Shae beamed, barely glancing over her shoulder. An invitation to breakfast the next day—their "welcome-home meal"—was included with every delivery, but her colleague didn't need to know that.

Shae was off the next day, but the Cardinals were starting a three-game home series against the Cincinnati Reds. Lately, it seemed as if her schedule and Rahn's were never in sync, but they were determined to squeeze in a few private moments before he took off again, beginning with their breakfast date.

As Shae saved the news copy she had just finished writing, she sensed a presence behind her. Twirling in her chair, she was surprised to see Diane still standing there, arms folded, studying the arrangement.

"Did you want something?"

Diane huffed and shook her head. "How do you do it?"

Staring at her, Shae was dumbfounded. Unless she'd zoned out like she sometimes did while thinking about Rahn, she was clueless as to what Diane was alluding to.

Perching her behind on someone else's desk, Diane made a production of fanning her arm in the air as if she was about to take a bow, then whispered, "You're dating this high-profile celebrity ball player, yet you act as if he's a regular truck driver—no, make that a delivery man for a floral shop."

Shae narrowed her eyes, waiting to see where this conversation was going.

"The man is hot and on the road, but you don't seem to have any concerns about trusting him. Has that ever crossed your mind?"

If Diane was trying to bait her to confide in her, then the woman was wasting her time. Shae had three sisters, one mother, two cousins, and Yvette for that. And her trust issues had vanished after Rahn's first road trip.

126

She wished she could boast that she didn't date men she didn't trust, but she would have to eat her words. The look in Diane's eyes revealed that she was more than curious. Taking a deep breath, Shae answered, "I trust God, and everything else falls in place. Rahn may be out of my sight, but he's never out of God's sight, and neither am I."

Diane shook her head. "You and your Jesus." She walked away, mumbling her own philosophy about dating.

Shae chuckled as she gave an imaginary high-five to her sister. She could hear Brecee say, "Good save."

⌒

Two days—two dates. That's exactly what Rahn and Shae had planned before his next trip. Both were determined to make a marathon out of it. Since Shae wanted to see a movie, Rahn took her to see 42, the story of how Jackie Robinson had helped integrate baseball.

Shae seemed reflective as they exited the theater and strolled through Plaza Frontenac toward Bissinger's Chocolate. His woman couldn't resist a taste of English Almond Toffee.

With her arm looped through his, she was still commenting on the movie. "So that explains why all the players on every team wore the number forty-two on their jerseys on April fifteenth. I guess that's one way never to forget the power of one—one man caught between the post-slavery struggle and the pre-affirmative action/equal opportunity era."

Shae had a way of sucking Rahn into her commentaries on various issues. It was part of who she was, and he wouldn't change anything about her—even her job—because that was her passion. Of course, God was first; Rahn was just glad he'd made the cut. He grinned to himself, then nodded to a few shoppers who clearly recognized him and were respectful of his off-time.

"What's your take?" she asked, pulling him out of his reverie.

"I agree with your conclusions." It took him a minute to remember exactly what she had been saying. "Uh, my parents, especially my father, made sure I understood the ramifications of the Civil Rights Movement and why it had to happen. I have to admit, at times, I've forgotten about those sacrifices and fallen short of my own expectations."

He could still recall his father's words of wisdom on the subject: *"Don't take the pleasures you enjoy lightly. Christ paid the price for our sins, and many of our ancestors paid the price of living proudly to be black and forcing the majority to open doors.*

Walk through them, Son, mixing humility with a bit of pride. Balance the two and make people of color proud."

"What's ironic is, Jackie Robinson broke the color barrier in the late nineteen forties for blacks to play in an integrated league, yet the number of African-Americans playing baseball has dwindled," Rahn added.

"And the reason is…?" Shae prompted him, switching to her reporter persona. The woman had to be the most inquisitive person he knew, and that was saying a lot, remembering his two rambunctious nephews. As they neared Bissinger's, Shae slowed her pace. She was an astute listener and gave him her attention.

"There could be a number of factors," Rahn mused aloud. "The League reaches out to more people of color who aren't U.S. citizens. For some African-American boys, baseball isn't the cool sport it used to be—not when they can get full-ride athletic scholarships for football and basketball. The reasons could be endless. But Jackie Robinson made sure the door would never be locked again—in theory. Society knows how to get around it."

Shae nodded. "But there will always be first blacks to open doors, like President Obama, who opened the door for other people of color to achieve the highest office in the land, or the ABC television affiliate in Utah that hired the state's first African-American news anchor in 2013. My hope is that doors will continue to open for people of color, especially blacks, where their opportunities won't be breaking news anymore but part of the norm. Now, let's get my toffee." Shae playfully dragged him into the store, knowing that he would go willingly anywhere with her.

"Beauty and brains…priceless." Rahn smiled and proceeded to do her bidding.

The day before Rahn and the team were set to leave, Shae wanted to do something fun and silly. She complained that eating out was adding inches to her waistline.

Definitely not true. "Woman, don't you change a thing that God endowed you with!" Rahn told her. "Whatever pounds we pick up together, we'll lose together. You and I are a team."

He liked her curves and her pretty baby-doll face, both of which could rival singer Beyoncé's. Her sleek ponytail and large sunglasses made a fierce-looking pose for any photographer.

After they shared a light breakfast, Rahn drove them to Creve Coeur Park, where a neighborhood carnival was under way. As always, Shae encouraged him to interact with his fans when they approached him, while she stood on the sidelines. No other woman he'd dated had displayed that level of patience. *"Sorry,"* he mouthed.

She made a production of removing her sunglasses, winking, and then sliding them back on.

Rahn knew when to call it quits whenever he spied male admirers engaging Shae in more than a cordial conversation. He reached out for her hand. "I have this lovely lady who wants to get on the Ferris wheel. Is anybody going to ride with us?" The children cheered and raced to line up. It was the only tactic Rahn could think of to keep the crowd of fans from growing.

"Good move, Mr. Maxwell," Shae murmured.

"This is our time." He squeezed her hand, and they strolled to join the others in line. Finally, when it was their turn, they climbed into the seat, and Rahn clicked the metal bar closed, securing them in place, before the attendant came to check it.

As the wheel lifted them in the air, one car at a time, Rahn relaxed and squeezed Shae's shoulders. The season was only halfway finished, and he didn't know how he would survive their dating schedule during the second half. "For the first time, I have mixed emotions about participating in the All-Star Game," he confessed.

She looked up at him. "Why? You deserve it."

"What?" He eyed her suspiciously.

"I voted for you for the outfielder position and rallied up the troops on the social networks." She beamed, looking proud of herself, as the wind ruffled the strands of hair that had come loose from her ponytail.

Rahn was speechless. It took a minute for him to register what she'd said. Finally, he found his voice. "Babe, it's important to me to honestly earn whatever accolades I receive."

"And you did. Your batting average is two seventy-five with fifteen home runs. Plus, this is your third appearance…"

"You amaze me." Every day he fell more and more in love with her. "You are really in my corner."

"Always," she screamed, laughing, as their car climbed higher and picked up speed.

"You're a jewel, you know that?" At times, telling Shae he loved her didn't seem to be enough. Two hearts beating as one was true of them.

After the Ferris wheel had made two or three complete rotations, the ride slowed, and the attendant began letting riders off. While Rahn and Shae were suspended at the top, he enjoyed the bird's-eye view of the park. He never would never noticed the small pond between the trees on the ground, or estimated the crowd to be so large.

As their car descended, Shae slipped her fingers between his. "Thank you," she whispered.

"You're welcome. I'm enjoying this, too."

"Not just the ride, silly, but forcing me to share that piece of cake with you..." She bit her bottom lip as he chuckled. "I didn't think I would take another chance, but falling in love with you...I can't even describe the magnitude of my happiness."

"I feel the same way." Rahn nodded. "Second chances have a way of making a man appreciate the blessings in front of him and stop chasing illusions that mimic happiness."

"Maybe I was chasing after the illusion of a good man. I tricked myself into believing Alex was the one." She looked away. "As an investigative reporter, I should have sniffed out the fact that something was out of order about him. I never would have guessed that jerk was still married."

Rahn used his finger to turn her face back toward his. "You're an excellent reporter. I've seen your skill and dedication. You said some of your stories have been nominated for awards, and I'm sure you'll win. As your number one fan, I'm here to cheer you on and make sure you're always happy."

"Keep loving me, and nobody gets hurt."

Where had that come from? He was about to laugh, but Shae didn't crack a smile. Rahn hated that her ex had somehow found his way into their conversation. "Consider it done," he said, then stepped off the ride.

25

$\mathcal{S}$hae had a front-row seat to cheer on Rahn's performance at the All-Star Game at Citi Field in Queens, New York City. She had taken off work and was glued to her TV. She sat on her sofa, decked out in baseball gear. From the Cardinals cap tilted on one side of her head to the socks on her feet, Shae was showing her love. Instead of pigging out, she snacked on a plate of veggies and dip. Despite Rahn's appreciation of her assets, she refused to add more depth to her curves.

Brecee sent her a text.

He is one fine man.

Shae giggled before texting back.

Yes, he is.

It was only one of many texts she had exchanged with her sisters complimenting Rahn's physique whenever he came to bat.

She also had to contend with her uncle's play-by-play phone calls after each inning. It was crazy but fun.

In the fourth inning, neither team had been able to score. With the American League at bat, Rahn signaled to the other outfielders that he could catch a fly ball to the center. Finishing off her bottle of water, Shae mentally fussed at the camera-person to do a better job of keeping the camera on her honey.

Somehow his acrobatic moves caused him to collide with the wall. When he slid to the ground, Shae cringed, as she always did when that happened. She held her breath and even began to choke, waiting for him to get up. She discarded her bottle and got within inches of her flat-screen TV.

"Run!" she yelled at the two managers strolling out to the field to tend to Rahn. Her eyes misted, and she put her hands in a praying position. "Jesus, please let him be okay."

After an agonizingly long period of time, they helped him to stand. With their assistance, Rahn limped off the field until he disappeared from view. His injury was soon forgotten as the game resumed.

"What? You've got to be kidding me. Viewers want an update—I want to know what's going on with the man I love!" She practically screamed, annoyed at the lack of information, then clicked off the TV. The game was over, as far as she was concerned. She didn't even like baseball unless Rahn was playing.

Uncle Bradford was the first to call. "Now, don't fret. Men get hurt all the time. He'll be fine."

As she listened to her uncle talk, Shae paced the space of her condo, from her front door to her bedroom to the dining room to the guest bedroom, ending at her bay window. She flopped on the cushion and looked out at the magnificent view. Normally a source of relaxation for her, it didn't provide comfort, only sparked more anxiety.

"They're back from commercial break. I'll call you back if they say anything. Rahn's tough." Uncle Bradford ended the call, and Shae padded across the living room to her kitchen.

She eyed a small box of vanilla cookies. "Lord, give me strength," she prayed, turning from the sweet temptation and resuming her intercession for Rahn.

Within a span of thirty minutes, she spoke with each sister, her brother-in-law, and both cousins. She even called Rahn's mother. "Hi, Mrs. Maxwell. I hope you're feeling well today," she said, getting the preliminaries out of the way.

"I'm doing well, sweetie. It's so nice to hear from you."

Eloise didn't mention her son, so Shae brought it up, but even then, she didn't seem too concerned. "His father used to get banged up all the time." With flair, she switched the subject, wanting to know when Shae would be visiting. Since Rahn hadn't said anything, Shae wasn't sure, and she said so.

Three hours had gone by before she heard from Rahn. "Don't ever scare me like that again!" She became frazzled once more. "I think I borrowed some of Mother's gray strands."

"Baby, I'm fine," his soothing voice cooed. "It's a little sprain. I'm in my hotel room with my leg elevated, nursing it with an ice pack. Players get hurt all the time."

"That's the same thing your mother said," she mumbled.

"You called my mother?" He chuckled. "There was no need to worry. If I don't need surgery, then I'm fine. And if I recall correctly, your mother doesn't have any gray hair, so I'm sure you're just as beautiful as you were before the game."

"Small technicality. Grays could be sprouting from my roots this very moment, for all I know." But his comment did calm her down. She even smiled at her own silliness.

"I can't wait to see the Carmens again," he said, steering the subject away from him.

Any other time, Shae wouldn't have let him get away with it, but she did miss her family and looked forward to their visit. "Me, too. They're really excited about coming next week to see you play. So, it's all about you staying in shape for my family and healthy for me…because I need you."

She didn't want to "need" a man, but seeing him hurt, even if it was a sprain or strain, forced her to admit that loving him entailed all of the emotions that made her vulnerable, including her neediness for him.

Rahn lowered his voice. "I've been waiting to hear you say that, because God knows I need you." A moment later, he winced audibly. "I'd better get some rest, baby. I have meds to keep the inflammation down, so I'm about wiped out. Love you."

She threw him a series of kisses before they disconnected, then asked and thanked God for His healing power.

A week later, Shae was excited to entertain the Carmens as they descended on St. Louis for the Phillies vs. Cardinals game. In attendance were her mother, sisters, brother-in-law, cousins, aunt, and uncle. Even Brecee was able to trade an overnight shift with a colleague in order to see her family and get a look at Rahn in person, as if she needed to see with her own eyes all of the wonderful things Shae had said about him. Then her sister was scheduled to fly back to Houston early the next morning.

"Spacious," Ted committed as they entered her condo. When he inquired about the sleeping arrangements, Shae couldn't help but rib him.

"Oh, I didn't tell you?" she said, trying to keep a straight face. "There's a sleeping bag in the kitchen, where you'll be close to the refrigerator."

Everyone hooted, even Ted. "That might not be so bad."

Stacy swatted him. "Don't get any ideas."

Shae had given up her master bedroom and the guest room for her mother and Aunt Camille and Uncle Bradford. Stacy and Ted would take the study, which she had converted into sleeping quarters with two hideaway beds. Victor and Dino would sleep on cots nearby, while she, Brecee, and Shari would share the large sleeper sofa in her living room. It brought a new meaning to "Carmens in the house." She was so full of emotions that it was worth having to camp in a sleeping bag for one night to spend time with her family all under one roof.

As was customary whenever they all got together, they harmonized on gospel songs while Stacy stroked the keys of Shae's electric baby grand piano. Later that night, the sisters had an impromptu pajama party in her living room. To keep from waking the elders, they whispered and giggled as if they were teenagers again, awake past their bedtime.

Although everyone wanted the latest on her relationship with Rahn, she was more interested in Shari's glow. Her older sister's unwarranted self-consciousness about her beautiful dark skin had given her a complex. The whispers behind Shari's back that she was "drop-dead gorgeous for a dark girl" did more harm than good, considering she was convinced she'd been picked over time and again for fairer-complexioned beauties. And then, Garrett had wooed Shari like Rahn had Shae, and her self-esteem had skyrocketed.

"I can't wait to meet Garrett." Shae sat cross-legged on the sofa, leaning in for the latest gossip.

"Oh, no," Shari said. "Our story is for another book. This is about you and Rahn." She leaned over and hugged Shae. "I'm so glad that Rahn is in your life and he makes you happy."

"Yes, he does." Shae beamed. The man gave her a feel-good emotion when-ever she thought about him. With all eyes on her, Shae stretched out and then pulled her knees to her chest, wrapping her arms around her legs. "He respects me."

"He better," Dino said, startling them on his way to the bathroom.

Like old times. Shae had missed her cousins' bodyguard treatment. Laughing, the sisters threw their pillows at him. Dino took their pounding like a man before ducking into her bathroom. Everyone was closed-lipped until he came out and disappeared down the hall to his assigned cot.

"Respect is worth more than money in a man's pocket, Sis," Stacy said, rub-bing her pouch. "That's a testament to how he was reared."

"Stacy," Ted yelled from the other room, "the baby needs to get his rest."

"I can't even enjoy my sisters?" Stacy huffed, rolling her eyes, then smiled. "That man knows we're having a girl." Although the couple was opting to be sur-prised on the delivery day, they went back and forth with their guesses.

"Maybe Ted's not talking about that baby," Brecee said, pointing to Stacy's stomach.

"Yes, my husband is the big baby." Stacy stood and hugged everyone good night.

"Night, night, good night," sang Shari, Brecee, and Shae in their best Three Stooges impersonation.

The next morning, Shae's mother was gushing with pride. "How cool is it that my baby is singing the national anthem at a major sporting event?"

The Redbirds' request was one of many that had come after Shae's impromptu performance at the MLK celebration. She had graciously accepted a couple of the invites, depending on the function, while regretfully declining many others.

But this invitation was one she couldn't pass up. She'd always loved hearing "The Star-Spangled Banner" and then seeing the F-15 fighter jets do their maneuvers over sports arenas. The show of military strength left her breathless.

An hour before game time, Rahn sent a limo to Shae's condo to transport her family to the stadium. Shae was the only one not dressed head to toe in Phillies attire. There was no way she was going to walk out on the field in the opposing team's uniform. Once they reached the VIP entrance at Busch Stadium, an usher guided them to their special seating. Yvette Evans and the children were already there, and Shae hugged her before making the introductions.

"You and your sisters all look alike," Yvette said. "I see the resemblance, even with your cousins."

"Strong Carmen genes," Uncle Bradford boasted.

Shae smiled, then excused herself. She followed the same usher to the lower level and down a tunnel that opened to the field. She took a deep breath to settle the butterflies in her stomach.

Rahn stood in the lineup, eagerly waiting for Shae to appear. When she strutted to the microphone, wearing his jersey, Rahn couldn't have been prouder. His heart beat wildly with excitement, knowing Shae's vocal gift would wow the fans.

"Ladies and gentlemen, please stand as we welcome KMMD Channel Seven news reporter and weekend anchor Miss Shae Carmen with our national anthem," the announcer's voice echoed through the stadium speakers.

Before glancing in the direction of the flag, Rahn peeked at Shae. She hadn't looked his way.

"Oh, say, can you see, by the dawn's early light..." Shae's voice burst with so much emotion.

Knowing that more than one camera was recording him, Rahn hid his smile. With a game face, he focused on the flag, holding his right hand over his heart. His left hand he kept behind his back, holding three long-stemmed red roses. Shae didn't crack a note under pressure, and Rahn thought again that she had missed her true calling, even if she was an excellent reporter.

"And the home of the brave...?" She held the last note, to the fans' thunderous applause.

While the players moved to get in position, Rahn jogged toward Shae, who was about to be escorted off the field. "Shae."

She twirled around, her eyes sparkling as she gave him that killer smile.

Stopping within inches of her, Rahn handed her the roses.

"You knew." She pouted.

Had she really thought that his teammates could keep it a secret? "Yes." Although he wanted to linger and talk to her, he had a job to do. Winking, Rahn turned and trekked out to center field. He was ready to play ball.

It was apparent from the first inning that the Phillies wanted payback, since the Cards had swept them on their own turf the previous month. By the third inning, the Phillies had matched the Cardinals with hits and runs batted in.

"I know you're good, but something tells me you're showing off because Shae's here," Marcus badgered him. Both were sitting in the dugout, waiting for the last out.

"A man's got to do what a man's got to do." He and Marcus bumped fists, then stood to take the field after the umpire called the third strike on David Freeman.

In another inning with the score tied, the bases loaded, and two outs, Rahn wasn't in any mood to play extra innings when a fly ball barreled his way. A hush spread across the stadium as Rahn made an adjustment to the right. He caught the ball with ease, and the fans went crazy.

Rahn stepped up to the plate at the bottom of the sixth inning, with two outs and the bases loaded. After a full count of three balls and two strikes, the pressure was on for him to make his last swing count. The pitcher sent a split-fingered fastball. Rahn anticipated the ball's dip, and his bat whacked the ball toward the upper deck. The sound seemed to echo throughout the stadium as the fans erupted in cheers.

The realization sank in…Rahn had hit his first grand slam. Marveling at the achievement, he pumped his fist in the air and circled the bases at a slow trot. "Thank You, Jesus." What better game to earn it in than one with his lady present?

Again he whispered, "Thank You, Jesus," as he crossed home plate and high-fived the three teammates who had scored because of his hit. In the dugout, Rahn was met with the same jubilation.

"*Show-off*," Marcus mouthed as Rahn took his seat next to him. "Maybe Shae needs to be at every game."

"Maybe." Rahn wiggled an eyebrow, then reflected on his first career grand slam. If only his father had been there to see it.

Despite the four-point lead going into the seventh, the Phillies threatened to even the score as their power slugger came to bat. An eerie hush came over the stadium as Cardinals pitcher Lars Leonard stood on the mound, struggling to get out of the jam. After checking on the runner on third base, Lars threw a curveball to Phillies' first baseman and St. Louis native Rob Hutchins and struck him out. It was a hard task, but Lars had come through. The Cardinals and their fans exhaled.

It was a repeat performance for the Cards at the bottom of the eighth inning, as the second Phillies relief pitcher had shamelessly loaded the bases again. As Rahn walked to the plate, he couldn't help but think about the inning where he had made history in the same scenario. As the Phillies' manager and back catcher converged on the mound, the only thing on his mind was that he couldn't leave his teammates stranded.

Minutes later, another pitching change was made, bringing in their third relief pitcher of the night. Rahn was familiar with the left-hander known for his incredible fastballs. As a right-handed batter, Rahn was certain to get at least a base hit to drive in one or two runs.

On the first throw, Rahn gave his bat so much force, it broke in two as he sent the ball with torpedo speed into the upper decks—again. He couldn't believe it. Cameras flashed, and fireworks exploded in the air. Had he done it again? It was the second grand slam of his career, in the same game as his first. Shaking his head, he ran around the bases to the roar of the crowd. He really couldn't believe it.

Your gift will make room for you, God whispered, bringing to mind Proverbs 18:16. *Never get ahead of Me.*

After that feat, the momentum was all in St. Louis's favor, and the Phillies couldn't recover. The Cardinals picked up another win, beating them by six points. In the locker room, the media shoved tape recorders and microphones in Rahn's face. He answered them quickly so he could shower, change, and get to Shae. As player of the game, he was expected to grant a live interview on the second level.

In record time, Rahn was presentable and detoured to get Shae before making his way to the broadcast booth. Her family and others vied for his attention to congratulate him. But it was the hug from Shae that he cherished. "I've got another interview upstairs. How fast can you walk?"

"Faster without heels," she answered, pointing to the athletic shoes on her feet.

"Let's go."

26

I may as well have worn heels, Shae thought as she tried to keep pace with Rahn's long strides. Her heart was pumping as beads of perspiration formed on her forehead. Thank God for twenty-four-hour deodorant protection. That's what she got for skipping her workout for more than a week. This was evidence that it didn't take long to get out of shape.

When Rahn noticed her panting, he slowed down. "Oh, baby, I'm sorry. My mind was caught up in the moment."

"You earned that moment, so no apologies necessary. I'm your cheerleader, remember?" *Just an out-of-shape one for today.*

Without words, Rahn's tender look conveyed his love for her. She had no further complaints, and she suddenly had a burst of energy to pick up the pace.

Sports announcer Lee Ramsey was giving the game highlights over the air when they slipped quietly inside the glass-encased broadcast booth. "Unbelievable— just an unbelievable game this evening at Busch Stadium, folks. Maxwell is playing incredible baseball this season, making history for himself and the St. Louis Cardinals…"

Lee paused as he glanced over his shoulder. "Well, here's our player of the game now, outfielder Rahn Maxwell, with Channel Seven personality Shae Carmen." He nodded for both of them to take a seat in front of the mic. There happened to be two unused pairs of headsets, and he motioned for both of them to slip them on.

Shae shook her head, declining the invitation, but Lee was persistent, so she obliged.

"What an amazing show you put on tonight, Rahn. If I hadn't seen it, I wouldn't have believed it. Two grand slams in one game by one player…whew." Lee's accolades were endless. "That'll go down in the record books for you. And this is the first double grand slam for the Cardinals in almost two decades."

During Lee's commentary, Shae watched as different emotions played across Rahn's face: awe, humbleness, pride, and—when he glanced at her—love.

"God really blessed me tonight," Rahn acknowledged. "My only regret is that my father wasn't here to witness my achievement."

"Understandable." Lee nodded and turned to Shae. "Miss Carmen, you pack a lot of power in that voice of yours. Wow."

Nodding her thanks, Shae didn't want to be dragged into any conversation that would take the spotlight away from Rahn. Just then, she saw movement in her peripheral vision. It was one of the photographers from her station, aiming the camera her way. Grady's actions encouraged the other camera crews to follow suit. Shae sighed.

"What was your secret weapon?" Lee asked Rahn.

Reaching for her hand, Rahn gave her a gentle squeeze. "This special lady was my inspiration tonight."

She blushed at his acknowledgment and touch. There was nothing she could do now to keep their relationship from making the news. At least it was good news about a Christian couple.

Lee chuckled. "The Cardinals may want to put Shae on the payroll. As you know, the player of the game receives a hundred-dollar gift certificate from Hamilton Jewelers. I guess you're taking Shae shopping."

Rahn smiled but didn't publicly comment as the interview concluded. Shaking hands with Lee, Rahn said his good-byes.

Instead of hustling back to the VIP section, where Shae's family was waiting, their steps were unhurried and more like a carefree stroll. Shae softly pinched Rahn's arm, and he protested with a frown.

"What did you do that for?"

Shae grinned. "To remind you that you aren't dreaming and that you're really everybody's hero tonight—well, except for the Phillies. But you're definitely mine. You showed me today that you can play a little baseball."

"A little?" Laughing, Rahn looped an arm over her shoulder and pulled her closer to him, then whispered, "So, when would you like to go shopping for a piece of bling? I think it's time we talked."

She stopped in her tracks. Buying a piece of bling was not the same as buying a wedding ring, which is where her thoughts had been leading. "I'm not good at reading between the lines when I'm not in reporter mode, which I'm not when I'm around you. What are you saying?" Shae held her breath.

"I think it's time we have a talk." His stare was so intense that it seemed like forever before he blinked, though Shae blinked first. "Come on," he said, and they continued on their way.

"What kind of talk?" She was impatient. "We've only been dating…I guess since February."

"Baby, how long does it take to know when you've found the one?"

Shae didn't respond; her family had noticed them and were coming to meet them.

"Rahn, I've had a most enjoyable evening watching my home team get beat up," her mother said with a smile, congratulating him again on his accomplishments. As a group, they headed toward the exit, where their vehicles were lined up at the curb.

"I really need to get me one of these." Ted tilted his head toward the limo.

Stacy shook her head at her husband's silliness, while Rahn snaked his arm around Shae's waist and whispered, "You mind riding with me?"

"You know I don't." Their time together was always short, so any seconds they could steal, Shae would snatch. Plus, as far as she was concerned, they weren't finished with their conversation. Once they were in his Audi, Shae rested her head on his shoulder and closed her eyes. She wasn't tired by any means. "Talk, Mr. Maxwell. You have exactly ten minutes before we get to my condo."

"That's not enough time." And Rahn wouldn't budge during the short drive to her place. The limo and Rahn's car arrived pretty much at the same time. Mr. Chapman waved as they all swept past him and crammed into the elevator.

In the five months since she and Rahn had begun dating, this would be his first time inside her condo. If it weren't for her family to act as a buffer, he wouldn't be crossing the threshold now. Although she and Rahn were willing to stay strong in their spirits, the Scripture didn't say the flesh was weak for nothing.

⌒

Nine chaperones. Rahn counted them in the elevator. They were all cordial, even her cousins this time. But Rahn wasn't in the mood to rehash the game or be subjected to any interrogation from her family about personal matters. All he wanted was overdue alone time with Shae. When the bell rang, announcing their arrival on the fourteenth floor, Rahn took a deep breath and exited the elevator with the others.

The hallway was decorated as exquisitely as the lobby. The wallpaper matched the beige marble tile that served as a doormat until their shoes sunk into plush maroon carpet that formed a T-shape at the end of a short foyer, indicating condos in both directions. Rahn veered right, following Shae.

Judging from the generous space between doors, the condo had to be spacious. It was good to know his lady wasn't living in cramped quarters at all. Stopping at the third door, Shae fumbled with her keys until she undid the lock. As the others rushed inside, Rahn took his time entering her home—her private world. He wanted to take it in slowly, allowing himself to admire Shae's mix of classy, elegant, and cozy décor. It fit her personality.

Immediately, he was drawn to the window where she had waved good-bye and thrown him kisses many a night. As if they were fly balls, he always caught them. The ivory baby grand piano in the corner surprised him. He couldn't recall Shae mentioning she owned one, only that her sister played.

Stuffing his hands in his pockets, Rahn peeped outside. Shae had a great view of Union Boulevard, including his car. He couldn't ask for a safer place for her to reside. The elite Central West End neighborhoods bordering Forest Park boasted of a handful of black politicians, doctors, attorneys, and successful entrepreneurs as their residents.

"It'll just take a minute to warm up the food," Shae yelled from the kitchen as the ladies kicked off their tennies and the men discarded the defeated team's attire.

"Sis, we can help," Shari offered.

"No, let me," Rahn said. "You're out-of-town guests."

His offer earned him lifted brows and approving smiles. The one called Brecee, whom he'd barely met back at the stadium, could have passed as Shae's twin. The doctor twisted her lips in amusement. Even Shae popped her head out the doorway. Her eyes twinkled as he walked closer. When he rounded the corner into the kitchen, Rahn was surprised at the size. "Incredible. This is a nice condo."

"Thanks. It costs a little more because of the area and space, but it was worth it. I feel secure. It's a good substitute for a home away from home." She turned her back to him as she tended to some food on the counter. "Mr. Chapman said this building used to have tiny apartments, but when the new owners did the renovations, they converted two- and three-bedroom apartments into spacious condos."

"I'm impressed," Rahn said, coming up behind her. He turned her around to face him, then began a slow appraisal, beginning with her bare feet on the marble floor. For some reason, neon green was her choice of toe nail polish. *Sexy.* His nostrils flared as if to cool off his attraction. He reluctantly moved back and gathered his wits. "Should I wear an apron?" he teased.

Shae bumped her hip against him. "No, but you need to wash your hands."

He did, and within minutes, they were working seamlessly as a team. Rahn easily found his way around her kitchen. He searched her cabinets and shuffled items in her refrigerator to do her bidding. Back in her formal dining room, they worked side by side to set the table as her family watched without a word. Since Shae could seat only eight at the table, she directed Rahn to her storage closet for the TV trays for the overflow seating in the living room.

During several trips back and forth to the kitchen, Rahn overheard comments like "They complement each other," "He treats her the way she should be treated," and "I like him." Whether they were meant for Rahn to hear or not, it inflated his ego that he had won them over for a second time.

Back in the kitchen, before joining the others at the table, Rahn trapped Shae between his arms at the counter. "You know I love you. Being apart is hard, but not coming home to you is harder. If you have trouble reading between those lines, let me know." He kissed her before she could protest.

27

If Rahn asked me today to marry him, would I say yes? The thrilling thought of being a bride, not a bridesmaid or a soloist, made her scribble "Shae Maxwell" on her reporter's pad. Scrutinizing the signature, she scratched it out and wrote "Shae Carmen Maxwell," then doodled over that. Decisions.

Anticipation of her talk with Rahn kept her from concentrating. Right now, Shae was supposed to be updating her story on an Amber Alert on a missing five-year-old boy whose noncustodial father had allegedly taken him across state lines. The good news was, the two had been found within the last ten minutes. The child had been returned to his mother, the father taken into custody—end of story with a happy ending.

Lord, am I about to get my happy ending? She blushed as her mind drifted to her first unofficial date with Rahn, when they'd shared a piece of cake; their first kiss; the first time they'd professed their love to each other; and the constant flow of flowers to remind her that he was coming home—as if she ever needed her memory refreshed. There were so many things about him that made her fall deeper and deeper in love.

Sighing, Shae propped her elbow on her desk and rested her chin in her palm. She didn't want to think about work but let her mind linger on Rahn...like the previous day, when they had decided on a matinee after attending church, since she'd taken off work, then had picnicked under the stars with Marcus and Yvette.

The double dating hadn't soured their romantic sparks. His presence was electrifying. But their bliss had come to an end that morning, when the Cardinals had left town for a ten-game road trip. Ten days! She groaned just thinking about his absence.

Someone cleared his throat, snapping Shae out of her daydream. Greg Saxon towered over her desk. "Have you seen the breaking news story in the sports feed?"

What she saw was the serious expression on the sports director's face. She immediately panicked, thinking about Rahn. "No. Why? What's going on?"

Greg leaned down and tapped her computer screen. "Click on the news wire." He straightened up, crossed his arms, and waited for her reaction.

Shae's jaw dropped. "What?" Her eyes couldn't read fast enough, but the headline said it all. *"Rumors surface regarding steroid use by some high-hitting baseball players. The allegations come after news that some sluggers have used performance-enhancing drugs to break records. Several teams are under suspicion, including the St. Louis Cardinals. The Major League Baseball Commissioner is alerting teams that players using steroids will be made an example of."*

The sinking feeling consumed her before she could blink. *The Cardinals—oh, no.* Shae fought to muster up the nerve to learn more. She kept reading.

"This comes after the release of the best-selling tell-all book from former slugger José Canseco, who says he was one of many players whose trainer injected him with human growth hormone. The list could grow. So far, no agents or players have issued a statement."

"Whoa" was the only word Shae could utter. This was big—really big. Baseball was considered America's pastime, and in the eyes of most sports fans, including adoring young children, athletes could do no wrong.

"This is hitting close to home," Greg said. "I was hoping Rahn would grant us an exclusive interview like he did with that ambush. He doesn't have to name names, just give his take on whether he thinks that doping stuff makes a difference."

Uh-oh. Greg was already writing his tease to lure viewers in. If his head were transparent, Shae would see his brain pulsating with excitement for getting the scoop. "You have his contact number—call him," she said nonchalantly, as her heart crashed against her chest. She was too close to this developing story.

"Yeah, but a lot of the players aren't talking to the media. Rahn might, if his girlfriend sweet-talks him into it."

Squinting, Shae tried not to fume, but she snapped anyway. "You want to use me to get to him?" She shook her head. "That's not going to happen."

Greg huffed. "It was worth a try." Walking away, he mumbled, "I was just asking."

Shae rubbed her forehead and closed her eyes. Taking a deep breath, she exhaled slowly to regulate her racing heart. Her mind was too jumbled to think clearly as she overdosed on local and national news feeds. There was more information than she had time to read as reporters continued to update the developing story.

The "I need a favor" request didn't stop with Greg. Other coworkers flocked to Shae, hoping for access to Rahn for a sound bite. Some of her colleagues even developed an attitude when she turned the tables on them with her "no comment" response, suggesting she had something to hide. The truth was, she didn't know any more than they did, and Rahn wasn't accessible. Even if he was, would she ask him what he knew? Would he tell her?

If only there was some other breaking news so she could go out in the field as a distraction. She was starting to feel claustrophobic at the station, as almost every reporter was covering a different angle of the doping story.

The devil seeped into her head, making her wonder about Rahn's double grand slam the other night—the second in Cardinals history. She refused to go there. *Lord, You know all things; nothing can be hidden from You. Jesus, help my mind from assuming the worst. In Jesus' name, amen.*

Needing to breathe, Shae slipped out to the patio off the break room on the second floor. The air was only as fresh as the cloud from the most recent smokers who'd congregated there. Thank God none was there now. She folded her hands, about to pray, when her smartphone alerted her to a text.

For the first time since she and Rahn had started dating, Shae was hesitant about talking to him, given her current runaway thoughts. She was going head-to-head with the devil, who was known to bring false accusation against the saints of God—including the man she loved. And though she hadn't seen the so-called tell-all book, she knew that former baseball player couldn't touch Rahn's good record.

With one eye closed, she glanced at her phone to see who had texted her. Shari. Shae exhaled as if she had taken a drag off a cigarette.

What's going on with the Cardinals? What is Rahn saying about all of this?

I don't know, Shae replied.

What do you mean, you don't know? Haven't you talked to him?

A call came through, saving Shae from responding. But it was her "uncle-dad"—the term she used for Uncle Bradford when she was in trouble. And, at this moment, for her to recall that endearment scared her. She knew he wanted to talk baseball, and that the conversation would have nothing to do with pitches or stolen bases. She answered.

"How's our Rahn holding up?" Uncle Bradford stressed *our*.

Shae sniffed to keep her tears at bay. Her day had gone from fabulous to horrible. She whispered, voice cracking, "I don't know, and I'm afraid to find out."

"Don't be. I've got good vibes about him. He loves you. I wouldn't tell you this if I didn't believe it. Humph. The media is always looking for smut on peop—"

"I *am* the media, Uncle Bradford," she said defensively, then apologized for her indignant tone. The news organization didn't wreak havoc in people's lives; they did it to themselves. Looking over her shoulder to ensure her privacy, Shae lowered her voice anyway. "My sports director approached me to convince Rahn to do an interview. My colleagues see me as the go-between." Shae huffed.

Her uncle was silent for a moment. He was either praying or thinking. "You're sure you don't want to call and talk with him for your own sake?"

"No. This is one of those instances where I need to hold my peace. I'll wait for him to call me."

"Don't wait too long. As you said, you are the media. Let him know you can separate your heart from your profession."

"Right." The pep talk was just the boost she needed. Moments later, she returned to the newsroom to focus on other stories besides sports.

28

Rahn couldn't believe José Canseco's gall. Sure, most players were aware that the former outfielder had released a tell-all book, but no one thought Canseco would name names. What was he trying to do, destroy lives?

The Cardinals didn't need this type of distraction during the home stretch of the season. As Rahn paced the floor of his New York hotel suite, he envisioned the media frenzy that would ensue. Journalists would be more interested in juicy details about the allegations that Cardinals players had used steroids than their chance in the pennant race, and even he wouldn't be above suspicion.

The media. Freezing in his footsteps, Rahn groaned and rubbed his face. What must Shae be thinking? Before he could call her, his smartphone played his mother's ringtone. Eloise Maxwell had bounced back to health, thanks to her meds, her diet, and her children harassing her. In essence, she was like a busybody on steroids. Any other time, her spunk would be welcome, just not now.

"How come I have to find out something this big from the news instead of from my own son?" she scolded.

Checking his attitude, Rahn answered in a respectful tone, "Hello, Mom. How are you feeling?"

"Don't sweet-talk me with pleasantries," she snapped. "What's going on with your teammates?"

"I don't know, and honestly, I don't want to know." Rahn continued to field her questions until Shae's text saved him. He prayed she wouldn't interrogate him, too. "I've got to go, Mom. Love you." He ended the call, then read Shae's message.

I love you.

The craziness of the day dissipated with her declaration. Calmness engulfed him.

I love you too. Can we talk later?

Always.

At that moment, Marcus walked out of the bathroom. "Okay, old man. The shower's yours." Picking up the remote, Marcus aimed it toward the flat-screen TV, then shook his head at the commentator discussing Canseco's book.

"Who made José mad?" his friend muttered. "I had to do some major Cardinals damage control with Yvette and other family members earlier about this."

In the shower, Rahn's mind wandered as he pondered Marcus's statement. Who had ticked off José? Performance-enhancing drugs weren't new. Their use could be traced back to the late 1800s, but the timing of José's book was suspect. While the hot water pounded his muscles, Rahn reflected on something his dad had said when he was playing with the Cardinals' Triple-A team, the Memphis Redbirds.

"Fools are born every day, and I'm not talking about at birth but when they're in a bind. You were born with a good name. Guard it to the grave." Then he'd imparted another piece of wisdom. *"How do you want your name to be remembered? Pud Galvin went down in the history books boasting that he used a concoction of the testicles of dogs and guinea pigs, which he called a testosterone supplement. There are no short-cuts to play fair."*

To drive the point home, his father had talked about Babe Ruth supposedly injecting himself with extract from sheep testicles and some quack doctor injecting Roger Maris with steroids and amphetamines. That year, Roger Maris had beaten Babe Ruth's single-season home run record.

"Have integrity, Son. God gives everyone talents. You have yours built into your genes. Don't be so lazy that you cave in to pressure to cheat." Those had been Ronald Maxwell's lasting words to keep Rahn on the straight and narrow.

"Let's go, man." Marcus banged on the door, sucking Rahn back to the present.

"Give me a minute," Rahn called out, scrubbing vigorously. It definitely wouldn't be a good day to arrive late at Citi Field to begin a four-game series against the Mets. He dried, dressed, and was ready in less than ten minutes.

"You know Mike's going to pounce on us in the locker room," Marcus said as they left the hotel minutes later. "He won't want José's book to mess with our heads and divide our team."

Although Marcus was right about their manager, it was too late. The book was all Rahn could think about.

"Rahn, what's going on?" Shae's heart pounded as the words rolled off her tongue. She had barely closed the door to her condo when she'd tapped his name on her smartphone to ring his number.

Throughout the day, the steroid story had refused to die. The news staff had scrambled to track down every sports medicine doctor, former athlete, and pharmacist they could—anyone who might be able to provide insight on how and why a player would basically use performance-enhancing drugs to cheat.

To say it had been a bad day would be an understatement. Her colleagues had repeatedly swarmed her desk, as if she held the key to the door with all the answers because of her ties with Rahn and one of the teams named in the allegation.

He seemed slow in responding. "Baby, before we talk about the breaking news of the day, can I get some love from my woman?" The tiredness in his voice was unmistakable.

Closing her eyes and taking a deep breath, she apologized, "Oh, I'm sorry. I'm really missing you right now." Shae didn't try to hide her emotional desperation that she needed him.

Rahn sighed heavily. "You have no idea how much I love you, miss you, and need you. My day went from—"

"Are you one of the Cardinals who have used—?" She covered her mouth in horror. *Where did that come from?* An uncomfortable silence hung between them, but she couldn't formulate an apology, because she honestly wanted to know. Shae counted to ten in her head, and Rahn still didn't respond. She closed her eyes and sniffed. *God, please let this day be a nightmare.*

"Who's asking, my baby or the reporter?"

"Me," she said softly. "The woman who loves you immensely is asking. I don't handle surprises very well." She thought about Alex's bombshell. "You once told me you didn't have any skeletons in your closet. This is not about me getting a hot tip to score points with the news director. I need you to confide in me." Why was she feeling as if she was pleading a case versus the other way around?

"As a sinful man of a forgiving God who has washed me clean, then yes, I've used them—past tense—against better judgment, and a couple of times when I first joined the Cardinals eight years ago. I can count the instances on one hand. I regret that indiscretion. Since then, I'm determined to give the game my all and never to look back at my mistakes."

When he paused, a tear streamed down her cheek.

Lowering his voice, he further explained, "I didn't think that was a skeleton that would ever resurface. God is my witness that I would never do anything to shame you. Actually, I didn't think of it again until hearing about the hype around

José's book and the players he threatened to expose." He seemed to run out of steam as he quieted, as if waiting for her judgment.

Still sniffing, Shae padded across the living room to the bathroom to grab some tissues. She had definitely chosen the wrong profession—one where integrity was supposed to mean everything. This was two strikes against men who had either already humiliated her or were about to. As Shae tried to digest the truth, her tears turned into sobs.

"*Shh*, baby. I'm sorry to disappoint you and everybody."

There is no condemnation in Me, God whispered to her, bringing to mind Romans 8:1. At the same time, she felt Rahn's concern and his helplessness.

Retracing her steps back into the living room, she flopped on the cushioned seat and looked out the window. Closing her eyes, she whispered, "I wish you were here." Her voice cracked as she struggled to compose herself, but silent tears continued to fall.

"Me, too," he admitted.

"I'm sorry; I just lost it. All I could think about was my crazy day, not realizing yours was probably worse, especially with the Cardinals breaking their seven-game winning streak tonight."

"I don't care about that winning streak! I care about you...us. I need you now, more than ever, to believe in me."

"I do."

"Thank you. I didn't want to have this conversation over the phone, but I didn't want to keep you in the dark for nine more days, either. If I were there, I would cup your face in my hands and look deep into your eyes..."

She imagined him doing that.

"I would tell you I'd experimented with drugs when I was in the minors because my performance on the field was nowhere close to what my father had achieved. I wanted us to be the next Ken and Ken Griffey Jr. or Cecil and Prince Fielder. When my father found out, he was livid. His disappointment cut me to the core, so I stopped. My dad passed away before I made it to the majors."

Her heart ached for him. Rahn had made a bad decision in his past that might come back to ruin his career. She had to be there for him. "If I have to imagine your beautiful brown eyes looking into mine, then imagine my smile. Thank you for confiding in me."

"I told you I would always, always, be honest with you. But there's more, babe."

Uh-oh. Shae could feel the blood draining from her face as she gripped the phone. Could it get any worse? Suddenly, his two grand slams from the other night came to mind. She refused to ask him. "Okay."

"When the Cardinals brought me up from their farm team, I had doubts about my abilities again. Everyone seemed to expect so much from me because of the Maxwell name. Against better judgment, and forgetting my father's tongue-lashing, I consented to the trainer injecting me with performance-enhancing drugs. After the second injection, I could hear my father shaming me from his grave.

"That was eight years ago, Shae—the beginning of my career as a Cardinal. Since then, I've been clean. When I had my good days, I celebrated. When I struck out or was charged with an error, I drank. When the disappointment in myself didn't cease, I prayed for help. Of course, it was out of desperation. I basically used God as my get-out-of-jail card."

"What's going to happen?" That was a stupid question. As a reporter, she knew: The baseball league would expand their investigation. Her colleagues would dig deeper and request every public document available, from kindergarten records to gossip from former neighbors.

The Major League Baseball Commissioner could rely on the media for supplemental information. There would be possible fines, suspensions, and drastic charges. In the end, careers would be ruined, reputations tarnished, and fans disappointed to learn they'd been deceived. The news media—her profession—was the watchdog of wrongdoing, with no exception, but this was personal. Her heart was on the line, and she wanted to protect Rahn. But how could she, in good faith, without compromising everything?

"I downloaded José's eBook," Rahn told her. "I've never been a speed reader, but so far, I'm not on José's hit list. No telling who's been feeding him information or what grudges are driving him to do this."

"Does Marcus or any of your other teammates know what happened?"

"No. Just you and my mother."

Shae's heart swelled with love, then deflated in pain. "I'll pray that God's will be done."

"And that's the scary part, because who knows God's will?" Rahn sighed.

"At times, when God does reveal His plan, we don't have faith enough to believe it." When Rahn asked that she lead them in prayer, Shae didn't hesitate. "Father, in the mighty, wondrous name of Jesus, we come boldly before Your throne, where we may obtain mercy. Lord, we thank You for the cross, where You already nailed our sins. Lord, You love Rahn more than I do, and I love this man. We need You in this situation. Give him wisdom and guide him, so that no matter the outcome, Your name will be praised. Whomever You set free is free indeed, in Jesus' name. Amen."

"Amen," Rahn repeated. "Knowing that you love me, and that God loves me more, I'm in safe hands. Good night."

"Night." The prayer had brought peace, but she knew the storm was coming. "Lord, only You can calm the hurricane-force winds heading his way."

29

The fact that Shae was in this with him gave Rahn comfort as he woke the next day more determined and encouraged than ever to play good baseball. As he and Marcus dressed, they discussed Ecclesiastes 1:9: *"There is no new thing under the sun."*

"The Commissioner set rules in place after the first scandal, years ago, so who would be stupid enough to try something as underhanded as that to tarnish our team and not think that it would be brought to light? I'm glad I don't know who it is, and I don't want to know." Marcus's disgust was evident.

Rahn felt as if he was back in grade school and the teacher had asked who had cheated on a test, hoping guilt would force the offender to raise his hand. What would Marcus's tune be if he was aware his best friend and fellow teammate was that stupid person? "You sound like my father."

Though your sins were dirty, I've washed them white as snow, Jesus spoke to his heart, bringing to mind Isaiah 1:18.

The comfort the Lord gave him made Rahn smile.

Marcus grinned, too, without knowing the reason. "Your dad was one bad third baseman and a pitcher's nightmare at the plate. At least you got your talents honestly."

If you only knew. Rahn had turned his back on honesty. He had been no different from the children of the kings of Israel. Whereas their fathers had done right in the sight of God, the generations that followed always managed to turn their backs on righteous living, just as Rahn had gone against his father's counsel.

But Rahn had repented, and God had just reminded him that those sins were washed as white as snow. As he and Marcus were about to leave their hotel room, Yvette called, and his friend stepped out on the balcony for privacy.

Marcus sounded so much like Rahn's father, it was almost eerie. "Lord, what am I supposed to do here—keep repenting, even though You've already discarded my dirty laundry?"

"Be still, and know that I am God." The Lord gave him Psalm 46:10 to meditate on as Marcus rejoined him and they headed out the door.

That night, the Cardinals bounced back with a vengeance at Citi Field, pounding the Mets 8–2. The following night, the Redbirds' pitcher shut out the New York Mets 4–0.

"We're back," the team chanted as the Cardinals kicked off another winning streak. But then, in Baltimore, the Cardinals took only one out of three games against the Orioles.

Despite the wins and God's reassurances, the devil taunted Rahn with his past when he least expected it. As he beefed up his prayer time with God, his nightly chats with Shae seemed to suffer. He could no longer depend on the pillow talks he had grown accustomed to.

"Well, I'm tired," Shae usually said just seconds after their conversation began. "Let's pray so we can get our rest." And Shae's prayers were powerful and soul stirring, but when she finished, he wanted more from her. Neither of them mentioned steroids.

As a matter of fact, Shae no longer wanted to talk about work when he inquired. "Oh, it was just another stressful day," she'd say.

One thing that never changed was the way she whispered, "I love you."

⌒

Whoever said "Silence is golden" didn't work in a newsroom. Shae had never withheld a scoop from her colleagues, and the secret was tearing her up.

It had been a few days since anyone had approached her for help in getting Rahn to talk, but that didn't stop the rumors from circulating, which made Shae feel like she was working in a cocoon.

"No player is above suspicion, including Rahn," her news director had the nerve to say to her. More than once he had voiced his displeasure about Shae's refusal to use her connections to help KMMD get ahead of their competitors on the story.

At least her colleagues were respectful enough not to make eye contact with her when they mentioned his name among all those on the roster during the afternoon news briefings. Even fires, murders, or car chases seemed to take a backseat to the baseball scandal.

How could Rahn expect her to hold in a secret of this significance? She had to talk to somebody. Shari came to mind.

Surprisingly, her sister answered on the first ring instead of the call going to voice mail, meaning Shari wasn't in the courtroom.

"Are you busy?" Shae asked. She never knew if Garrett was nearby, on the other line, or on his way to take her out for lunch, shopping, or a movie.

"Never too busy for my sister, so what's up? Plus, I'm done with court for the day, and I have a few hours before I meet Garrett for lunch."

Shae smiled. No surprise there. She couldn't just blurt out what was bothering her, so she rambled, stalling. "Are you working on any interesting criminal cases?"

"Is this for a story you're working on?"

"Nah, it's a slow news day for now," Shae explained. "You know that can change any second."

"Oh. No, nothing big, just cookie-cutter cases of women who would rather add to the fastest-growing segment of the prison population by defending the losers in their lives."

"What are you talking about?" Shae frowned.

"These silly women—some girlfriends, others wives or mothers—are willing to go to jail to cover for their drug-dealing men." She sighed heavily into the phone. "I can't believe how many women are stupid enough to be willing to leave their children and sit in jail for their men. Eventually, both parents will be incarcerated. Where does that leave the children? It's not easy being their attorney. My job is to keep the innocent out of jail."

Stupid was such a strong word, though it was probably accurate. But Shae's situation wasn't exactly the same. Rahn hadn't broken any laws—had he? When did that steroid ban go into effect? Shae wasn't faced with taking the rap and going to prison. She swallowed. Still, holding secrets was hard.

Shae was proud of her sister's code of ethics, which made her not only a great Christian but also a dynamic attorney.

"Honey, I would snitch in a hot minute," Shari went on. "What kind of example is a woman setting for her children if both parents are criminals?" Shari's cell phone chimed in the background. "Hey, that's Gee. Can we talk later?"

"Sure. Enjoy lunch. Thanks for your insight."

"I will. I love you, and tell Rahn all of us Phillies fans say hi." They shared a lighthearted laugh. Shari hadn't asked her for an update on the steroid scandal.

Shae took a deep breath when the call ended. Well, that confirmed it. It was too much to ask her to stay silent, considering she worked in the news business. Rahn didn't have to wait for the ball to drop as more players' names surfaced every day. Surely, if he came clean about something that happened a long time ago, the public would understand. Wouldn't they?

30

*S*hae's heart didn't flutter like crazy as it usually did when Rahn's next bouquet of flowers arrived at the news station. As a matter of fact, her heart ached. The doping scandal may have been old news, but with the team back on home turf, the buzz was about to grow louder.

"Okay, listen." Diane approached her desk as if they were already in the middle of a conversation. "We don't have to put you in an awkward position to interview Rahn. One of us can ask him the questions. What's the harm in convincing your boyfriend to help us out? Unless…" Diane let her words fade as she placed her skinny hips, uninvited, on the edge of Shae's desk. Licking her lips, she eyed her. "Come on, what do you know that you ain't telling?"

"I won't use my relationship to advance this story." Shae repeated the same spiel she had given her other coworkers ever since the news broke, then changed the subject. "Have we heard back from the committee for the Emmys?"

"Nope, but there's still time for a late entry. You could add this to your repertoire, if—"

"Let it go." Shae put her hand up. "You and everybody else are welcome to dig up the dirt, but I've drawn the line in the mud on this story."

Standing, Diane shrugged, then smiled. "Oh, we will." It didn't sound like a joke but a veiled challenge.

Shae released the breath she hadn't known she'd been holding. She didn't even want to think about the day when her colleagues would unearth Rahn's secret that Shae had been sitting on all along. *Lord, I need a distraction.*

"Shae, we've got a house that's cookin'. You and Jeff need to get there ASAP!" the news director yelled across the room from the assignment desk area.

Thank You, Jesus! She scrambled to her feet while gathering her purse and tablet.

"All companies evacuate the building…all firefighters evacuate the building," came the dispatcher's urgent warning over the EMS/fire scanner.

Not good. That could only mean the structure wasn't secure and might collapse any minute. Shae and Jeff raced out of the newsroom. In the news vehicle, Jeff weaved in and out of traffic to get to the location. When they made it to the scene, EMS workers were loading victims into ambulances. One was a firefighter. Shae surveyed the residence. One side of the upper floor had indeed buckled.

Jeff heaved the camera onto his shoulder. Shae waited for him to adjust his focus before she conducted the first interview in a crowd of bystanders.

"Sir, can I get your name, and will you spell it?" Shae asked a man, holding the microphone to his mouth.

"John Brody." He was an elderly gentleman with dingy overalls, curly gray hair, and several missing teeth. "That's B-R-O-D-Y."

"Mr. Brody, can you tell me what happened?"

"It's a shame that somebody's been setting fires in these vacant houses. I knew someone was going to get hurt. Sho'nuff. See what happened." He pointed to the dwelling that was still sweltering.

Thanking him, Shae moved on as others vied for her attention. She tried to keep the interviews to a minimal length, looking for the best sound bite. Then she went in search of the neighbors whose houses were threatened by the blaze.

The situation turned out to be more complicated than she had first assumed. Most folks believed victims were trapped inside. There was no way she could piece together a coherent story in the short amount of time allowed. She called the station for a backup writer, dictating the main points, so a script could be typed while Shae continued to gather information in the field.

Too soon, the five o'clock producer advised Shae through her earpiece to stand by. The fire was the lead story, and she had secured an official on the scene who was willing to speak on camera.

Shae positioned her microphone and looked into the camera as she listened to the station's theme music and waited for the anchor's introduction. Then, on cue, she began. "Firefighters discovered two people inside a house while battling a blaze in the fifty-seven hundred block of Clemens on the city's West Side. Captain Royce Kavanaugh, can you tell me what happened?"

The exhausted fire chief wiped his brow. "The house appeared vacant, but after the fire was extinguished, we found two victims near the kitchen area. They're in extremely critical condition."

Jesus, please help them, she silently prayed. "Any idea who they are and how the fire started?" she prompted him.

"The fire is still under investigation, but preliminary findings suggest the man and woman may have been squatters. We did find traces of some accelerants, so the fire marshal has been called."

"Could this fire be connected to the other recent blazes on adjacent blocks?"

"We're not sure at this time."

"Thank you, Captain Kavanaugh." Shae faced the camera. "Many questions remain, but KMMD will stay on top of it to give you the answers. Reporting live on the West Side, I'm Shae Carmen for Channel Seven News."

She waited until Jeff said they were clear before she relaxed her stance. They remained on the scene to give live updates on the ten o'clock news.

Back at her desk in the newsroom, Shae wrote notes for the morning crew to follow up on the story. As she signed off and gathered her purse, she eyed the flowers from Rahn, which were a symbol of his love—and a reminder of the secret she carried because of that love. With her purse on her shoulder and keys in hand, Shae said good night to the handful of lingering staffers and then headed home.

"No," Shae whispered. Rahn's car was parked in front of her building when she arrived. Any other time, his presence would have been a welcome sight, but tonight, she felt the uncertainty about what would happen to him—and them— while the steroid investigation dangled over their heads. She sighed, feeling defeated in her spirit. Rahn was already coming out of the door to meet her. Once she captured his swagger, Shae smiled.

All it took was one look into his soulful brown eyes, then being swallowed up in his strong arms, and Shae dismissed any reservations. She involuntarily protested when he released his hold. His cologne was drugging. "You smell good."

With a chuckle, he squeezed her again, then brushed a kiss against her cheek. "And you smell like my favorite perfume mixed with smoke. God knows I've missed you, woman."

"I've missed you, too, but I've needed you here with what's going on."

"I know." Securing her hand in his, he turned and guided her inside. "The press was at the airport."

Waving at Mr. Chapman as she cleared the door, Shae steered Rahn to the lounge area in the lobby. Her condo was still off-limits to him, with no chaperones around. Finding a more secluded spot, they sat and snuggled together. Shae stared out the window.

"Talk to me, baby."

Angling her body, Shae faced him. His loving smile made her words more difficult. She admired the beard and mustache that outlined his full lips. Shae exhaled at the long lashes that were the envy of any woman. She continued her assessment. Rahn's skin was void of any razor mishaps, making it smooth to the touch. But Shae already knew all of that. Why was she stalling? "This is hard. I don't like secrets, and—"

"Shh."

Shae's eyelids drifted closed as Rahn brushed his fingertips on her lips.

"Me, either," he whispered. "But we could be worrying over nothing. If my name doesn't show up on the radar, then it remains in the past." He sounded hopeful.

Opening her eyes, she gritted her teeth. "I hate to be the bearer of unpleasant news, but your name is already being circulated around my newsroom."

Rahn's body stiffened. "What do you mean, 'circulated in your newsroom'? Please tell me you didn't mention anything we talked about." He squinted as his nostrils flared.

His apparent attitude caused her to develop one of her own. "Of course not!" Did he really think she would betray him? His accusation stung. Yet, Shae tried to shake it off as she reasoned with him. "Just think about being proactive, babe. Don't wait for someone to run your name in the mud. Beat the devil to the punch, so you won't have to look over your shoulder when this story resurfaces. I guarantee you, this isn't going away."

Bobbing his head, Rahn glanced around the quiet lobby. That gesture proved he was at least thinking about what she'd just said. Then he said quietly, "And my reputation will be tainted forever for a stupid decision I made. I can't believe you're suggesting this. I refuse to look back. I've repented, and God has forgiven me. It's a done deal. I'm guiltless."

He frowned. "What's the real motive here? Will my admission make you look good among your peers?" Rahn didn't wait for her response. "I don't know what's going on inside that beautiful head of yours, but if you broadcast any word of what I've confided in the woman who professes to love me…" His mouth twisted; Rahn was quiet as he avoided eye contact with her. "I'll deny it."

Surely, she hadn't heard right. She blinked as her heart sank. Was he basically daring her to say anything, and had he no qualms about backsliding so easily into a lie? What kind of Christian man was this? Alex's face flashed before her eyes. *Not again.*

Girl, don't take that! the devil taunted her.

In this instance, Shae took the devil's bait. Getting to her feet, she stared at Rahn. The hurt, the love, her faith in him—all the emotions battled for dominance. She opened her mouth to call him a coward, and a few other choice words she would never utter to the man she loved, so she closed her mouth and took a deep breath. "Good night."

With her head held high and her heart sinking low, Shae carefully measured each step to the bank of elevators without a backward glance. Otherwise, she would collapse, coming to grips with the fact that she had lost again. This time, there might not be a recovery.

31

$\mathcal{R}$ahn shook his head. *What was I thinking? Why did I say that?* Standing, he stuffed his hands into his pants' pockets and watched Shae's beautiful, retreating figure. That wasn't the homecoming he'd wanted or expected. What she was asking of him was career suicide. How could she even suggest that he put himself out there unnecessarily?

Once the elevator doors closed, Rahn rubbed the back of his neck and stormed out of the building. He passed Mr. Chapman as if he wasn't there. The tranquility of the stars twinkling in the night sky did nothing to calm him. He fought the temptation to turn around and count the floors to her window for that beacon of light.

Was this their first argument? He had too much on his plate to think about an apology. Rahn got behind the wheel of his Audi and pulled into traffic. The drive back home seemed twice as long with the constant instant replays plaguing him: what she had said, what he had said, and what she had said again.

He had to question himself: "Am I willing to lie?" He shivered in disbelief of his statement and actions. "Pitiful. God, what kind of example am I of You?" His vision blurred temporarily.

As he accelerated to change lanes on the interstate, Rahn continued to berate himself. This was not how he had anticipated his Christian walk to be. Wasn't life supposed to be easier?

Many are the afflictions of the righteous, but I will deliver you out of them all. God made His presence known, reminding Rahn of Psalm 34:19.

Can You, Lord? Can You get me out of this web I've gotten myself tangled in? Rahn wanted to believe Jesus could.

A construction sign about an upcoming detour caught his eye. As he passed the exit, Rahn thought it appeared to be legit, but so had the one the night of the ambush. "Lord, it seems my life has been a constant detour for more than a week."

Rahn had no one he could confide in. He had already upset his mother and angered the woman he loved; and after Marcus's speech, Rahn had begun to pull away from him, too. This had become a nightmare. Who else did he have?

You have Me. Come unto Me when your burdens are heavy, and I will give you rest, God urged him.

He had read that in Matthew somewhere, but how could it be that easy? "Lord, why would You even have anything to do with me? If I'm so quick to sin, maybe You haven't saved me." He couldn't shake the doubt.

Do you not know that I call many but choose few? God reasoned with him from that same book in the Bible. *Once I speak something into existence, My Word shall accomplish that which I please. Your salvation is sure and shall prosper. Read My Word in Isaiah 55.*

The Lord's voice ceased as Rahn reached his estate. He was in awe that God still loved him, but he hungered for more time with Jesus. Inside his house, Rahn walked straight to his home library and retrieved his study Bible from his desk. At this point, he needed all the Scriptures to make it through and out of this mess.

Feeling like a fool, Rahn called Shae to apologize, but he wasn't surprised when he got her voice mail. He debated whether to leave a message when he wanted the real thing. They had had spats over silly stuff, but never had they hung up angry at each other. "I know this is a strain on our relationship and a test of our love. I'm sorry. I shouldn't have said those things to you. I'm still struggling about what I should do. Keep praying for me, baby. Night."

She never called back.

⌒

Shae rolled over in bed and used the pillow to both drown out the ringing and catch her tears. Her head was still pounding after her argument with Rahn. "Why torture yourself?" she asked as she reached for her phone. Then, she held her breath as she listened to his voice mail.

He was wrong about one thing. It just didn't feel right in her spirit to accept his decision on this matter.

The next morning, her phone rang again. Lethargic from a lack of sleep, she knocked it off her nightstand first, then grabbed it before it went to voice mail. The name on the caller ID was blurred as she answered. "Hello?"

"Okay, what's going on?" Shari was on the other end, speaking in her attorney tone.

"I'm trying to sleep." Shae moaned, hoping her sister would catch the hint that this wasn't a good time.

"Wake up. I'm hearing rumors that the list of players using steroids is growing. Is Rahn one of them?" She never beat around the bush.

Blinking until she was fully alert, Shae sprang up into a sitting position. There was no way she could answer that. Rahn had already accused her of being a snitch. That hurt more than his threatening to lie. "What are you talking about?"

"Stupidity doesn't run in our family. My advice—as your sister first and then as your attorney—is to distance yourself while this is front-page news, or, as your profession would say, the top story. Your credibility as a journalist could come into question if the public finds out that you knew something but failed to report it. Next to us attorneys, the media is supposed to stand for justice and be unbiased."

"I love him," Shae whispered, still evading the question.

"Sis, I like Rahn. The entire family does. I know you love him, but you've been through the fire before with a man, and you were a hot mess when you came out. Stay out of the fire and protect your heart and image first. This is his trial. Let the Lord fight his battle."

But alone? Shae sniffed as uncontrollable tears trickled down her cheeks. When her sister began to pray, Shae listened silently. "Thank you."

"Anytime. I'll have my clerk bill you for the consultation."

That remark made Shae crack a smile until laughter exploded from within her. Shari joined in. Once Shae was quiet, Shari threw her a kiss, then hung up.

It was mid-morning on her day off. Any other time when Rahn was at home, they would be sharing breakfast, exploring the city, or relaxing at a matinee. None of the above. Not today. Her sister had been right to verbalize what was going through the back of her own mind. Would her colleagues view her silence on the scandal as guilt by association?

Rahn had made a choice. "And I have to make mine," she decided, right before calling him back. When he answered, the deep richness of his voice made her tongue-tied. Her heart fought her resolve. He didn't rush her as they waited to see who would be the first to speak.

"I'm sorry, too," Shae finally whispered.

His heavy sigh sounded like one of relief. "Baby, this shouldn't have come between us. I need your support on this. Agree?"

This was more than a simple "agree to disagree" argument. She shook her head before answering, "No, I don't agree. The devil will ride your back every time someone else releases a new book or someone else is caught and wants to bring others down with him. I disagree, and I'm a nervous wreck. I love you, but I need to—"

"What? Walk away?"

She didn't like his tone. "No…not be so visible, so up-close and personal. I can be your cheerleader from afar."

"Shae, why skirt the issue? I need a woman by my side through thick and thin. I thought you were that woman." Rahn disconnected without saying good-bye.

What? Her jaw was still slack as it registered he had hung up on her—the ultimate no-no. Now she was really mad. Hurt, too, but madder that he'd had the nerve to end their call so rudely.

The next few days proved very difficult to love Rahn from afar, especially with the team playing at home. Not that Shae attended all of his home games, but she tried. Suddenly, she couldn't wait until his next road trip. She needed the distance between them, because knowing they were so close but not together was almost unbearable. She exhaled when he left town for a long road trip.

It was upon his return that Shae ignored—or tried to ignore with dignity—the whispers at work on speculations why Rahn's flowers had stopped coming to the station. When her colleagues asked about Rahn, Shae's reply was short and sweet: "We're not together anymore." Her tone indicated there would be no further Q&A, but that didn't stop her news director from prying.

"Perfect." He grinned and leaned on her desk with both hands, almost panting like a puppy. "What do you know?"

"Excuse me?" *I care about this man, and you're ready to destroy him!* she wanted to scream. "Nothing that I could pass on." She held her ground. Rahn had confided in her, and she loved him enough to honor his confidence, even if she couldn't honor his decision.

32

$\mathcal{R}$ahn had voluntarily submitted to a drug test along with hundreds of other players. The results would hopefully bring an end to the controversy and quiet the allegations against him. He hadn't spoken to Shae since the day of their disagreement.

"The poor girl. That's way too much to put on someone in her position," his mother said, defending Shae's actions. "The only reason I can't disown you is because I birthed you."

"That comforting," Rahn said dryly. "Thanks." *So it is what it is.*

Despite the chaos around them, the Cardinals held on to their lead in the National League Central Division against the Atlanta Braves by seven games. The heat the media and the Baseball Commissioner put on the team only served to fuel the players' determination to prove they were worthy of all accolades. A week before the playoffs, the Baseball Commissioner announced a press conference. Marcus and Rahn were in the hotel with their eyes glued to the flat-screen television.

After fumbling with the microphone, the commissioner steadied the device, looked sternly into the camera, and apologized to sports fans. "We want baseball to remain the pastime of American sports. In order to do that, we must uphold the integrity of the game.

"Unfortunately, we keep revisiting this infesting issue within our organization. In two thousand and two, when we started testing players for performance-enhancing drugs, we thought the fines and penalties would deter further unethical activity. Players had five chances to get their act together. There was a ten-game suspension after a first positive test result, a thirty-game suspension after a second positive result, a sixty-game suspension after a third positive—that's one-third of the season—the fourth was one full year, and then the fifth was a penalty at my discretion. Yet that was not enough." He shook his head with a look of disgust before continuing.

"Besides the players who have come forward, whether or not they were named in Mr. Canseco's book, *Juiced*, we took the initiative to expand our investigation.

We now have evidence that proves the following players have abused the system currently and/or since we first set the guidelines on banned substances…" Cisco was named, along with another current Cardinals player, before the commissioner moved on to another team.

"Cisco?" Rahn was shocked. It was by the grace of God that Rahn hadn't been singled out, even though it had happened long ago.

When the commissioner refolded his paper, Rahn couldn't contain his relief. It was over. God was good. Leaping off the edge of his bed, he pumped his fist in the air. "Yes!"

His reaction caused Marcus to give him the oddest look. He didn't comment on his behavior, but his face slowly registered the reason for Rahn's reaction. Without saying a word, he turned back to the television.

"The buck stops here!" The commissioner slapped the podium. "Players will have three strikes and you're out. A first positive test result is a fifty-game suspension. Double that for a second positive offense. If a player is foolish enough to stay on that destructive and dishonest path, he will end his career with a lifetime suspension from Major League Baseball. I hope not to address this again." The man scowled, then opened the floor for questions from the media.

"Robert Blake, Associated Press," the first reporter identified himself. "Are you only going after players who have tested positive for substances currently or those rumored to have abused the system since the new guidelines were established a decade ago?"

"We will continue our random drug testing to keep the game clean. We tested many, many players—involuntary and voluntarily. I released only the names of those who failed," the commissioner replied.

"Greg Saxon, KMMD-TV, St. Louis. The investigation focused heavily on the St. Louis Cardinals players. Since only two players were named, is that an indication that all the other players tested negative?"

"That's exactly what it means, Mr. Saxon—"

"I've heard enough." Aiming the remote at the television, Marcus muted the press conference. Reclining in the corner chair, he rested his ankle on his knee, folded his hands, and calmly addressed Rahn. "Let's talk."

Marcus was six months older than Rahn, but at the moment, he came across as much older. Nodding, Rahn braced his arms on his thighs.

Marcus glanced away, appearing to struggle to find the words to speak. Then he looked back at Rahn, his expression unreadable. "Why?"

It was Rahn's turn to avoid eye contact. He huffed. "Stupidity, insecurity, competiveness…"

Shaking his head, Marcus leaned forward. "Besides me, who else knows?"

"My mother." He paused. "And Shae knows."

"Ah, Shae." Marcus nodded. "That explains a lot. Yvette and I were wondering what was going on between you. Shae hasn't been easily accessible when Yvette has tried calling her, and when they last met to go shopping, Shae refused to talk about baseball or mention your name." Marcus rubbed his chin and squinted.

So, Shae had not only cut ties with him but with his best friend's wife, too? There was no hope to keep alive. It was over. If only she had waited it out with him.

"Is that why you two broke up?"

Taking a deep breath, Rahn stood and paced their hotel room. "It was her call." He didn't look at Marcus. It was a weak argument, but he had to convince himself that she had walked away willingly and not because he had forced her hand. "I told her I would deny the truth if she said anything to the media." He cringed, recalling her wounded look, which had turned into an indignant expression before him.

Marcus covered his eyes with the palms of his hands. "You threatened her? Ah, man." He shifted in the chair. "Are you double crazy? You've messed up big time, and I do mean big time. I thought the doping was big, but letting go of the woman who really loves you? Insane!"

"I know that!" Rahn raised his voice. "I experimented with some concoction while in the minor leagues—one time." He demonstrated with his finger. "My dad was hot when he found out. My excuse was trying to measure up to him. Although I knew about the ban when I started with the Cardinals, a bout of insecurity returned, and I tricked myself into believing I wouldn't get caught, so I agreed to the injection—"

"Was it Dr. Davidson?"

Rahn confirmed it with a nod.

"I never trusted him." Marcus grimaced. "I was glad when the organization gave him the boot."

"While I had no guilt the first or second time, a random drug test made me come to my senses, when I realized the magnitude of what I could lose. When my results came back negative, I used that as my wakeup call. I haven't used anything in almost eight years. Everything I've achieved on the field since has come from hard work and body conditioning."

"I believe you." Marcus stretched out his legs and leaned on his elbow. "What are you going to do about your relationship with Shae?"

"There is no relationship. She wanted to walk. I let her strut her fine self away. I refuse to beg, man."

"Admitting you're wrong, saying you're sorry, and kissing and making up is far from begging," Marcus said, checking off his examples one finger at a time.

"I *did* apologize." Rahn grunted. "I love her, but I'll lose some respect for her if she tries to run back to me now that I've been cleared. It's best we both move on." His ears tingled, hearing him say that.

"If you say so. Come on. We'd better get to the stadium."

33

Everything should have been all right in Rahn's world, but it wasn't. He wasn't surprised he hadn't heard from Shae, but it seemed as if God wasn't talking to him, either. Stretching out in his home theater, Rahn clicked off the movie that he hadn't been watching. He rubbed his head. "God, what's wrong with me? I thought I would be happy that my secret was kept."

He needed God to speak to him. His mansion seemed still—not even a tick of the clock invaded from the background—yet Rahn didn't hear a whisper from the Lord. Restless, he wandered into his home library for his Bible.

Sitting behind the desk, he bowed his head and prayed before opening it. "I should've asked You, Jesus, what Your game plan was up front. Then maybe I would have some peace."

Come unto Me with your burdens, and I will give you rest, God advised. *Read Matthew 11:28 in My Word.*

"Lord, I did, so why can't I shake this uneasiness?" he asked in frustration. His eyes were still closed, his hands still folded.

"*Confess your faults one to another, and pray one for another, that ye may be healed.*" The words from God were swift, but they echoed as if a light wind had carried them away.

Opening his eyes, Rahn glanced around the room. Everything seemed intact, but he felt God's presence again. What more was there to confess? He opened his Bible to James 5, trying to understand why God would tell him to confess—what and to whom?

Be a witness, the Lord stated instead.

That night, before climbing into bed, Rahn prayed a lengthy prayer. He tossed and turned but couldn't sleep. He needed help in decoding God's messages. Why did the Lord have to speak in riddles?

The next morning, Rahn opted to fast—a spiritual practice Shae had taught him—so he could get some answers. He ached to call her, to ask her for some spiritual direction, but she'd made it clear she didn't want to be a part of his dirty laundry. "It's me and You, Lord. Open my eyes and ears to Your Word."

Rahn anointed his head with holy oil from the small bottle the altar workers had given him at Bethesda after he had received his water and fire baptism. Then he strolled throughout his mansion, praying and reciting passages from his Bible. As his body weakened from the lack of nourishment, his spiritual endurance grew stronger. He seemed to be more in tune with God's Word and better able to decipher it than even a few days earlier.

At nine that night, he broke his fast after finally getting a basic understanding of what God wanted him to do. Initially, Rahn had resisted God's request, but Jesus told him to trust Him, reminding him of various times when God had protected him before and after the carjacking incident. Once he had accepted his fate, he called Marcus and shared what he was about to do.

"Are you sure God is directing you on this?"

Marcus's reaction surprised Rahn. "I thought you would agree, as my Christian brother and close friend. I have no doubt. As a matter of fact, I have peace with it."

"As long as you're sure this is God's will, I'm with you. You know the devil has a way of intercepting messages like he did in the Old Testament."

"I fasted and prayed earnestly. I know this is God's will because there is no way on His earth I would do this, even for Shae."

"Okay. I've got your back, bro."

Early the next day, Rahn had his agent, Fred Klass, advise the media that he was holding a press conference before the Cardinals took off for one of the last road trips of the season.

The press packed the room in the Cardinals' clubhouse. Cameras flashed and conversations ceased as he walked to the podium. Standing nearby were the Cardinals' owner and manager, as well as Fred Klass and Marcus.

Because of his own experience of being fined twenty-five thousand dollars and suspended for fifty games, Cisco had tried that morning to talk Rahn out of going public and committing career suicide. But Rahn couldn't be deterred. He stood on Acts 5:29: "*We ought to obey God rather than men.*"

Rahn scanned the crowd. The media would always remind him of Shae, and she had been right all along. "Thank you all for coming," he began. "As you are aware, the Major League Baseball Commissioner released the names of players who admitted to and/or tested positive for using performance-enhancing drugs."

Bowing his head, he whispered a prayer, then lifted his chin. He felt no condemnation as he told the truth: "I violated the anti-drugs guidelines the first year I joined the organization. I agreed to two injections from the late former club physician, Dr. Davidson. I'm asking my colleagues and the fans to forgive me for cheating. I have no excuse for my lack of judgment. I've shamed the Maxwell name.

If my father were still alive, he would be the first to tell me that. Although I didn't test positive, I'll accept any fines and penalties placed upon me by the commissioner for whatever stated time period." With the truth out, his burden seemed light. "Are there any questions?"

Greg Saxon lifted his pen. "Why did you do it in the first place?"

He had his own question for Greg. *How is Shae?* Rahn cleared his throat to keep his mind from wandering. "I'm a second-generation ball player. For me, it was about chasing my father's record. Although I proved myself capable to be on the Cardinals' roster, in the back of my mind, I doubted myself and sought out steroids, which I thought would make me worthy. Guilt forced me to cultivate my God-given ability."

"Mike Bledsoe, Fox Sports," the next reporter identified himself, as if Rahn didn't already know him. "You mentioned why you felt you needed to use steroids, but what is your motive for going public, subjecting yourself to possible fines and suspension during a crucial time for your team?"

This was the part he hoped would give God His glory. "It's part of Jesus' redemption plan for me. As you know, earlier this year, my life was spared in a car-jacking ambush. That caused a chain reaction in my life led to my surrendering to Christ. If I want to walk freely with Him, it means I have to admit my mistakes—which Jesus has forgiven—so the devil won't have power over me."

"One last question." He pointed to an unfamiliar face.

The man identified himself as a local radio sports commentator. "You've been linked romantically with media personality Shae Carmen. Did she know?"

"Yes, I told her off the record. As a reporter, she honored that. To my knowledge, she never influenced her colleagues one way or the other about reporting on the topic."

"Are you and Miss Carmen still together?" asked an unfamiliar woman from somewhere in the back.

He was not about to let Shae's name be tainted with his dirt. "Listen," he said, not trying to hide his irritation, "this news conference is about my actions. I have no comment about my relationship with Miss Carmen."

Rahn walked out of the room with Marcus and Fred by his side. "Well, it's done. I'm at the mercy of the commissioner."

Fred slapped Rahn on his back and gripped his shoulder in a comforting gesture. "Although I'm disappointed, I have to respect you for coming forward when you didn't have to. I hope the commissioner will take that into consideration."

"Me, too." Rahn exhaled, then watched as the two men got in the limo that would take them to the airport so they could join the team for tonight's game.

Although the commissioner hadn't banned or fined Rahn, he felt Rahn would be a distraction if he played immediately following his announcement—so, in a sense, the punishment had already begun. Rahn understood. *Lord, no matter what happens, I know I have You.*

Be content. I will neither leave you nor forsake you, the Lord whispered, then gave him Hebrews 13:5–6 to read.

On his way back home, Rahn thought about the last reporter's question. Shae's career would always take precedence over their relationship. He knew it had to have been hard for her not to say anything, but what about the next time there was something big that pertained to his world? "I guess I'll never know," he mumbled. He and Shae were history.

34

Quietly rejoicing, Shae blinked back her tears. The way Rahn had conducted himself at the press conference was proof that God had given him perfect peace. If only she could borrow some of his.

Shae wished he had commented on the reporter's question about the status of their relationship: "Absolutely over," "Maybe," or "We will definitely reconcile." She missed him terribly, but it didn't feel right to go running back to him once the smoke had cleared. Two relationships, two strikeouts, she was done.

Seeing her news director heading her way, Shae took a deep breath and tried to achieve a blank expression by the time he made it to her desk. "I'll give Rahn Maxwell credit. That took guts to risk everything to do that."

No, it took the peace of God to do that, Shae wanted to correct her boss.

"Me, personally? I would've kept my mouth shut. Since your name was mentioned, I think you should make a statement."

Excuse me? "Don't you think that would become too much of a tit for tat?" She didn't want to make the tabloids by allegedly lodging derogatory insults at Rahn. Regardless of the fact that their relationship had fallen apart, they still respected each other. "Can't we monitor the social media tweets and posts?" she countered.

He seemed to give it some thought. Once Martin made a decision in his mind, it was the law, so she awaited his response. It was slow in coming. "We can try that, but be prepared to make a statement, if necessary." When he walked back to his office, Diane rushed to the spot he had vacated.

"Girl, how did you hold that in for all these months?" She playfully shoved Shae's shoulder.

No one would ever get a quote out of her just because Rahn had let everything out in the open. In hindsight, she didn't know which was worse: holding his secret close to her heart or shutting him out of her life. Shae merely shrugged and smiled.

"Well, you did the right thing—getting out of that mess before your reputation tanked," Diane went on. "Although I do miss the flowers. We had the sweet-est-smelling corner of the newsroom. So that's why you were so tight-lipped. You handled it better than I would have. Whatever he told me off the record, I would put on the record for an upcoming fall sweeps series—"

"I have a conscience. I didn't get into this business to be ruthless," Shae interrupted Diane's rambling. "It wasn't my story to tell. It was up to you and my other colleagues to do the digging and force his hand. I guess you guys lost your edge on this one." Actually, Shae was glad they had. Otherwise, Rahn would have missed the opportunity to show others that he had made the decision to come clean as a testimony to God sparing his life.

Leaning her elbow on her desk, she stared at Diane. "Have you ever been in love—really, head over heels in love—with any man, even the one you married?"

"No comment." Diane lifted a brow and positioned her fists on her hips. "Stick by your man," she mumbled before walking away.

Whoa. Shae must have hit some nerve. But her coworker's off-handed remark made Shae feel guilty. She hadn't stayed by Rahn's side. Shae exhaled and gnawed on her bottom lip. What if she called Rahn? Surely he would think she was shallow. Alone with her thoughts, she bowed her head and whispered a brief prayer. "Lord, You knew about these fiascos in my life before the foundation of the world. I bounced back after Alex in Nebraska, but my recovery after Rahn isn't going so well. I'm hurting, God. Please mend me, in Jesus' name. Amen," she hurriedly concluded when she heard voices nearby.

"Shae." The assignment editor strolled to her desk. "I forgot about an East St. Louis forum on neighborhood gun violence. Nothing else newsworthy is going on, so will you and Jeff check it out?"

"Sure." Anything to keep her mind focused. Shae could write the generic script with her eyes closed: *A neighborhood watchdog group is rallying the public to put a stop to gun violence. A spokesman is calling on police to beef up patrol…* It would be the same story, just a different location involving different people.

She and Jeff made it across the Poplar Street Bridge into the Metro East in no time. As Shae conducted her interviews, Rahn's "no comment" remark continued to revolve in her mind. Had he erased her completely from his memory?

The thought sparked mixed emotions. What did the man expect her to do? KMMD paid the bills and added to her social security benefits. *That was my career that could've been damaged!* she wanted to shout. He used to cherish her with his love, but now he merely added to her anxiety.

The next morning, on her day off, instead of jogging on the trail in Forest Park, Shae opted to use the gym equipment in the condo exercise room on the sixth floor. She had just returned from her workout when her phone rang.

"How do you feel about what Rahn said yesterday?" Shari asked.

Her sister's directness never offended Shae. "I admire him. He put everything on the line to tell the truth, shaming the other wrongdoers with his confession." She had hoped a good workout would clear her head of what Rahn had said, but Shari's question only caused the previous day's events to resurface.

"Or to get you back…" Shari sounded as if she was in the courtroom, prompting her on a witness stand.

I wish. Rahn had done exactly what she had suggested as far as nipping the problem in the bud before it could grow; but clearly, it had been God's timing, not hers. "I want to reach out to him, but to say what? 'I love you'? That sounds like a mockery, but it's the only thing I want to say."

Shae wandered through her condo until she finally rested on the familiar window seat in her living room overlooking Union Boulevard. She admired the foliage of the trees against the backdrop of pricey homes.

How many times had she waved good-night to Rahn from that very spot? She frowned, then blinked. Was wishful thinking causing her eyes to play tricks? What were the odds of someone besides Rahn who drove a black Audi coming to visit someone at her address? Craning her neck, she squinted to see if the driver was still inside the car.

Shari's chatter faded as Shae's heart pounded, wondering if Mr. Chapman would buzz her to alert her that she had a guest in the lobby. Several seconds passed, but nothing happened. She peeked out the window again. The car hadn't moved.

She had to get downstairs. "God will work things out. I'll call you later. Bye." Racing into her bathroom like a madwoman, she freshened up as best she could, though she would have preferred a shower. Then she snatched the first piece of sweat-free clothing she could find from where she'd thrown it over a chair.

Getting to the lobby ASAP was her mission. She couldn't chance a shower, coordinating an outfit, applying makeup, or making sure every strand of hair was in place. She didn't care how she looked. Well, almost. All she wanted was Rahn's strong arms around her; his smooth voice telling her that they could work it out.

Hopping on one foot and then the other, Shae slipped on her flats. The phone rang again. She reached for it, hoping it was Rahn. She didn't hide her disappointment when she heard Brecee's voice on the other line.

"You know, I was just thinking about Rahn's 'no comment' from yesterday—"

"Yeah, me, too. Hold that thought. I'll call you back." Again Shae rushed off. She finger-combed her curls as she raced to the elevator. On the ride downstairs, she tried to tame her nerves. When the door opened, she stepped off and scanned the lobby. There were only a few residents hanging out, and there was no sign of Rahn.

She nodded at Mr. Chapman as she hurried to the front entrance. There were two vacant parking spots. The black Audi was gone. Her heart dropped. Had Rahn changed his mind? In a slow twirl, Shae retraced her steps.

"Did I have any visitors?"

Mr. Chapman shook his head as if he knew what she suspected. "For a moment, I thought that was Mr. Maxwell's car, too. I wanted to commend him for coming forward and saying what he did." He shrugged. "Anyway, the driver took off without ever getting out."

There was no use denying her purpose. Embarrassed and humiliated that she had acted like a desperate woman, she thanked him, then returned to her lonely abode.

Back in her condo, Shae berated herself for her behavior. She swiped up her cordless phone and called Brecee back. "Sorry about that."

"So, where was the fire you had to hang up on me to cover?"

"No fire." Shae sighed and flopped into her chaise in her bedroom. "I thought I saw Rahn's car parked down below. It was wishful thinking on my part that we could pick up where we left off—end of story."

Brecee balked. "Right. I sense there are still a few more chapters left before you close the book on Rahn," she stated with a yawn. "Okay, well, I need to crash, but all things work together for our good..."

Shae finished Romans 8:28 with her, but how was another broken heart for her own good? For the remainder of that day and all of the next, she didn't leave her condo. She cleaned, did laundry, and got caught up on her social media accounts. She dared to read what viewers had said about the way her relationship with Rahn had ended.

On Facebook, Mzz Lady commented: "A woman's got to do what a woman's got to do. Men have to understand that!" Mzz Lady had ten likes and one share.

BradleyLookinggoodpapa wrote: "A good man is hard to find, or so women say. I think Shae should have stuck by him through thick and thin, for better or worse."

The man's comment had generated some backlash on his wall. Some had criticized BradleyLookinggoodpapa for quoting sacred vows that didn't apply to any relationship but marriage.

"Humph. My point exactly," Shae mumbled with a nod.

With more than a hundred posts, her Facebook friends seemed just as torn as she as to whether she had done the right thing. On a good note, it didn't seem as if she had lost any ground professionally because of her decision.

Most people seemed to believe she was still a great reporter and had done what she felt she had to. Rahn's actions also seemed to have garnered a mostly positive response. He was receiving more radio and television air time than he had for the attempted carjacking incident. Good for him.

On Twitter, Shae was surprised that #baseballandreporter was still trending with so many retweets. Some were positive. @shaecarmennews7 said: "They should find their way back to love." Another tweet read: "They should work it out. I like both…Rahn, you see how fine Shae is, & Shae, you see that body? Doesn't anybody believe in love anymore?" Still another tweet was touching: "Shae and Rahn were my heroes…"

"But we're two ordinary people who were trying to find our way," Shae whispered. A tension headache was building, so she logged off. As she lay down for a nap to rest her mind, she whispered, "Lord, what's Your tweet?"

35

The verdict was in. The Major League Baseball Commissioner didn't like to be made a fool of, and he had said so himself in a statement released to the media: *"While I and others in the baseball league are disappointed by Mr. Rahn Maxwell's actions, we must also commend him for coming forth and telling the truth. Despite his good intentions, Rahn did break the rules, albeit a long time ago, and he must be subject to the same penalties as anyone else…"*

Fred Klass informed Rahn of the verdict. "You're being slapped with the fines and penalties that were in place in two thousand and two, when the incident occurred, instead of the harsher ones that Cisco got hit with. That means a ten-game suspension and a five-thousand-dollar fine."

Since the Cardinals' season had ended and they had been eliminated from the playoffs, Rahn would be suspended for the first four games of the following season. Rahn was grateful.

He retreated to Richmond for a few days to check up on his mother. While there, he had time to reflect on the highs and lows of the past year. He missed Shae like an addiction. Her smiles, her hats, all the things they had talked about, even her urging him to go public… In the end, he'd done just that. Had that been the only purpose behind Shae's being in his life? He refused to believe that.

"There you go again—drifting." His mother had been watching him like a hawk, as if she was looking for signs of a smallpox outbreak or the side effects of an overdose on baby aspirin or something.

"How can I be drifting when my eyes are open and I'm watching ESPN?" He had stopped by to visit and helped himself to the dinner she had prepared. Now, they were relaxing in her study. She had no objection watching sports programs, stating that it was in her blood after dating and marrying an athlete.

"No, you're staring at the TV, but I can tell by your expression that your mind is elsewhere. It looks like you have some unfinished business." Her eyes twinkled with mischief. She made it no secret that she loved Shae. The two women had spoken only a few times before and after his mother's health scare.

177

"You were stupid once. Don't repeat it. Go after Shae's heart with everything you've got."

Am I that much of an open book? he wondered. Unfinished business meant he needed a business plan, and that was the problem. He didn't have a plan—yet.

"Might as well listen to me." She shrugged. "I'm the mother, and Momma knows best."

Rahn didn't argue. She was right. He let Eloise Maxwell have the final word.

A month later, Shae welcomed her family back to St. Louis. The Carmens were the best distraction. Not only had three of her stories been nominated for recognition at the annual Salute to Excellence awards gala, but someone on the committee had heard her sing the national anthem at Busch Stadium and had asked her to perform one or two selections to kick off the party following the ceremony.

Initially, Shae had declined. Her heart just wasn't in it. But then, for some reason, she'd had a change of heart and called back. "I would like to accept, if the offer still stands."

"Absolutely. It would be such a treat." The organizer had sounded delighted.

She had smiled. "I have one favor to ask. Would it be all right for my sisters to accompany me?"

Once the woman had agreed, Shae had called Brecee to tell her to bring her guitar, then phoned Shari and instructed her to bring her sax. Shari had revealed a surprise of her own: Garrett would be tagging along. Finally, Shae would get to meet Shari's Prince Charming. The only person who would be missing was Rahn. *"I plan to be right there beside you,"* he had once said. His words flooded her mind more and more as the ceremony drew near.

When the night of the shindig had come, Shae sighed as she spied the gown flowing from the satin hanger in her walk-in closet. She loved the chiffon fabric; she liked how the two coordinating shades of deep blue and ocean blue created an unusual, eye-catching shade.

Again she thought about Rahn's reaction when she'd modeled it for him—which she'd done more than once, per his request. His eyes had sparked before he'd stood and walked toward her, his look of passion holding her captive, as she'd mentally counted his steps. When she'd reemerged from the fitting room dressed in her everyday clothes, she'd discovered that Rahn had already paid for the stunning piece from the Jovani collection. "I want you to turn heads when I escort you that night," he had said.

Shaking the recollections from her mind, Shae tried to regroup. She had to get ready. Her family was waiting on her.

Not so fast. Her mind refused to comply as one more memory slipped out. She could hear Rahn's deep voice complimenting her: "*Hmm-mm. When you walk, it flows. It's beautiful on you.*"

Enough! She battled for mental dominance. If she broke down and cried, she wasn't sure if she would be able to stop.

Shari strutted into Shae's closet. "I would definitely wear this." Her sister fingered the intricate silver beading that crisscrossed below her bust in a continuous loop around her waist. "Even if you didn't pay for it."

Shae gnawed on her lip, still undecided. "It will only make me remember how much I love him," she admitted softly.

"You love that man, whether you put that dress on or not," Brecee stated from her perch on Shae's bed. "No one else will know your benefactor." She uncrossed her legs, stood, and joined her and Shari at the mirror.

Shae was almost persuaded, but she still held back, looking for other options.

Her mother, who had been standing silently on the sidelines, came into the walk-in and hugged Shae. "It's beautiful, and that's probably the same beauty he saw in you. Wear the dress, or we'll be late for this premiere St. Louis black-tie banquet you've been telling us about for weeks." Then she followed Shari to the living room to join Stacy and Ted and to greet Shari's boyfriend, Garrett, who had just arrived. He was staying at a nearby hotel.

"You heard Mother. Let's do this thing." Brecee fussed as Shae slipped into her gown. "Don't mess up your hair. Do you realize the artistic skill it took to get every spiral curl in place?"

"I know. I feel like I'm wearing a cap made out of bobby pins." Shae patted the crown of her hair—all hers, no more weaves. She liked the look of her hair piled high on her head, even though it was likely she would pay for her fashion statement with a headache the next day.

Brecee zipped up the dress as Shae admired its beauty in the wall-length mirror. It hugged the curves Rahn had raved about when Shae had said she thought she could stand to lose five or ten pounds.

Soon Shae and her family entourage traveled the short distance to the Renaissance Hotel downtown, with the men carrying the cases holding Shari and Brecee's instruments.

Everyone attended: the local celebrities, the self-proclaimed famers, and the politically influential. It was the one day out of the year when the media was honored for its work. It wasn't about showcasing the bad but exposing the ills of society, so that, eventually, the good could triumph.

The ambiance wowed the Carmens as they entered the ballroom. The gigantic chandeliers cast a glow of elegance throughout the large hall. An usher welcomed the group, checked their tickets, and guided them to their assigned table.

Along the way, Shae was stopped by fans and colleagues. Everyone was genuinely cordial. Some whispered their support of Shae's decision to take a stand. *Right.* She nodded, not wanting to think about the love she'd found and lost.

Garrett and Ted pulled out chairs for the Carmen sisters and their mother before they took their own. Shae relaxed, if only physically, and took in the sights around her. Watching the other guests sashay through the door was like attending a fashion show. She was glad that her family had convinced her to wear the dress Rahn had bought her, even though it made her think of him. *God, will I ever stop missing him?* Releasing that thought, Shae concentrated on the here and now, post-Rahn Maxwell.

Glancing around the table, Shae smirked when she noticed her brother-in-law rubbing her sister's stomach.

Ted winked. "Caught me."

Shae shrugged. "If she's enjoying it, don't stop on my account," she teased. Everyone around the table chuckled.

Next, her gaze was drawn to Shari and Garrett, who were huddled together in their own private world. This was the first time Shae had witnessed their blossoming love. The man was pure Hershey's dark chocolate wrapped up in a Godiva wrapper. A dimpled chin gave him a boyish look when he grinned. He was handsome, but not "hold your breath and don't blink" handsome like Rahn.

At least two out of the four Carmen sisters had found happiness. What Shae had heard was true—Shari and Garrett really did complement each other. What Shae wouldn't give to be a fly on the wall and watch Garrett woo her sister.

With his arm poised protectively on the back of Shari's chair, Garrett squeezed her shoulder, then kissed her cheek. "She's beautiful, isn't she." It wasn't a question.

"That she is." Pulling her attention away from the lovebirds, Shae looked around, waving at more colleagues who were seated nearby. KMMD-TV was well represented, with ten guests each at three tables. Their presence was reassuring, considering she was one of only three African-American reporters out of a staff of twenty-five employed at the station.

Too bad people didn't see affirmative action as an equal-opportunity mechanism. Without question, she had to work extra hard to be noticed, but praise God that she'd found favor on her job.

Shae leaned over toward her mother. "There have to be hundreds of people in here."

"A thousand easily, sweetie." Her mother smiled and tugged on one of the spiral curls dangling against Shae's forehead. "You look like a princess," she added, beaming.

On the other side of Shae, Brecee nudged her and whispered, "How is it possible for all these gorgeous men to swagger in here by themselves? Once I finish my residency, I may need to start my practice in St. Louis."

"That would be great. I'll help you pack. I could use some company here, and Stacy and Shari already have each other in Philly."

"Yep, they're taken. It's just you and me," Brecee mumbled as a fine brother snagged her attention.

Out of nowhere, Rahn's "no comment" remark resurfaced. Shae's mind dug farther in its memory bank and pulled out his plan to celebrate her victory. He had an amazing amount of faith in her abilities as a broadcast journalist, considering his fear for her safety when she was filming on location.

"*Of course you're going to win, babe. You are the best. While the weather is still warm, we could take a ride in a hot air balloon during the annual ballroom race,*" he'd said, his brown eyes holding her captive as he'd apparently conjured up a celebration she would never forget. "*I want to treat you to a day at the spa and then a quiet dinner, just the two of us. I know of a restaurant that will shut down for the right price and cater to the needs of my lady and me. Would you like that?*"

Closing her eyes, she sighed. When would she stop hurting? She quietly sniffed. This was her night, and she had her family. The Carmens were a united front.

Promptly at seven, the four-piece band serenaded the attendees as the servers began placing salads before the guests. After her mother had blessed the food, all conversation ceased, and they enjoyed the meal, which included chicken Marsala as the main course.

As the platter of assorted finger desserts tempted each table, especially Shae, the mistress of ceremonies stepped up to the microphone. "Welcome, everyone, to the thirtieth annual Salute to Excellence awards banquet." After greeting the audience, she told a few jokes to warm up the crowd, then wasted no time in reading off the categories and nominees. As names were called and awards handed out,

Shae wasn't surprised by the winners from competing stations. St. Louis had some well-seasoned reporters.

Antsy, Shae shifted in her seat when the emcee reached the category of hard news. Brecee took one of her hands, her mother took the other, and they squeezed in solidarity. "This category is fierce. The nominees are KZTY Channel 3 reporter Todd Green and the St. Louis City Hall Midnight Basketball Scandal; KCCV Channel 10 reporter Jason Bender and the Flood Wall Sabotage in Alton, Illinois; and KMMD Channel 7 reporter Shae Carmen and Burying the Dead: Drive-by Shootings."

The emcee fumbled with the sealed envelope. "And the winner is...Shae Carmen."

Shae slapped her cheeks and nearly screamed. She had won. Shouts, cheers, and applause erupted throughout the room; coworkers at nearby tables whooped their excitement. As she edged out of her seat, a couple of whistles pierced the air.

When Shae stood, Ted pushed back his chair to escort her to the stage. Her eyes played tricks on her heart when she imagined Rahn stepping out of her memory and materializing into the flesh-and-blood man she loved.

Then her nose tickled at the scent of musk cologne that preceded Rahn as he intercepted Ted. With a grin, her brother-in-law stepped aside and muttered, "About time."

Shae didn't move or exhale as she welcomed Rahn's invasion of her space. His custom-fit black Armani tux yielded to his muscular build, and his unbreakable stare made her shiver. For a moment, she forgot about her coveted award.

He cradled a bouquet of long-stemmed pink roses. "Congratulations," said the baritone voice that had lulled her to sleep many nights."For you." He presented her with the flowers.

She wanted to cry at his thoughtful gesture. A hush swept throughout the room. Shae no longer felt she was the center of attention—she and Rahn were.

As Brecee took the flowers from her, Rahn acknowledged her family with a nod. Then he cupped Shae's elbow, and she followed his lead to the front, as if they had rehearsed their steps.

"I'm so sorry, baby," he whispered.

Relishing their private moment amid the public scrutiny, Shae wanted to escape to a place where no one could find them. As far as she was concerned, her award could be mailed to her address because she had her prize walking beside her.

36

The sparks between Rahn and Shae ignited with ferocious power with one touch. He wanted to whisk her away from the public eye. Stopping at the bottom of the stairs, he met her gaze again. "Whether you still love me or not, I love you."

"*I do,*" she mouthed.

"It's good to see St. Louis Cardinals outfielder Rahn Maxwell escorting our award-winning reporter tonight," the mistress of ceremonies said, invading their secret place. As she applauded, many people in the audience gave them a standing ovation. Rahn gave a slight wave, then handed Shae up the stairs. He waited at the bottom in a military stance.

Shae looked mesmerizing with her hair gracefully swept up on her head. It wasn't often that she showcased her slender neck. And she had worn the dress—the one he had picked out and purchased because it teased his senses. Rahn groaned. Her sexiness was torture, causing him to succumb to a slow death. Whichever way she turned, her skin sparkled under the soft light, which accented the silver beads across her bodice and softened her features.

There had to be a Scripture about the consequences of being a fool. Only his pride could have kept him away this long. *Lord, please help us to work out our differences, in Jesus' name, amen.*

A few nights moping at home in Richmond had compelled him to pull out his sketch pads. The images his mind had conjured up had proved to be too much for him to stay away. Although Rahn had conceded that he had unfinished business, he was still working on a plan. How would they mend their broken hearts?

That's when he'd consulted Marcus and Yvette, and they'd told him it was a no-brainer: He needed to attend the awards banquet, as originally planned. They doubted Shae would make a scene or protest talking to him.

"You said it meant so much to Shae to be nominated," Marcus had said, reminding Rahn what he'd told him weeks earlier. "Yvette and I will even go along to cheer on Shae and have your back."

His friends had kept their word. In their usual fashion when it came to fundraisers, they had purchased a table and invited others to help fill it—a feat that was never a problem, thanks to their celebrity status.

Shae accepted the crystal trophy and admired it for a few seconds. "I'm honored, I'm humbled…I'm speechless." She choked.

Rahn smirked at the irony of a woman who talked for a living yet couldn't find the words to speak. "And you're beautiful, baby," Rahn mumbled under his breath. It was a good thing that she hadn't come with another escort. If she had, it definitely would have caused a scene, because he wasn't backing down until they talked—tonight.

She glanced at him momentarily, as if trying to read his thoughts, then looked back at the audience. "Thank you, St. Louis, for welcoming me to your city and letting me come into your homes every weekend and on weeknights at five, six, and ten. Special thanks to my colleagues and photographer Jeff Craig, who edited my story. And much love to my family, who came all the way from Philly. Say hey, family."

A chorus of "Heys" floated from the table, sparking another wave of chuckles around the room.

"And last, thanks to my escort, Rahn Maxwell." Shae turned and glided across the stage to a few whistles and shouts of "Yeah!"

"Congratulations, baby," Rahn said, reaching for her hand to assist her down the stairs. Linking his fingers through hers, Rahn gave her hand a gentle squeeze before the pair weaved their way through the maze of tables back to her seat. "I've missed this closeness between us," he whispered as he forced himself to relinquish his prized possession. "I'm sitting not far away, and we need to talk, okay?"

She teasingly scrunched her perfectly shaped nose in response. He'd missed her little gestures, too. Rahn would not be rushed away from this moment; he took his time planting a kiss on her cheek, to the *oohs* and *aahs* around them. After reluctantly letting her go, he made it back to his table. Yvette and Marcus were grinning like silly cartoon characters when he resumed his seat.

"Job well done," Marcus said, slapping him with a handshake.

"You're going to love the kissing and making up part." Yvette giggled.

"Yeah, I'm looking forward to that." As far as Rahn was concerned, nothing that might come between them was worth keeping them apart. He hoped Shae felt the same way.

Rahn adjusted his chair at an angle to have a better view of Shae, albeit an obstructed one. She was seated seven tables down and one over—yes, he had counted them. Now that he had expressed his feelings to her, he was impatient to follow through. Huffing, he alternated between checking the time and glancing at the program. He needed closure—for both the ceremony and the issues that stood between him and Shae.

Ignoring what was happening around him, he willed Shae to glance back and find him. Just then, she did, and graced him with a warm smile. He winked.

More awards were called, and Shae's name was mentioned among the nominees, but others had beaten her out. *Foul*, Rahn wanted to cry out in her defense. Although she had received one award, he wondered how she felt about not having been chosen for the other two for which she had been nominated.

"Before we get this party started, you may have noticed a new category—more of an honorable mention," the mistress of ceremonies said. "One person has changed the look of weekend news in St. Louis. KMMD's secret weapon on Sunday night to steal the ratings is Shae Carmen and her hat of the week, which she dons at the close of every broadcast." She chuckled along with everyone else. "Ladies and gentlemen, this year's number one weekend anchor is Miss Shae Carmen, dubbed The Hat Lady." She clapped and beckoned Shae back to the stage to get a plaque.

Rahn made a beeline to her as if he was trying to steal a base.

"I'm getting an award for my hats?" The look of genuine surprise on her face was endearing and picture-perfect.

"You deserve it, honey."

He took her by the hand and led the way to the stage once again. After Shae had thanked everyone, Rahn returned her to her table.

"That brings the awards portion of the ceremony to a close, and it's time to kick off the after-party. Our Hat Lady has another talent. If you missed hearing her sing the national anthem before one of the Cardinals games this season, it's your lucky night, because Miss Carmen will now sing a selection of her choice, accompanied by her sisters."

The applause was deafening…or maybe it was Rahn's whistle.

⌣

The sisters had been planning to sing a rendition of the classic Staple Singers' "I'll Take You There." People generally loved the R&B sound of the classic gospel song. But Rahn had changed everything. When Shae's sisters stepped onstage, Shae whispered a different song in Stacy's ear as she slid onto the piano bench, then did the same thing to Brecee as she adjusted her guitar strap, then Shari, who caressed her alto sax, ready to play. Each of them smiled at the news and seemed not at all surprised.

Shae adjusted the microphone, then introduced her sisters. The lights dimmed in the room, so that she couldn't see where Rahn was seated, but she felt his presence no matter the distance. Closing her eyes, she swayed to the Caribbean beat while her sisters harmonized the opening line to "I Wanna Be the Only One," arranged by one of her favorite gospel artists, BeBe Winans, and Eternal. It seemed appropriate, since Rahn had sent that saxophonist to serenade her with the same song during their phone lunch last spring. She hoped the words of the song would convey that she wanted to be his only one—always.

As her eyelids fluttered open, she guessed where Rahn might be sitting, then belted out the lines in that direction. Immediately, folks were out of their seats, clapping. Others made a beeline to the dance floor just below the stage. As the sisters sang the last chorus, Shari capped it off with a brief sax solo.

Despite the sophistication of the event, chants of "One more song" mingled with the applause, and soon it seemed that more people were on the dance floor than sitting at the tables.

Shae looked to her sisters, who shrugged, leaving the choice up to her. She walked across the stage and asked the drummer's permission to use his sticks. Nodding, he handed them over, then adjusted the seat for her. Once she was settled, Shae looked to Brecee and mouthed, *I'll Take You There*, which began with a guitar introduction. Stacy picked it up on the piano. Shae kept the rhythm on the drums, and Shari wowed the crowd with her artistic ability on the sax.

They ended the selection to more thunderous applause and whistles. Forgoing another song, Shae thanked the musicians. As the sisters exited the stage, Ted and Garrett were waiting for them…and so was Rahn.

He immediately wrapped his arms around Shae. "Thank you for the song—"

A photographer Shae recognized, who worked for the St. Louis Black weekly newspaper, *The American*, interrupted them. "Shae, Rahn, can I get a picture of you two?"

Rahn answered for them by snuggling her closer for a pose. Shae sank into his arms. Her smile was one of bliss.

"Does this mean you two are back together?" the photographer asked.

Shae contemplated how to answer that question, considering nothing had been resolved, but Rahn didn't hesitate. "No comment. We don't hold press conferences on our personal life." After twirling her around on the dance floor, Rahn guided her to a vacant table.

While waiting for Rahn to speak, Shae familiarized herself with everything she had missed about him—his beard, eyes, hair, build…everything.

His hands caressed hers, then brought them to his lips. He gazed steadily at her. "You do know I'm going to ask you to marry me."

Shae blinked at his serious expression as his words sunk in. "You do know, Mr. Maxwell, you're not supposed to tell a woman that you're going to ask her to marry you. You're supposed to just do it in a way she'll never forget."

Rahn displayed the killer smile that had wooed her the night they'd shared that piece of cake. "True, but in this case, considering how insensitive I've acted, I wanted to give you a heads-up to think long and hard about your feelings toward me—the good times only. I plan to ask you one time, and I don't want a long engagement. It has to be before I leave for spring training. When I come home, I need a wife…"

Shae pressed her finger to his lips. "You have a lot of demands, for a man who hasn't asked anything." She giggled. There was nothing to think about. Her answer would be yes, but, like any woman would, she was going to make him work for it.

Then again, with all the love that shone from his eyes, maybe not.

37

It's been two weeks—where's my proposal? Shae wanted to ask Rahn that question every time his brown eyes distracted her, but he never brought it up again. Was he really trying to pull off a surprise? She was beginning to rethink her demand. She would love to be Mrs. Maxwell. Shae had started to scribble that name again as her mind wandered.

"Enjoy the making-up part," her sisters and mother had encouraged her.

"Especially the sweet kisses," Shari had added, then giggled when their mother cleared her throat.

Since the day they'd given her those words of encouragement, Shae had been praying for patience. She was grateful for each moment God gave her to spend with the man she truly loved.

Shae had even apologized one Saturday night when she'd had to decline attending a function with Rahn. "I know that my profession can be hard on a relationship, but working weekends is hard on dating."

"Baby, I'm not complaining." The way he'd looked at her had made her a believer. "Baseball season is over, so I'm available at your beck and call, any hour, day or night." He'd capped it off with a wink.

So, she and Rahn maintained a kind of schedule. After attending morning worship on Sundays, they enjoyed brunch together before he dropped her off at work. "You know, you don't have to do this every week," she always fussed.

"I love you." Rahn's answer was just as predictable as the dinners that arrived like clockwork at the station on Sunday evenings. Shae could never guess what would be on the menu. The real treat was Rahn showing up early enough to sit in the studio and watch the ten o'clock newscasts. Shae wondered if he planned to surprise her with an on-air proposal. Public engagements done on live TV were becoming overrated and cliché. But then she chided herself. Any declaration from Rahn would be meaningful, no matter when, where, or how. When the assignment editor called her name and instructed her to head to the scene of a car crash, Shae tucked away the sweet memories.

A few days later, she and Rahn enjoyed a romantic dinner of fondue at the Melting Pot. "I noticed the annual balloon race is this coming weekend. I think it would be fun to go."

The night before the Great Forest Park Balloon Race, the pilots fired up the burners of their balloons to create a rainbow glow. The balloons were mesmerizing as the hot air pumped them to life, to the delight of children and adults alike. Shae stood and watched in awe, her hand linked with Rahn's.

"Excuse me, Mr. Maxwell and Miss Carmen." A woman emerged from the crowd and approached them.

"We're going to have to change that," Rahn murmured into her ear. "You won't be 'Miss Carmen' for much longer."

"I'm glad you two got back together," the woman told them. "I love your hats, Miss Carmen. And Mr. Maxwell…can I get an autograph?" She pulled out a piece of paper. "It's for my son Tommy."

Shae's eyes misted. The fallout from Rahn's confession had not been as devastating as either of them had anticipated. Granted, some people had said they would never forgive him. Yet more seemed to respect him all the more, calling him courageous for setting the record straight. That was God's grace.

The next day, Shae took off work so that she and Rahn could return to the park and experience the entire feel of the event dubbed the "hare and hound" race. It was considered the most prestigious one-day balloon race in the world, and Shae was thrilled to attend.

More than seventy balloonists from across the globe gave chase to the Energizer Bunny Hot Hare Balloon. Folks who dared not brave the swelling crowd had a bird's-eye view from upper-floor windows, nearby balconies, and penthouse decks.

To Shae's surprise, Rahn had paid for them to ride in the Purina balloon. Her heart pounded with the excitement of her first balloon ride—and with the man she truly loved.

Their pilot, a short man with numerous wrinkles and a thick gray mustache, gave them a bit of advice before taking off: "You do understand there's no telling where the wind may take us and might land? Sometimes it's in people's backyards or in a parking lot, but we shoot for open spaces, like parks." Rahn nodded as he assisted Shae onboard.

As the fire ignited, Shae rested her back against Rahn's strong chest, glad to have his arms securely around her waist. With the wind under their feet and the gentle swaying of their carriage, Shae closed her eyes and sighed.

Rahn squeezed her. "Happy?"

"Yes." She felt breathless. Turning in his arms, she smiled, drawn in by his serious expression. "I'm in tune with you, Mr. Maxwell. I praise God that you're in my life."

"I plan to stay in it."

Was that his prelude to his proposal?

An hour later, the hot air balloon landed. The experience was so exhilarating, she almost didn't care that she had been wrong—again—in thinking he was about to pop the question.

⌒

Rahn was ready and definitely willing to make Miss Shae Carmen into Mrs. Rahn Maxwell, but there were some loose ends that had to be tied first. Shae may have perfected patience, but there was only so much temptation a practicing Christian man could endure with a beautiful woman. One thing was sure: Shae was worth the preparation he was putting into his proposal package.

As they dined at Fleming's Prime Steakhouse, Rahn watched different emotions play across Shae's face. "Okay, you're distracted. What's going on in that head of yours?"

She pouted, making him imagine the young daughter—or daughters—they might have one day. "I want to get back home to Philly before the fall sweeps rating period kicks in. Nobody can take off in November." She chuckled. "The joke is, unless you have a scheduled date with death, you're expected to be on board. I haven't been home in a while, Stacy's going to have her baby soon, and I miss my home church. I just miss Philly. I guess I'm in a venting mood."

Rahn reached across the table and squeezed her hand. He recognized homesickness when he saw it. A quick trip could be to his advantage. "Let's plan a visit next week on your day off. You haven't officially taken me 'home' yet. Although I've met your family—twice—it's always been on my turf."

"I'd thought about going on my day off but decided against it, because I would rather spend it with you. But having you along would make a short trip worthwhile. I'd love to show you around." Shae closed her eyes, as if inhaling the moment, just as she always did whenever she was excited about something.

"I would certainly appreciate a tour of all the things that molded you into the woman who has me wrapped around her finger."

Shae made a soft grunt, as if she thought he was exaggerating. If only she knew he would do anything to make her happy and would always treat her as his queen.

A week later, the two cleared security at the airport through the preferred customers' line. Rahn kept his hand possessively around Shae's. He couldn't tell if the men staring at them were fans wanting to approach him for an autograph or jealous males gawking at Shae. Just in case it was the latter, he pulled her closer.

When they landed in Philly, Stacy and Ted were waiting for them outside the terminal. Ted shook Rahn's hand and slapped him on the back as the sisters embraced. He caught a glimpse of Shae rubbing her sister's abdomen, trying to feel the baby kick. Ted grinned with pride. Rahn looked forward to the day when he and Shae would be the ones expecting. Finally, without success, Shae gave up and looped her arm through Stacy's. The four of them then made their way to baggage claim.

After Rahn had retrieved their bags, the four of them climbed into Ted's vehicle. When Rahn mentioned that he would have been happy to rent a car, Ted feigned insult. "Rahn, the last time you were here, you didn't get a chance to visit Philly. We're more than the Liberty Bell, just like St. Louis has more than the Arch." He grinned. "Think of me not only as your driver but also your tour guide."

Stacy groaned and shook her head. "Here we go. Why Ted studied engineering in college is beyond me. If my husband ever needed extra money, I'm sure he could find a job as a spokesman for the City of Brotherly Love. He could be a career trivia contestant."

Ted threw his wife a kiss. "Hey, can I help it that we have history? We were the first in the country to have a zoo, public library, and school for woman doctors," he said, exaggerating his Philadelphia accent. Rahn barely detected it in Shae's manner of speaking.

"Brecee will tell you that MCP, or the Medical College of Pennsylvania—now part of Drexel University—inspired her to go into the medical field," Shae said, snuggling against Rahn. "You never know how the things you're exposed to as a child will influence your future." He loved the feel of her squeezing his bicep.

"True," Stacy agreed. "After Brecee finishes her residency in Houston, she'll be a board-certified pediatrician—the first doctor in our family." She glanced over her shoulder and gave Shae a high five.

The gesture reminded Rahn of the moment his father had learned that Rahn had been handpicked for the Cardinals' farm team.

"Me," Stacy paused, "I always wanted to be a teacher. History was my passion ever since our parents took us to the Johnson House on Germantown Avenue. Harriet Tubman used it as a safe house along the Underground Railroad."

"My father was my role model. He played baseball, so I wanted to play baseball." Rahn nudged Shae and kissed the top of her head. "Okay, babe, your turn. What made you want to get paid to be nosy?"

Ted hooted, and Stacy playfully swatted his shoulder.

"Humph." She jutted out her chin in feigned insult. "The news business is a profession that keeps people informed. My inspiration came from KDKA, one of the oldest commercially licensed stations in the country. And while it isn't located in Philly, it's still in my home state, since it's in Pittsburgh."

"A teacher, a lawyer, a doctor, and a reporter...your parents did something right," Rahn said.

"Our parents sacrificed so much to ensure a prosperous future for us, including sending us to the Germantown Friends School. It was prestigious then, and it still is," Shae explained.

Ted was able to get a few words in, pointing to landmarks and explaining their history as the foursome entered West Mt. Airy. "Now this is Gorgas Park. It's known for its summer concerts and its farmers' market, and a lot of people have their wedding photos taken here."

Was Ted fishing for information? The man couldn't force Rahn's hand, so he said nothing as Ted turned onto a nearby street bearing the same name.

W. Gorgas Lane was a clean tree-lined block. The cottage-style homes seemed almost identical, with white tuck-pointing between faded chunks of stone of various sizes, yet each home had its own personality with its unique placement of bay windows and side patios. Some were one-and-a-half stories; others were twos. Rahn smiled at the white picket fences that sectioned off the properties. It reminded him of the backdrop of some 1950s sitcom.

When Ted parked, Shae was out of her seatbelt within seconds and practically deserted Rahn as she hurried through the gate and up the short pathway to the porch. Annette Carmen stood in the doorway with open arms. The women hugged once and then twice before her mother turned her attention to him. Rahn had lagged behind, taking in the feel of the neighborhood.

"Rahn." She welcomed him with a tight embrace, and he kissed her cheek.

From the moment Rahn crossed the threshold, he was entertained by the Carmen sisters' baby pictures and tales of many of Shae's mishaps, to her embarrassment. Before long, they were summoned to the table for a light lunch. Rahn noted that the kitchen had been updated with the latest appliances, while the living room and sun porch retained the feel of old memories that never faded.

After the meal, the ladies went to visit a few family friends who wanted to see Shae while she was in town. Ted snacked on sandwiches as if they hadn't eaten lunch less than half an hour ago. Shae's brother-in-law had a comical streak in him without having to try.

Ted finished off another slice of German chocolate cake, then cleared his throat. "You know, man, you got my respect after you put yourself out there about the doping…"

Rahn hid his cringe. He didn't like that term, but it was what it was.

"I don't know if I would have confessed like you did when you could've kept quiet."

"Don't think I didn't consider that." Rahn didn't want the accolades. "That's why Shae broke off our relationship. Man, I missed her." He shook his head at the memory of watching her walk away that night. Rahn never wanted to experience that loss again—ever. "But it was all God," he went on. "He told me to trust Him. I was relieved to come clean. I don't think there would have been a chance for Shae and me if I hadn't."

"How serious are things between you and my girl?" Ted spoke as if he was the patriarch of the family.

"Very serious," Rahn affirmed. "Speaking with Mrs. Carmen about our status is on my to-do list."

Ted bobbed his head. He seemed thoughtful. "I can get rid of the Carmen sisters while you do that."

"How?"

"Shopping with my MasterCard."

Rahn laughed, and they bumped fists. Ted would make a fine brother-in-law.

38

$\mathcal{R}$ahn was convinced that Annette Carmen had multiple personalities. She was not the sweet lady full of smiles who had greeted him at the door the day before, or the other times they met. The woman sitting stoically in the plush suede rocker seemed downright intimidating. She had yet to crack a smile.

Clearing his throat, Rahn began the "proposal" protocol. "Mrs. Carmen, I love your daughter." Those words would make any mother smile, right? Apparently not. Shae's mother merely watched as he stuttered, squirmed, and cleared his throat countless times, struggling to get through his spiel.

"This is not a cliché—she really does bring out the best in me. I care about her happiness, spiritual and physical. I'll take care of her until my last breath. I'll be a faithful and prayerful husband…"

Feel free to stop me anytime. He tried to send her a telepathic message. Rahn had never prayed so much in his life. "I would like your blessing to marry Shae." He held his breath.

Lifting an eyebrow, Annette folded her arms. "You had my blessing the day I met you after the baseball game."

What? Rahn exhaled. "Then why did you let me suffer through this?" He wiped some perspiration from his forehead.

"I like to see you sweat." She laughed at his discomfort, then leaned forward with a serious expression on her face. "Storms will come in between the sunshine, but no matter what, you still have to cover her. That's called protecting her heart."

"If this is about the steroids—"

Annette Carmen held up her hand. "It's not. It's about temptation in heels and a size thirty-eight cup and synthetic hair."

Rahn wanted to laugh at her choice of words, but he doubted she would see the humor, judging from her no-nonsense stare, so he responded like his mother had taught him to as a child: "Yes, ma'am."

She nodded, and her smile returned. "Then you may proceed with Shae." Then she switched gears before his eyes again. "And if I hear about you doing something as stupid as using drugs, I'll join forces with your mother and give you a spanking that you'll never forget." She stood. "Let's get us a snack from the kitchen. What do you say?"

The Lord knew Rahn had worked up an appetite. Exhaling, he got to his feet and followed her.

⌒

"If you weren't here, Shae, I wouldn't be able to splurge like this. My husband is showing off," Stacy said giddily as she stuffed Ted's credit card back in her wallet after purchasing three maternity outfits at Nordstrom. "He thinks what I wore at three months will still fit at five and seven months."

Shae exchanged a bemused glance with Shari. It was a known fact that Stacy didn't need a reason to shop. The King of Prussia Mall was a shopaholic's paradise with about four hundred stores to feed the addiction. Stacy was a bargain hunter, unless there was something she really wanted—like designer maternity outfits. She always dressed meticulously. Right now she wore a pair of fashionable, low-heeled pumps and a two-piece pearl-gray skirt and blouse set that could easily be worn after the baby arrived. She had begun to wear her long hair swept up and twisted into a bun on top of her head, a style that gave her a youthful look.

"I want to get Rahn some cologne before I'm bogged down with shopping bags," Shae told her sisters.

"Let's go to Bloomingdale's," Stacy suggested.

As they passed Kay Jewelers, Shae's heart pounded. They paused at the window display and admired one diamond piece after another. Stacy absentmindedly said, "I thought both of you would be engaged by now."

"Me, too," Shae admitted with a sigh. It hadn't been quite a month yet since Rahn's declaration. The weekly anticipation was making her wish he hadn't said anything.

"That won't be happening with me." Shari didn't crack a smile.

Now Shae exchanged a confused look with her oldest sister. "Huh?" the two said in unison.

"Something tells me this discussion is going to drain my energy," Stacy said. "I'd better feed my baby first." She rubbed her stomach.

Turning around, Shae led the way toward Café Court. As she eyed the beautiful water fountain from the upper level, she wondered what had happened between her sister and Garrett. Claiming a vacant table, the three set down their purchases and settled into their chairs. Stacy and Shae looked at Shari, waiting for her to explain her earlier statement.

Shari's carefree demeanor was definitely gone as she blurted out her bomb-shell: "Garrett and I broke up."

Shae's mouth dropped open, but no words came out. Shari had been Shae's Cinderella story since she'd met Garrett. This was not the ending she'd expected.

"When did this happen? Weren't you two together just last night, or the night before, and you were fine?" Stacy quizzed, crossing her arms. "Clearly, I missed something. Sis, every couple has disagreements."

"Clearly, I know about that one," Shae mumbled, looking away.

"That hasn't stopped since Ted and I got married," Stacy added. "I'm sure you two will kiss and make up."

Making up had been the best part of Shae and Rahn's relationship, just as Shari had predicted when the two of them had been trying to patch things up. Since the steroid scandal, they had communicated more than ever in order to ward off any possible misunderstandings.

"I can't and won't talk to him. How could I have been so wrong about a person?" Shari looked like she was about to cry.

Shae stood, scooted around the small table, and was at Shari's side within a couple of blinks. Stacy leaned over and wrapped her arm around Shari's shoulder.

"Should I ask what he did?" Stacy asked cautiously.

A tear fell as Shari shook her head. "Worse than what Rahn put Shae through."

"Uh-oh." *Lord, please don't let it be that serious*, Shae prayed. "It sounds like we may be here awhile. I'm going to grab us something to eat."

Stacy nodded. "Good idea."

Getting up, Shae scanned the food court. There was a crowd at every station. She joined the long line at a sub sandwich shop. As Shae inched closer to the clerk, she couldn't help but wonder if all four sisters would ever be in sync when it came to love. What had Garrett done?

Finally, Shae made it back to their table, balancing a tray of food. At least Shari wasn't crying. She wasn't smiling, either, but she had regained her composure.

"Is everything okay?" Shae retook her chair and divvied up the sandwiches as she looked from one sister to the other.

"It's something Shari needs to pray about." Stacy eyed Shari with her eyebrows raised in a look that said, *You had better comply.*

Shari shrugged, seemingly unsure. As an attorney, she was big on confidentiality, so if she'd said anything to Stacy, it must have been big.

Stacy bowed her head to say grace, and Shae and Shari followed suit. "Amen," they said in chorus.

After taking a bite of her sub, Stacy focused on Shae. "So, what's going on with you and Mr. Maxwell?"

"I'm in a holding pattern." Shae nibbled on her turkey club sandwich, then swallowed. Her family already knew what Rahn had said to her at the awards banquet. "It's driving me crazy, trying to figure out when he's going to ask me. Now I'm wondering if I made him change his mind."

"He's here, isn't he? Humph. I doubt if Rahn's changed his mind. Every man should take a basic course on how to go about surprising a lady. You never give a heads-up." Stacy rubbed her stomach. "If we're revisiting this conversation one year from now, then you should be worried. It's been only a month since he said something, so give him a few more days." She grinned.

"A year? Please." Shae sipped her water. "Rahn doesn't want me to have to go John Legend on him."

"What?" Stacy asked, frowning in confusion.

"John Legend's fiancée threatened him that he had until the end of the year to marry her, or she was leaving him." Shae sighed. "I'm just trying to get engaged."

"Whoa!" Stacy cringed.

"What?" Shae panicked at her sister's tortured face.

"Your niece…or nephew…kicked me. Now she's moving." Stacy took Shae's hand and placed it on her stomach.

The feel of the baby's movements wowed Shae. What a miracle. She looked at the blissful expression on her sister's face.

"Did it work?" Shari asked.

"Huh?" Shae was irked by her other sister's interruption. "What?"

"John Legend's fiancée. What happened?"

"Let's just say John Legend was caught cheating a few months later." Shae shivered.

"Humph." Stacy shook her head. "Never give a man an ultimatum. Although I did hear the singer and his supermodel girlfriend tied the knot."

Rahn was one step closer to proposing. It was time to return to St. Louis so that Shae could anchor the newscast that evening. Before leaving Philadelphia, Rahn accompanied Shae to a service at her home church, Jesus Is The Way. With their hands linked, she introduced him to her longtime circle of friends as someone special in her life.

Pastor Ellis acknowledged Rahn among the visitors that day, telling everyone that he was a Gold Glove outfielder with the St. Louis Cardinals. "He is a guest of Sister Shae Carmen." The congregation applauded heartily, and Rahn thanked God for His grace that allowed others to accept him despite his mistakes. "Sister Shae, will you come sing a song to the glory of God?" the pastor asked.

Without hesitation, she stood, strolled up to the pulpit, and ascended the steps. Stacy was already sitting at the organ. Shari was in the band, holding her sax. Rahn was surprised to see Garrett there, too, also with a sax. He briefly wondered if Ted played an instrument, also, or if taste testing was his primary skill.

Rahn admired his lady's mustard-colored suit. She was beautiful, but it was her choice of a black hat with a tilt to one side that made her look stunning. And to think that God had saved her just for him. Rahn almost wanted to shake the other guy's hand and thank him for Shae before landing a punch to his jaw for hurting her. He quickly banished that scenario from his imagination.

"Praise the Lord, everybody! It's good to be home." Shae bowed her head and prayed, then opened her mouth and, in the sweetest angelic voice, sang forth the opening line of "How Great Is Our God." She gave Stacy a hand cue, and her sister struck a note on the piano.

As the congregation got on their feet, Rahn stood to praise God and support the woman he loved. When Shae hit the last note, Garrett and Shari manipulated the musical scale on their saxophones, holding the highest pitch as if they were in a duel. The sanctuary burst into worship after that. Rahn shouted praises to God, and Shae joined him once she returned to his side.

Soon, the pastor resumed his place at the podium. Jude 1:24 was the text for his message, "Stop Looking for a Loophole in the Bible to Sin."

"There isn't one," Pastor Ellis warned. "God is not to be mocked. Whatsoever a man sows, he'll get paid for it. There are consequences for sin. There is no such thing as a little lie, a big fat lie, or an almost lie. It's the same way with sin. There is no middle ground. If you want to make it to heaven, look to Jesus, and He will keep you."

He wrapped up his sermon in less than an hour, to a standing ovation. The altar call followed. "God wants to save you today. No appointment is necessary. If you want to start the process of salvation, take the first step: repent. God knows your dark, hidden secrets anyhow."

"Yes, He does," Rahn mumbled in agreement.

"All you need to do is acknowledge you're a sinner." Pastor Ellis paused. "Step two is to get prayer from one of our ministers who are waiting for you at the altar. Don't go halfway with God; go all the way and be baptized in the name of Jesus for the remission of your sins. The Lord will fill you with the Holy Ghost and speak to you through tongues of fire." He stretched out his arms. "Won't you come?"

Many did. Most received prayer only. Others who desired to be baptized were ushered through a door. Rahn had witnessed ten souls go down in the water, in Jesus' name, by the time the benediction was given.

After the service, while Shae received hugs, some people approached Rahn and asked for his autograph, which he gave freely. Then an elderly woman wearing a pillbox hat wobbled toward him. She beckoned with a crooked finger for him to come closer. He obliged.

"God showed me you're the one."

Rahn frowned, wondering what she meant, as Shae walked up to him. Together, they watched the woman scurry away faster than she'd come. "Oh, I see you've met Mother Stillwell. Be wary of whatever she tells you."

"I think she was on point with this one." Rahn laughed, encircling her waist with his arm. "Come on. Let's go so we can make our flight."

39

Two weeks after the trip to Philly, Shae flew to Virginia with Rahn to meet his family. Halfway through their flight, Rahn angled his body in his seat next to hers. "Nervous?"

"Why?" Shae squirmed.

"Because you've asked me more than once about your appearance."

"Oh." What woman wouldn't be self-conscious as she prepared to come face-to-face with her boyfriend's mother? She and Eloise had gotten along fine on the phone. Shae just hoped she would pass inspection in person.

Rahn scanned her attire. "Believe me, you've never looked so pretty." Leaning forward, he brushed a soft kiss against her lips. The touch relaxed her, and he knew it, too, judging from his cocky grin.

And the "Rahn effect" wasn't limited to his touch. The intensity of the way he looked at her made her feel desired and admired. And his respect always shone through.

His appearance was perfection with precision, from his facial features to his height, from his build to his cologne and clothes; but the most endearing thing was that he loved Jesus. That was the icing on the cake. Shae smiled, remembering the slice of actual cake they had shared, back when they had barely known each other. Now, their love was secured, so she had stopped worrying about when Rahn was going to propose—almost. Whenever that happened, she would be ready to say yes.

Once they landed in Richmond, Rahn retrieved their luggage and picked up a rental car. Shae was speechless at the wealth and beauty surrounding her as they entered Moseley, Powhatan County. She mentally calculated the probable worth of the nearby estates at well over half-a-million dollars. "These are breathtaking."

"Can you see yourself living in one of these?" Rahn asked with a serious edge to his tone.

Without looking his way, Shae could only shake her head. "I've never dreamed this big."

"Dream, baby, dream." He turned onto Fox Creek, and the mansions became even more majestic, with landscapes that showcased meticulous detail.

Frowning, Shae did a double take. Were those bushes that had been manicured into the shapes of Mickey and Minnie Mouse near a swing set? *Really?*

"We're here."

Rahn hardly needed to point out the house. The luxury cars parked along the perimeter of the large property and jammed in the long driveway were a telltale giveaway. "This must be some afternoon tea," Shae muttered, referring to what Eloise had said—that she was inviting "a few friends" over to meet her.

"Small means big to Mom, and big means grand. These are old friends and some family. Consider this a welcome party, babe. Be yourself, and everyone will see why I love you." He chuckled.

Shae bowed her head and whispered a short prayer. When she opened her eyes, Rahn gave her a tender smile. "Amen."

The calming effect of that one word eased some of the tension as Rahn parked behind a black Bentley. Then, holding hands, they strolled up the circular cobblestone drive, Rahn identifying the various guests by their vehicles. They hadn't made it to the porch when a beautifully carved oak door opened.

A petite, exquisitely coiffed woman graced the doorway—Eloise Maxwell. Rahn had her same engaging smile. Ignoring her son, Eloise stretched out her arms toward Shae. "Shae, we finally meet face-to-face. You're gorgeous," she said, eying her up and down.

Shae blushed under her scrutiny. Eloise looked stunning herself, especially considering her recent health scare.

"Welcome to Richmond." Eloise gave her a hug that made her feel right at home.

"Thank you."

Rahn cleared his throat. "I hope you'll have some love left over for your favorite son."

His mother shushed him. Laughing, Eloise took her time and kissed Shae's cheek, then turned to Rahn. "I left a little for you." She gave him a brief squeeze. "Come on in. Everybody's waiting."

The grand entrance was impressive, with wood molding everywhere. The spiral staircase looked like something out of a classic movie, but the gleaming hardwood floors looked newer. Shae felt sorry for the Persian rugs that were taking a pounding from the guests who filled the foyer or peeked around the corner from one of two sitting rooms on either side of the hall.

With a hero's welcome, Rahn received hearty hugs, cheers, and even toasts, but he didn't release her hand as he made the introductions. Some of the men had no shame, blatantly flirting with her in jest.

However, not everybody approved of Rahn's decision to disclose his steroid use when he didn't have to. That's when Shae came to his defense, linking arms with him. "Rahn has made some unfortunate decisions in the past regarding his career, but the good thing is, he whom the Son has set free is free indeed—talking about Jesus' acquittal. How many people are willing to admit their mistakes and face public humiliation? He's my hero."

Rahn's gaze was tender as he leaned in and brushed his lips across hers, to the *aah*s of those looking on. "Thank you, baby," he whispered.

She was somewhat surprised by the applause.

"Uh…that sounds like a woman in love now, but I don't recall your presence when this was happening," boomed a tall, distinguished-looking gentleman as he approached them. Rahn stiffened beside her and loosened his hold of her hand.

"That's enough, Uncle Joseph," Rahn warned him.

Shae wasn't about to back down. She tightened her grip on Rahn's hand. "You're correct. I made the decision to love him from afar, but I loved him nevertheless. I had to separate my personal life from my profession."

A stylishly dressed older woman elbowed Uncle Joseph in the side as she asked, "Would you do it again?" She then identified herself as Aunt Gertrude.

All eyes were on her, including Rahn's, as everyone waited for her answer. So, this was how an ambush felt. She and Rahn had reached an understanding that she had a right to protect her career. *"After all, that's what our argument was about—me trying to save my career,"* he had said during the first long talk they'd had following the awards banquet. *"I never should've threatened you, saying I would lie, or disrespected you. I was wrong to treat you that way, especially since I loved you."*

After reflecting on that conversation, Shae knew her response would not be a surprise to him. "I would."

"Good for you. If you don't stand for something, you'll trip over nothing," Aunt Gertrude stated with her own version of a cliché. She winked at Shae, then eyed Rahn with a serious look. "Marry this girl!"

That's what I'm saying. Shae blushed but didn't say a word.

Rahn stared at her with an unreadable expression. "I think I will."

This was it. Was he about to propose? Was this the moment Shae had been waiting for? Her heart pounded wildly, and she had to catch her breath. Then she frowned. Rahn wouldn't asked her in front of his family without having her family present, too—right? False alarm—again—which caused her to be annoyed.

Barreling out of another room, two mini-versions of Rahn smothered him, vying for his attention. He put a halt to their questions as he made the introductions.

His nephews eyed her, giving away no hint as to what they were thinking. Seconds ticked by before the boys waved and, in a practiced manner, politely said, "Hi."

Shae chuckled as Rahn rubbed one's head and then the other's. It wasn't long before she met the twins' parents. Rahn's sister, Phyllis, was down to earth, and the two hit it off right away.

"Lunch is being served," Eloise announced, directing her guests to the buffet tables set up in both sitting rooms.

Shae had never seen so much food at a gathering in someone's home. "You want me to fix your plate?" Rahn asked her.

"Please, thank you."

Rahn was attentive as he catered to her every request. When he vacated his seat, his sister stole it. Smiling, Phyllis sipped on her punch, then whispered, "Don't let Uncle Joe get to you. Aunt Gertrude keeps him in check. You passed. We've met a few of Rahn's previous dates, and they seemed interested in saying and doing whatever necessary to keep him."

I'm not one of them, for sure. Shae smiled. "Don't get me wrong—I truly love your brother—but I have a conscience, and I can't go against it. When I made the decision to break up with him, I accepted my fate that I had lost him." She closed her eyes, recalling her bouts of loneliness. "But God worked it out."

"I'm so glad. You make my brother a better man. He loves you. I heard it in his voice the last time he was here, but seeing you two together, I can feel it."

"Me, too."

The two chatted like old girlfriends. Phyllis entertained Shae with stories about Rahn's childhood, and she had never laughed so hard. The "afternoon tea" continued into the evening. At sunset, Rahn guided Shae onto the veranda for some time alone.

They were content to just sit there. Finally, Rahn revisited her remark to his uncle Joseph. "Thank you for loving me from afar, but I plan to keep you so close, you won't ever have to make that decision again."

Snuggling deeper in his arms, Shae shook her head. "I didn't want to leave you."

"I know, baby. You followed your convictions. How can I not love you for that? I always will." After saying good night, Rahn prepared to head to the house he owned nearby, leaving her in the care of his mother. "Baby, if you need anything..." He was clearly reluctant to leave.

"She won't. Good night, Son." Eloise shoved him out the door, laughing.

The next morning, Rahn gave Shae a tour of his historic hometown. They visited the Richmond Slave Trail, which documented the history of the largest slave-holding state, as well as the state capital. They also shopped. Their last stop was a restaurant inside the Virginia Museum of Fine Arts, where they had made dinner reservations.

Both seemed to shut out the world and focus on each other. "You know I love you." Rahn appeared more interested in her than the meal they were sharing by candlelight.

Enjoying his attention, Shae scrunched her nose at him. "As a matter of fact, I do know that," she whispered. Her heart pounded, just as it did every time she heard him say that.

"I did tell you that I wanted us to get married before I left for spring training, right?"

"Are you asking me?"

"Almost."

Shae lifted her eyebrows. "What do you mean, 'almost'?" The man was killing the ambiance. Now she knew how other women felt when men strung them along. "Wouldn't it be something if I decided I wasn't ready to get married?"

"Woman, don't play." Rahn's nostrils flared.

She leaned close enough to get a whiff of his cologne. "Then stop playing with me and my heart!" She had lowered her voice but didn't try to hide her irritation. "It's October, Rahn. Are you planning on asking me before this year is out?" she snapped.

"Yes."

Okay. Shae calmed down and exhaled. She wouldn't have to make a John Legend threat. *Now I know.*

40

$\mathscr{B}$ack in St. Louis, Rahn relayed his conversation with Shae to Marcus as they shot pool in Rahn's game room. "Can you believe she basically challenged my intent to ask her to marry me and asked me when?" Rahn had to chuckle at the absurdity. "And this coming from a woman who wants to be surprised."

Marcus *tsked*. "It's a good thing Shae is too ladylike to smack you for teasing her. Yvette would have dragged me to the jeweler if I had mentioned the *m* word without the ring."

"You know it's about more than the ring. Shae is my heart, and I'll protect my woman as my wife at all costs."

"Personally, I think you're going for overkill." As Marcus racked up the balls to play a new game, Rahn chalked the tip of his cue. "You and your surprises." Marcus shook his head. "You better hope she doesn't walk away—again. 'Marriage' and 'babies' are fighting words to women, and they don't play when their biological clock is ticking."

The weeks rolled into November before Rahn got the call that everything was ready and done to his specifications. "I've got to fly home to take care of some business," he informed Shae as he bid her good-bye at the elevator in her condo lobby, "but I'll be back before the week is out."

"Is everything all right?" she asked. "Do you want me to go with you? I'm off tomorrow, and I can fly back in time for my shift on Saturday."

Rahn loved that she was always concerned about him. He hadn't factored in the possibility that she would want to go along. Ever since they had mended their relationship, they had agreed there would be no more secrets between them, so he stuttered as he answered. "Uh, no, baby, but I'll be home as soon as possible."

She eyed him warily. "Is everything all right?" she asked again.

"Perfect." He winked.

"O-okay." She kissed him. "I love you. Be safe."

"I love you, too." He waited until she stepped inside the elevator and the door closed. Whistling, he saluted Mr. Chapman and strolled outside. He pivoted on his heels and looked up. The light in her condo came on minutes later. Within seconds, she appeared in the window, waved, and blew him a kiss. As if he was wearing his baseball glove, Rahn lifted his arm and caught the imaginary jewel.

Then, smiling, he swaggered to his car. The next time he saw Shae, they would be engaged.

The next day, Rahn boarded the plane with his one-way ticket. When he arrived at his mother's house in Richmond, she chewed him out. "It's about time. You made Shae wait long enough. I won't be surprised if she tells you no."

"Don't put any ideas in her head, Mom." Rahn kissed her cheek, then left to pick up Shae's presents. Once her engagement ring had passed his inspection, his next stop was a car dealership owned by his friend Harold, aka Hamster. The pearl-white Jaguar had been custom-made with reinforced windows able to withstand close-range gunfire.

"Do you know how long it took to make armor-plated doors for a Jag that wouldn't take away its sleek look?" Hamster said.

"But your men did an outstanding job." Rahn strolled around the vehicle, giving it a close examination. It had been worth the wait for them to get it right. When it came to his wife's safety, he refused to compromise.

With everything in order, Rahn bid his family good-bye and began the solo drive back to the Midwest. Thoughts of Shae—her smile, her laughter, and the sense of completeness he felt when he held her in his arms—occupied his mind. He grunted. "I'm really going to do this."

Two days later, although it seemed like forever, Rahn was an hour away from St. Louis when snow started to fall. Despite the perilous road conditions, he was able to arrive at Shae's before she got home from work. He hoped it would be a slow news night so that she could leave the station on time.

Sitting behind the wheel in anticipation of what he was about to do, Rahn prayed, "Lord, thank You for putting Shae in my path…" Just then he noticed headlights in the rearview mirror.

Shae's modest car appeared through the backdrop of the snow. Rahn slid down in the seat while he waited for her to pass, then scooted up again. He watched as she parked and then carefully climbed out of her car.

She made a camera-perfect model in her off-white wool coat. As her features came into view, Rahn selected her name on his smartphone and waited as she fumbled through her purse. Shae pulled out her phone and answered just when he thought it was about to go to voice mail.

"I've made it home," he whispered. He didn't have to imagine her smile; he got to witness it.

"Praise God! I could've picked you up from the airport, but you never gave me your flight information. Listen, the snow is coming down a little heavier. Let me call you back once I get upstairs."

"Okay, baby, but no woman can wear white like you. You're stunning in that fur hat." He smirked as Shae touched the top of her head. "As a matter of fact, you become more beautiful every time I see you."

She froze. "You didn't see the newscast, did you? Wait a minute." Her head jerked around. "I wasn't wearing a fur hat on the news." Shae put her gloved hand on her hip. "Rahn Maxwell, exactly where are you?"

Rahn stepped out of the Jaguar and crept up the street toward her. "Look behind you, baby."

⌒

Shae felt like a character in a Christmas movie as she hurried toward Rahn. He swept her off the ground with one strong arm around her waist, and she wrapped her arms around his neck. "You're here. You're really here." She peppered his face with kisses as he laughed.

Despite the snowflakes gathering on her eyelashes, Shae took the time to study the silky black beard that outlined his full lips. Tears escaped her eyes as Rahn tightened his hug. The silhouette of his unbuttoned black wool coat and coordinating hat gave him a mysterious look that contrasted against the backdrop of falling snow.

"Yes, I'm here—all six feet three inches of me," he whispered, releasing her. He cupped her cheeks. This time, it was his turn to shower her with affection. He kissed her eyes, her nose, and finally her lips—a gesture that was sweet, soft, and too short. "I brought you a wedding present." He dangled a set of car keys before her eyes.

Confused, Shae watched him turn and press the button, activating the alarm of a white Jaguar parked a few cars behind hers. The interior lights blinked, the horn chirped, and the parking lights illuminated the majestic luxury vehicle.

A Jag? Rahn had to stop this madness, playing charades with her heart and making her guess when he was going to propose. She jammed her fists on her hips and tapped her boot on the snow-covered sidewalk. "Come back when you're ready." She turned to go inside, but Rahn's strong hand twirled her around. He drew her into his stare while he slowly dropped to one knee in the snow.

His puppy-dog expression tugged at her heart. Oh…this was it. Rahn was proposing! She dusted the snowflakes off of his face.

"Shae Carmen, I have loved you from the first time I saw you. When I'm with you, I am simply me—not a celebrity or a man of means; just an ordinary man blessed to have a special woman in his life. I love you so much, but I had to have everything in order before I asked you." He paused, reaching inside his pants' pocket. His hand seemed to move in slow motion as it emerged with a black velvet box.

Shae sucked in her breath as tears streamed down her cheeks. When Rahn flipped the lid open, the diamonds sparkled. She covered her mouth.

"Will you marry me?"

The words echoed. Either Shae's head was spinning or her brain was frost-bitten. Her answer was stuck somewhere between her stomach and throat. She nodded.

He shook his head. "That's not going to work. You're a broadcaster. I need you to broadcast your answer."

Her voice was coming up her throat like a slow-moving choo-choo train. Finally, "Yes" slipped out. She sniffed as Rahn removed her glove and tenderly slipped the ring on her finger. Then he admired his gift before kissing her hand.

Before she could blink, Rahn had stood, scooped her up in his arms, and carried her to the entrance, where Mr. Chapman was holding the door open for them. No doubt he had witnessed the scene.

"I'm an engaged man," Rahn boasted to anyone within hearing range.

"So it appears." Mr. Chapman chuckled, rubbing his chin. "I guess this is breaking news."

Rahn carried her to the sitting area, where a roaring fire beckoned them. Unwilling to break their contact, Shae nestled in his lap and admired her ring. Suddenly she started sobbing.

"Baby, what's wrong?" He nudged her off his chest to look at her.

Shaking her head, Shae sniffed, then whispered her confession: "I thought you were never going to ask."

"Then you really don't know me." He paused, wiping away her tears. "You deserve the best, and I refused to give you anything less than that—the ring and your armor-plated car."

She blinked. "That Jag is armor plated?"

"Yep." Rahn's lips curled into a smirk. "Wait until we go house hunting."

Joy filled Shae until she had a giggle fit. Rahn laughed with her. Once they recovered, the reality hit her, and she straightened. "It's snowing outside."

"It has been for some time. What's your point?"

She stood and pulled him to his feet. "What's my new car doing out in this weather?" She escorted him—more like pushed him—toward the door. "It is a Jag, after all."

After stealing a kiss, Rahn howled his amusement on his way out the door.

"Don't let anything happen to my car!" she yelled after him.

"What about me?"

"Oh, yeah." She beamed. "Or to you, either. You're my most important cargo." She couldn't wait to go upstairs and call her sisters. They had a wedding to plan.

41

Two months till the start of spring training, Rahn paced the men's dressing room at the church, counting down the minutes until Shae would arrive in the limo he'd sent for her. He had lovingly placed her wedding bouquet on the seat with an envelope that included a sketch of them and a message: *I'll always love you.*

"What's going on? I was supposed to be a married man seven minutes ago. Where are Shae and the others?" Rahn didn't want to entertain any of the worst-case scenarios trying to get into his head.

Marcus smirked. "Hold on to your suspenders, if you're wearing them. I'll try to reach the limo driver." He punched in the number on the card Rahn pulled out of his wallet. "The line's busy." He finally got the driver after two more tries. When Marcus was about to say 'hello,' Rahn snatched the phone out of his hand.

"Where are you and my wife?" He would make amends for his rudeness later.

"Fiancée," Ted interjected. "It's not official yet." His attempt to lighten the mood seemed to work on everybody but Rahn.

He was not amused. He refused to spend a night in jail for strangling his future brother-in-law. He turned his attention back to the phone. The limo driver was explaining the delay. "An accident…?"

His good humor gone, Ted yanked the phone away from Rahn, his eyes watering. Rahn grabbed it back, and the two of them battled, Ted with shaking hands. "Are they hurt badly?" he shouted into the phone. "Oh." He frowned as the other groomsmen gathered around, concern etched on their faces.

Ted scowled like a pit bull at Rahn. "The bridal party wasn't in an accident. There was a fender-bender in front of them, and the police are letting one lane of traffic through at a time. Don't you ever scare me like that again, taking years off my young life. They will be here in less than ten minutes."

Rubbing the frustration from his face, Rahn apologized.

"I wouldn't have really hurt you…not until after the honeymoon." Ted gave him a bear hug, then patted his back.

Marcus offered to go to the sanctuary to inform the five-hundred-plus guests of the reason for the delay. He spoke into a microphone, so Rahn could hear him.

"Ladies and gentlemen, the bride didn't run off." Some guests laughed. "She's tied up in traffic but will be here in a couple of minutes."

"Otherwise I'm going looking for her," Rahn muttered as the remaining groomsmen nodded in agreement.

〜

The limo driver glanced over his shoulder. "Miss Carmen?"

Three women answered.

Shae smiled. She had four attendants: her sisters and Rahn's sister, Phyllis. "I think he's talking to me."

Her mother patted her hand. "Not for much longer."

The chauffeur chuckled. "Mr. Maxwell sends his love and nervousness."

Serves him right for keeping me on pins and needles, leaving me to wonder when he was going to propose, Shae said to herself, even as she laughed along with the others.

Soon the driver was able to maneuver the limo around the traffic accident. The wedding coordinator—a petite woman with salt-and-pepper hair—was waiting for them at the church door, looking frantic and flustered. "We are behind schedule. Oh, dear," she fretted before hurrying Shae into a small dressing room to wait. Everything seemed to accelerate before Shae's eyes. The next thing she knew, her mother and then Rahn's mom kissed her cheek, then turned to their escorts, ready to make their way up the aisle.

The organist struck the first chord, signaling that the procession was about to start. Shae glanced at her reflection in the mirror. Her makeup had never looked better. As the music played, she imagined her bridesmaids gliding down the aisle, followed by her matron of honor, Stacy, and finally by the two flower girls littering the runner with pink rose petals.

The soft tap on the door was her cue. Shae was feeling a mixture of anxiety, excitement, and some other emotions she couldn't name. After taking a deep breath, she stepped out of her bridal chamber. At the same time, she heard Rahn's twin nephews ringing silver bells and crying out, "Here comes the bride...here comes the bride," which sounded more like "Here comes the broad."

This wasn't a dream. Rahn had indeed asked her to marry him—finally—and she'd accepted. "I'm the bride," she whispered to herself.

"I was wondering who I was going to walk down there." Uncle Bradford patted her hand before resting it over his forearm. "I believe Rahn will make you happy."

"He already has."

The double doors opened, and the wedding planner beckoned them forward. Feeling like Cinderella in glass slippers, Shae stepped into the sanctuary. Everything blurred except for Rahn, who came into focus immediately. When she was midway to the altar, Rahn left his post in a comfortable swagger toward her.

"You're more than beautiful. I'm so honored."

Through her veil, Shae looked into the eyes of the man to whom she was about to vow her faithfulness and love forever. "Thank you."

Uncle Bradford gave Rahn a stern expression before shaking his hand. No words were exchanged, but Rahn nodded. Evidently, the two had come to some type of understanding that she wasn't privy to.

Then, with a loving gaze, Rahn refocused on her. "Let's do this."

"*I would love to,*" she mouthed as they continued to the altar.

Bishop Archie cleared his throat. "Dearly beloved, we're gathered together here in the sight of God…"

Rahn caressed Shae's hand as he repeated his vows with such tenderness in his voice and love in his eyes. She became teary eyed when he slid the wedding band that matched her pink gold engagement ring on her finger. When it was her turn, Shae's hands shook as she pledged her love and faithfulness, surrendering to him as the head of the home. His eyes moved from her eyes to her mouth, and Shae finally exhaled once she'd pushed the band onto his thick finger.

"Inasmuch as you have each pledged to the other your lifelong commitment, love, and devotion, I pronounce you husband and wife, in the name of our Lord and Savior, Jesus Christ," Bishop Archie proclaimed. "Those whom God has joined together, let no man—or woman—put asunder. Rahn, you may kiss your bride."

Leaning forward, Shae closed her eyes. Their first kiss as a married couple was powerful and romantic. The audience started clapping and whistling. Once Rahn had stepped back again, he scooped her off her feet—which was good, because she was getting dizzy—and dipped her backward.

Hooking her arms around Rahn's neck to hold on, she whispered, "If you drop me…"

"If I can catch a fly ball in center field, I can definitely hold on to my wife."

EPILOGUE

Shae Maxwell loved Jesus, she loved her husband, and she loved married life, especially after spending ten wonderful days in Italy on their honeymoon. The bliss continued when she returned to work to find a glorious floral spread on her desk.

Plucking the sealed envelope out of the arrangement, she smiled as she opened it.

To my wife. Thank you for marrying me, Mrs. Maxwell.

Not long after that, she found a piece of mail from the St. Louis Cardinals' promotions department in her mailbox at the station. The organization wanted her to be in one of their commercials that would run before the upcoming baseball season. Although she thought it would be fun, Shae called Rahn to ask him to weigh in on the decision. She wanted to make sure they consulted each other on important matters.

"If you want to do it, babe, do it, not because you're married to me."

"Of course, that's the only reason I would want to do it—because I'm married to a fantastic husband." She frowned. "They don't want you in there, too?"

"I'm not as cute as you," Rahn cooed in her ear. He was at home, packing up some personal items in preparation for the big move next week. Besides the Jaguar, her husband had gone overboard in selecting their first home based on some off-handed comments she had made regarding what she wanted in a home: cubbyholes, bay windows, and a home office.

When she'd mentioned that she *might* start sewing again, Rahn had requested a custom-built sewing room be added to the blueprint and stocked with thread and other notions for whenever the mood hit her. Then, there was the matter of the five bedrooms for the children he expected to enjoy. They would definitely have to negotiate that.

So, Shae agreed to be in the commercial. One week before Rahn and his teammates were set to jet off to Florida for spring training, Shae stood on the pitcher's mound in an empty Busch Stadium. Although the weather was warm for February, it was still chilly, so she'd dressed in several layers of clothes beneath Rahn's baseball jersey. The filming wasn't supposed to last more than twenty minutes, so she figured she would be warm enough.

"We want you to relax and have fun. That's what baseball is all about—fun," the producer explained, as two camerapersons—a man and a woman—set up their tripods. "You and Rahn are our newest local celebrity couple. We'll keep the camera rolling for a few minutes before we shoot another angle."

"This is exciting." Shae grinned and closed her eyes, imagining that she was standing in the middle of a tied game before a sellout crowd. She took a deep breath, then exhaled slowly. She was ready to role-play as a pitcher. After agreeing to do the commercial, Shae had tried to read up on different pitches: the curveball, the slider, and the knuckleball. In the end, she'd decided it wasn't that big a deal for a commercial that was supposed to portray her as carefree and natural.

Cocking her Cardinals cap to the side and popping her bubble gum, she eyed all the positions from her vantage point as if the bases were loaded. The field was huge. It was an amazing feat that her husband could catch anything in this wide-open space.

"Okay, Shae, we're sending out your first batter," the producer said, breaking her reverie. "Remember, just act natural."

Then her husband, sporting his uniform, walked out of the dugout and strolled to the plate, wearing a silly grin.

Lifting a brow, Shae smirked as she rested her fist on her hip. "Really?" She gave her first pitch all she had—to no avail. The second one was even wilder than the first. Rahn started laughing, and soon even the producer was snickering.

"Throw me something I can hit, woman!" Rahn taunted her.

Shae scrunched up her nose and concentrated. Honing in on her target, she released the ball, and this time, she didn't miss. Throwing her hands in the air like a football referee, she yelled, "Home run!"

"Ouch!" Rahn cried as the ball deflected off his arm. He stormed the mound with a scowl.

Giggling, Shae left her post and took off running. It became a game of tag as she ran one way, then turned and darted in another direction. At this point, Shae didn't care about the commercial. She *was* caught up in the moment. Then Rahn tackled her from behind. Shae screamed but never felt the impact, as his sturdy arms cushioned her fall.

"Don't you know you're an easy catch?" Rahn kissed her before she could answer.

"That was great!" the producer shouted in the background. "Cut. That's a wrap."

Rahn didn't stop kissing her, and she wasn't about to make him.

BOOK CLUB DISCUSSION QUESTIONS

1. Have you ever had a tumultuous relationship with someone else in the church? How did it affect your relationship with God?

2. An embarrassing situation compelled Shae to "run away from" Nebraska to St. Louis, where she carved out a prestigious career and met the love of her life. Have you ever "run away from" a problem, only to discover that it was part of God's purpose all along?

3. The idea for an attempted carjacking of Rahn was sparked by an interview I saw with Michael Irvin years earlier. Do you feel that athletes and other celebrities seem to be exempt from various perils in their lives because of their status?

4. Until he decided to go public about his drug use, Rahn maintained that what he had done in the past should stay in the past—it was forgiven and forgotten. Do you agree or disagree with this viewpoint?

5. Was Shae right to choose her career over her relationship with Rahn?

6. What was the most memorable scene in the story for you? Why?

7. Do you have a Mother Stillwell figure in your church? Has her presence had a positive or negative impact on your faith?

8. Who is your favorite celebrity couple? Why?

9. What Scripture from the story seemed to resonate with you the most?

10. Shari and Garrett's story is the second in the Carmen Sisters series. What do you think Garrett could he have done that would be worse than Rahn's scandal?

A Preview of Book Two in The Carmen Sisters

Coming Spring 2015

1

$\mathcal{S}$harmaine "Shari" Carmen's smartphone chimed as she climbed out of her black Cadillac SUV. She fumbled with her purse and briefcase before pinching the device between her ear and shoulder without checking the caller ID. "Hello?"

"I need you." The raspy voice sounded desperate.

Lifting an eyebrow, Shari adjusted the items in her arms, then squinted at the screen of her phone to see who was calling. *John Whitman.* Her lips curled up in a mischievous smile. "Does your wife know?" she whispered huskily as she strolled up the pathway to her childhood home, where she lived with her widowed mother.

"Who do you think put me up to this?" he snapped.

Shaking her head, Shari burst out laughing as she inserted the key in the front door. John—the band leader at her church—and his wife, Rita, were known pranksters. The only thing more notorious than their antics was their campaign of matchmaking schemes directed at members of the band and choir at Jesus Is The Way Church. The pair seemed to have a gift, not necessarily from God, to sense a potential couple's compatibility.

And don't think church folks didn't keep score. The Whitmans' record was better than that of Mother Ernestine Stillwell, an elderly woman known for her "hope chest" prophecies. So far this year, the Whitmans were leading her by five couples to Mother Stillwell's one. The senior citizen maintained that her last three fiascos had been false starts.

"You Whitmans have no shame," Shari said. "Whatever it is, my first and final answer is no."

"Hear me out, Sharmaine…"

She was surprised John didn't attach attorney to her given name. His request was probably a doozie. "It's a favor for a close friend, a new church member, a band member…" he empathized.

"Hmm." She entered her second-floor bedroom. Although Shari could afford a nice piece of real estate in Mt. Airy, she liked her mother's company. Plus, her other three siblings, all sisters, had moved away—two of them to different states.

But Shari loved the historic feel of Philadelphia, the cultural events the city had to offer, and her church.

Shari's older sister, Stacy, a teacher, lived across town with her husband, Ted. Shae, Shari's younger sister, was a TV reporter in Nebraska; and her baby sister, Sabrece, aka "Brecee," was in Houston to compete her pediatrics residency.

Shari would probably remain a home girl, just like Stacy. Staying in Philly allowed her to keep tabs on her mother. Kicking off her four-inch heels, Shari wiggled her toes as she flopped on the bed.

"Brother Garrett Nash is in a bind."

Now, that name gave her pause. Shari recalled the formal introduction of the three new band members—all male—at the last practice she'd attended. She doubted any of the brothers had given her a second glance. There were too many single sisters skilled at getting a man's attention within seconds of meeting him and then staying on a prayer chain to keep it. "Why bother?" was her motto.

However, Brother Garrett Nash's dark complexion and handsome features could rival Djimon Hounsou, the West-African actor. One glance, and he could make any lady smile—even one with cataracts.

"So, what does that have to do with me?" Somewhat curious, Shari took the bait.

As he launched into a long-winded explanation, she stared in the mirror, scrutinizing her dull black hair screaming for a shampoo. As soon as she got off the phone, she planned to tend to it. It was Friday, and she was tired after a long week spent defending clients with colorful criminal portfolios in court.

"Garrett asked if some band members wouldn't mind traveling to Boston for his grandparents' fiftieth wedding anniversary party," John explained. "Apparently, something went down, and now he's in a bind to find a musical talent for the program. He's covering the transportation costs, so there's no expense on our part. Please."

Shari wasn't opposed to the travel aspect. The five-hour road trip would be a piece of cake. Her church's gospel choir and band participated in competitions all the time, and the music department also accompanied the pastor to preaching events. Almost any invitation was accepted, as long as the group could make it back to their home church in time for Sunday services.

Her lips were forming an *o* for "Okay" when he dropped the bombshell.

"I need you to play 'Thank You' for the ceremony," John stated, then rushed on. "Terrell was going to play his sax, but he's down with the flu. Rod could manage it on his guitar, but, as you know, the horn rules on that song."

John had wasted a call. He knew she wasn't going to do it.

Shari felt no shame in turning him down. "Sorry, no can do."

The last time she had played the timeless Walter Hawkins tune had been at her father's funeral. Now, twelve years later, just the mention of that song quickened bittersweet memories.

Shari's mother always remarked how much she reminded her of her father, Saul Carmen. Out of the four daughters, Shari liked to think of herself as a bona fide Daddy's girl. She even shared his same rich, dark skin. It was actually because of her skin, which was the color of God's earth, that she'd needed her father to wipe away many of her tears and remind her how beautiful she was, even though she didn't think so.

All the Carmen girls were noted for their long hair, which came courtesy of their African and Italian heritages. Their mother always called hair "a woman's glory." Stacy, Shae, and Brecee were fair like their mother. They could have passed the brown paper bag test in order to be accepted into certain social clubs or sororities.

Her first cousins, Victor and Dino, shared her darker hue and seemed to understand her complex. Both had taken it upon themselves to become better protectors and bodyguards than the fiercest of any big brother.

"Please, Sharmaine. I need you," John continued pleading. "Garrett is a perfectionist. The horns kill that song, and you're the only one who can pull it off. I asked everyone else I could think of, but now I'm desperate. Face your fear. Jesus can help you overcome…"

Which fear? She had more than a few. Although Shari exuded confidence inside the courtroom, when the suit and heels came off, she easily faded into the background—the woodwork, really.

Without a social calendar, Shari filled her life with family, work, and church. She overindulged in the latter two areas. She gladly accepted a heavy client load and had more than a few commitments to various auxiliary groups, including her church's prison ministry with its monthly visits. That explained her absence from Saturday band rehearsals for two weeks straight. But her first love was music, and as a child, she'd learned from her cousins to command the sax. She loved to play, and the band leader knew that.

John must have taken her slight hesitation as a cue to forge ahead. "The attire is black…"

Yes! She grinned, glad that she had nothing suitable to wear. "I just dropped off an armload of clothes at the cleaners yesterday, and they won't be ready until Monday." Hopefully, she had grabbed every black garment in her closet.

"That's no excuse," said John's wife, Rita, taking over the conversation. "Pick your poison: I can go shopping with you or for you. Sis, you really are one of the best on alto sax. Let's pray that God will give you a cheerful heart toward that song for this festive occasion."

Shari gnawed on her lip. Wasn't that what every saint of God wanted—to be delivered from spiritual bondage?

"Do it for Brother Garrett, and God will bless you."

When would God bless her in other areas of her life? She was twenty-nine, with no relief in sight from her singleness. Even Mother Stillwell—the church busybody whose greatest pleasure was tracking down sisters and proclaiming they were next in line for a husband—wobbled in a different direction when she saw Shari coming. It didn't matter. The older woman didn't even have a fifty-fifty accuracy rate anyway.

When Shari had heard enough of John's whining and Rita's pleading, she caved in. "All right, all right. I guess I'd better find something to wear for this cross-country trip you've suckered me into."

"Yes!" the Whitmans exclaimed in unison.

"The bus leaves the church at nine in the morning," John added.

"Thank You, Jesus," Rita said. "We love you, Shari!"

With the call over, Shari exhaled, then chuckled at the Whitmans' flair for persuasion. "How did I let them break me down like that?" Inside her walk-in closet, she started a scavenger hunt for a dark skirt.

A knock on her door interrupted her task. "Hey, sweetie. I don't know if you're hungry or not, but I made pot roast…" Her mother's voice grew louder as she peeked inside Shari's bedroom. "What are you doing?"

A former Miss America beauty contestant in her heyday, Annette Carmen was the only woman Shari knew who could cook and clean, then step out the door at a moment's notice looking youthful and refreshed. But what Shari really admired was her mother's calm demeanor, which few people could rattle. That was a quality she wished she had inherited.

"I've been duped by the choir couple." Shari threw her hands up and came out of her closet. It appeared that all her black clothes were indeed at the cleaners.

Releasing a melodious strain of laughter, her mother came further into the room and folded her arms. She happened to be a fan of the Whitmans. "For what event? When and where is it?"

Shari gave her the details, then confessed, "My heart really isn't into going."

"Why?" Her mother positioned herself on the bed and cuddled a throw pillow.

Shari recapped her conversation with John and Rita. "Mother, I buried that song with Daddy."

Her mother shook her head. "Your father wouldn't have wanted that. We thank the Lord for him every day. Play the song to God's glory. The memories you have will never fade. Plus, you need to get out more. You're young."

Shari used to keep track of the number of times she heard that saying. When she was a child, her parents had nicknamed her "house kid" because of her preference to curl up in a corner chair and devour a book while her three sisters went outside and played with the neighborhood children.

"Okay, let's take a deep, cleansing breath. Oxygen is good for your heart and brain." Her mother stood and exercised what she was preaching. She resembled a yoga instructor as her eyelids drifted closed. Seconds later, her eyes popped open wide. "Now, what's priority?"

"I have to wear black, and all my conservative clothes are at the cleaners."

Her mother never failed to remind her to be consistent with her dress in and out of church because God was omnipresent. But that's where Shari rebelled. Church was church, business was business, and outside of both, feeling flirtatious in her clothes was her personal fantasy, as long as they weren't revealing or suggestive.

Sitting back on the bed, Annette squinted at the closet from her spot atop the overstuffed white down comforter. "I see a black skirt in the back on the right-hand side...hmm. It may be a little short, but I'm sure it's respectable."

Who said eyesight diminishes with age? Shari mused. After a search and rescue, Shari tugged the skirt off the hanger. A few minutes into the negotiation, Shari manipulated the sleek fabric over her hips, then braved a glance in the full-length mirror. "Yep. I see where the five pounds settled from Aunt Camille's earthquake cake, your pecan pie, the cheesesteak from lunch..."

Her mother sighed and rested her hands on her hips. "Ah, to be so generously endowed."

"It isn't always a blessing."

"Tell that to a skinny woman," she stated. "What else?"

"I need to change my oil," Shari said.

"I thought you took care of that last week."

"I meant my hair."

They laughed. "Problem solved. I'll wash and set it with plenty of curls so there'll be less fuss when you get there. Next?"

Four hours later, with all the tasks complete, Shari drifted off to sleep after praying, "Lord, let me be a blessing to Brother Garrett's family."

⌣

Garrett Nash's homecoming was bittersweet. If it wasn't for his grandparents' monumental celebration, he wouldn't be there. Musically, everything had been in order for the event when he'd left Boston. Personally, his life had been in disarray.

He had been settling into his new life in Philly when he'd gotten the news that the band he had hired to play at the party had backed out. Thank God for old college roommates like John Whitman, who'd stepped up and offered the services of the music department at Jesus Is The Way Church. The band members would arrive the next day, and John had assured him that the musician who could blow "Thank You, Lord" was flawless on the sax. Garrett prayed so, because when it came to music, his family members were perfectionists. At this late date, however, he would take whatever he could get to save face.

Garrett sighed as he glanced out the window of his bedroom in his childhood home in Roxbury, Massachusetts. It seemed like yesterday that his maternal grandfather, Moses Miller, had called that infamous family meeting. Whenever trouble stirred, the family elders called for a fast. The old adage "The family that prays together, stays together," was the bond that made the Miller clan a team.

"Did you get an answer from God?" his grandfather asked, his weary eyes reflecting the same heaviness Garrett felt in his heart.

"Yes, sir." Garrett's voice shook as he made eye contact with his grandparents, his parents, and his two sisters. They had just concluded a two-day fast with a family prayer. God had spoken through a family member in tongues, with Garrett receiving the interpretation. "I can't stay."

His baby sister, Zion, initiated the protest, wailing like a toddler. No one would have guessed that she was a twenty-five-year-old college graduate.

Tai, the eldest sibling at thirty-two, was outraged. "It doesn't make sense. Why does my brother have to leave? His fiancée got herself pregnant."

"Granddaughter, my spirit bears witness, and God's decision is final," their grandfather stated.

Their grandmother, Queen—a classy, garrulous grand diva who was appropriately named—seemed to age in seconds. Sniffing, she held her peace as she linked her arthritic fingers with her husband's.

"This pregnancy is not only an embarrassment to our family but a humiliation before God. There's no excuse for any sin, and sexual immorality…" Moses shook his head.

Garrett listened as his grandfather spoke of the Miller name and what was expected of each descendant, male or female. Garrett had never imagined being basically banished from his hometown.

Now thirty, he had been born, reared, and educated in Boston, completing his undergraduate studies at Boston University. Everything had been going smoothly, until, through no fault of his own, a night of passion—one that never should've happened— had altered his life forever.

"Married or unmarried, that child will have Miller in its blood, and we take care of our own," his grandfather explained unnecessarily. "All the years I've talked to you and your cousin Landon—my only grandsons—about walking upright before God and not touching a woman unless she's your wife. I'm so disappointed. Your ex was bewitching from the start, but God can forgive instantly, as each of us is a work in progress. Look at this as a blessing in disguise."

Zion snorted. "A blessing, Grandpa? I see it as Ivette dolled up in a church disguise."

Their mother, Phoebe, frowned and shook her head. She was long-suffering toward her children until they stepped out of place.

"Before the night is over, we need to revisit Genesis thirty-seven and the story of Joseph and how his brothers sold him into slavery in Egypt," Grandpa concluded.

One thing the Miller men didn't do was shed tears, but the river had flowed in the room that night months ago. It was probably for the best. The fault didn't lie with Ivette alone. Regardless of his sister's outburst, Ivette hadn't gotten pregnant by herself.

ABOUT THE AUTHOR

$\mathscr{P}$at Simmons is a self-proclaimed genealogy sleuth. She is passionate about researching her ancestors, then casting them in starring roles in her novels, in hopes of tracking down distant relatives who happen to pick up her books. She has been a genealogy enthusiast since her great-grandmother died at the young age of ninety-seven in 1988.

Pat describes receiving the gift of the Holy Ghost as an amazing, unforgettable, life-altering experience. She believes God is the Author who advances the stories she writes.

Pat has a B.S. in mass communications from Emerson College in Boston, Massachusetts. She has worked in various positions in radio, television, and print media for more than twenty years. Currently, she oversees the media publicity for the annual RT Booklovers Conventions.

She is the multi-published author of several single titles and eBook novellas, including the #1 Amazon best seller in God's Word, *A Christian Christmas*. Her awards include *Talk to Me*, ranked #14 of Top Books in 2008 that Changed Lives by *Black Pearls Magazine*. She is a two-time recipient of the Romance Slam Jam Emma Rodgers Award for Best Inspirational Romance for *Still Guilty* (2010) and *Crowning Glory* (2011). Her best-selling novels include *Guilty of Love* and the Jamieson Legacy series: *Guilty by Association*, *The Guilt Trip*, and *Free from Guilt*. *The Acquittal* (2013) kicked off her new Guilty Parties series. Given the success of the Jamieson men stories, Pat is elated to introduce the Carmen women in *No Easy Catch*, book one in her latest series, The Carmen Sisters, published by Whitaker House.

In addition to her hobbies of researching her roots and sewing, she has been a featured speaker and workshop presenter at various venues across the country.

Pat has converted her sofa-strapped, sports fanatic husband into an amateur travel agent, untrained bodyguard, and a GPS-guided chauffeur. He is also constantly on probation as an administrative assistant. They have a son and a daughter.

Readers may learn more about Pat and her books by visiting her at www.patsimmons.net; on Twitter, Facebook, or LinkedIn; or contacting her at authorpatsimmons@gmail.com or P.O. Box 1077, Florissant, MO 63031.